SING JESS, SING

Tricia Coxon

Published in 2013 by FeedARead.com Publishing – Arts Council funded

Copyright © The author as named on the book cover.

The author or authors assert their moral right under the Copyright, Designs and Patents Act, 1988, to be identified as the author or authors of this work.

All Rights reserved. No part of this publication may be reproduced, copied, stored in a retrieval system, or transmitted, in any form or by any means, without the prior written consent of the copyright holder, nor be otherwise circulated in any form of binding or cover other than that in which it is published and without a similar condition being imposed on the subsequent purchaser.

A CIP catalogue record for this title is available from the British Library.

CONTENTS

Acknowledgements

Chapter 1	Discovering Mr Vivaldi	5
Chapter 2	Journey	16
Chapter 3	Arriving in Venice	24
Chapter 4	Life at the Pieta	48
Chapter 5	Meeting Angelo	71
Chapter 6	Christmas Time	93
Chapter 7	Meeting Jude	111
Chapter 8	Jane Eyre	133
Chapter 9	Solo Singing	159
Chapter 10	Betrayed	163
Chapter 11	Run Jess, Run	169
Chapter 12	Sanctuary	182
Chapter 13	Learning About Love and Other Things	200
Chapter 14	Fire	245
Chapter 15	New Life	260
Chapter 16	Telling	271
Chapter 17	Preparation	280
Chapter 18	Leaving the Sanctuary	286
Chapter 19	The Stones	326
Chapter 20	Arrival	337
Chapter 21	Grandmother Naming Ceremony	355
Chapter 22	Return	365
Chapter 23	Home	381
Chapter 24	Filling in the Gaps	385
Chapter 25	Ceremony Two	390

ACKNOWLEDGEMENTS

Thank you to all the friends and family who have read drafts, offered advice and support.

Thank you to Lilli and Steph in my writing group for listening and encouraging.

Thank you Do for technical support.

Thank you to Rebecca Harris for editing support.

Thank you to Dorien, curator at The Lady Waterford Hall for allowing me to access art work.

Thank you to Michael for cover design.

Thank you to Marika for photograph of The Pieta.

Chapter 1

Discovering Mr Vivaldi

If Mr Vivaldi was to do today what he did then, he would need to have a CRB check. He took all those abandoned little girls and taught them to sing. I wish I had been abandoned when I was a baby, it would have saved a lot of pain, foster parents, visits to the accident and emergency unit, all those hurts. But I wouldn't have been found by Mr Vivaldi, would I? Not in Newcastle.

Anyway I found him. I was flicking through the television stations in yet another care home that was supposed to contain me, care for me and somehow rehabilitate me. I don't know how you get rehabilitated from my early life. It certainly didn't happen in the care home. Not for me.

So, there I was flicking and I saw all these women singing in a church behind some railings. Something made me want to listen to them. And that was how I got to know about Mr Vivaldi. He found abandoned little girls and he took them off the streets and fed them and then he taught them to sing in every way possible until they made this beautiful sound.

I could sing. It helped. I didn't talk much to people. When it mattered they didn't listen. So I sang. This teacher at school said I was very gifted with my voice and I should speak to a music teacher. But then I was excluded and music teachers were in short supply where I spent most of my time.

The voice of the woman telling the story got to me. The sounds of the women singing behind the railings pierced my mind. They blanked out the nightly commotion in the corridor of the care home. The screams of a girl who, like me, in her own frustrated way, was trying to make sense of her life.

The voices stayed with me. The singing and the railings. I decided to find out more. I knew about the library at the end of Northumberland Street. I had legged those walkways that went past it many a time in the middle of the night. Running away. I knew it was open at night. That would be the best time to go, so no one would see me. "Doing a little night work are we?" That's what the other girls said. They could say what they liked.

The library man knew lots of things. He knew about Mr Vivaldi. In the middle of the night he showed me on a map where the church with the railings was. It was called the Pieta and it was in Venice. He was so clever he found that very same programme for me on a computer. I watched it over and over again till the story and the music was all in my head. All I knew about was how to survive so there was a lot of space in my head. I could fill it all up with the sound of the voices and the pictures of the church with the iron railings. That was the start of my journey.

What a journey. I slept during the day. I did think I would tell the workers in the hostel where I was going but things might have been said that spoiled it for me. I didn't want it spoiled. If it was, I might want to stop learning about it. This way it felt safe. Who would be interested anyway? They were only interested in the X Factor.

I watched his face. I studied it. I got to know every bit. I could see nothing wrong in it. His eyes were seeing. His mouth was kind. I fell in love with Mr Vivaldi not just because I thought his face was so wonderful but because he put the seeing together with kindness and lifted those little girls into song.

I sat by the river and sang. There were places you could go where no one could hear. One day I went into the big glass building beside the river where they have concerts. I sneaked in through the door and climbed up onto the stage and sang. The sound went right up to the ceiling and I just kept singing and singing and that made me think about me and who I was. That I could do one big thing in this world. If I died doing, it it didn't matter. Who would care? I was going to the Pieta.

When I told the library man what I was going to do he shook his head. "How will you manage? How will you get there? Where will you live? Have you got any money?"

I was so excited I didn't let any of his questions bother me. There was nothing else in my mind. "Will you be alright?" He went on and on. I tried to make him understand that I had never been alright. Where did he think I came from, Darras Hall where all the footballers live? He didn't know that I had never been alright. That it didn't matter, being alright.

I asked him to help me plan my journey. He said he wasn't allowed to help me but he could point me in the right direction. Show me all the books that would help me.

"Would I like a bus timetable? Did I have a passport? What about money? Did I understand about foreign money?" My nights were spent with piles of books on the library table.

I had to do a little night work but that was no great hardship. I hid the money away. And then I filled in a form for a passport. When it came, the staff were very curious. I just said I fancied one. I might go on holiday some day. They didn't say anymore.

    I went to listen to the choir in the cathedral because the library man thought it might be a good idea. I didn't even know there was a cathedral and I asked the man in charge if I could join the choir. I had to sing in front of the choir master and he liked my voice. He said I could join the choir. Some of the people in the choir were a bit snooty. I could tell they thought what's a little rubbish like her doing here? I didn't care. I knew what I was doing. The choir master said I had a voice like a diva. I didn't know what that was but I wrote it down. The library man was impressed. He said he could find some music for me to listen to that was sung by divas. I listened to it in the library and realised that I did have a voice like a diva. More importantly, I had a voice. In the choir I learnt what to do with it. My mind soaked up the learning. But I didn't stay. I was on my journey.

I got the bus on a Monday. It was a pity that I'd had a tussle that weekend; there were two bruises on my arm and a cut above my eye. Somebody had sussed I had some money. I would have fought to the death to keep that money.

I'd never been out of Newcastle that way before. The bus went over the bridge and past the building where I had sang on the stage and then I left the city where nobody had cared for the little girl who needed a sanctuary. I saw the Angel a bit further down the road. It was huge. It spread its wings over the whole of Newcastle. Now, when I looked at it through the window of the bus, I wanted to believe that it was spreading its wings over me and protecting me on my journey.

It might seem like a weird thing to do. Going to a strange city with little money and not a friend in the world except the library man. Going to a church to see where the women sang. Because I wanted to sing there too. Because I saw it on the telly. It was my epiphany moment somebody told me later. I didn't know what that was then but I do now. Not everybody has them.

The bus went to London. I looked out of the window and saw different buildings and parks and houses all along the way. I didn't think anything about them. It wasn't my concern. I had to focus on what I was doing and where I was going. I had to keep myself safe. I didn't want to look like I'd never been further than Tynemouth beach. I didn't know what to do with Tynemouth beach when I got there so it wasn't a great success. On the bus I sang in my head the songs I had learnt. I sang them in my way and I would play with the sound. That way I was keeping the songs fresh in my mind and it kept me alert. I thought that if anyone thought I was a bit unsussed about this travel thing, they might take advantage of me and I couldn't afford that. I was on my journey and nothing had to stop it.

The coach station in London was big and confusing but I had done my homework and I found the right stand. I sat on the top of my rucksack staring at the buses coming and going. There were thousands of people moving around. I stayed still. I had found the right stand and there I sat. I didn't eat and I didn't drink. Just sat watching for the bus. That was all I needed to do. So I didn't like it when I heard a voice speaking to me.

"Is this the place to get the Milan bus?" I nodded. Then I heard her say. "Good, you going there too?" I nodded again. Silly cow, I thought, don't talk to me. She was persistent.

"Good. Me too," was the next thing. I looked up and gave off a bad look. She didn't take any notice. She put her case right next to me and sat on it.

No, not good, I thought. Go away from me. I couldn't afford to let down my defences. It had never worked before. Letting down my defences meant pain. And that might interfere with my journey. So I didn't give her any reason to think that we were going to buddy up. She could buddy up with somebody else as far as I was concerned. She didn't get the message.

"I'm Becks. I'm going to see my man. He's working in Italy."

If I yawned would she get the message I thought? I could give off a pretty strong message when I wanted. It usually worked but not with this one.

"Are you going all the way to Milan?" Another question.

"All the way," I answered.

"Great. Like I said, I'm Becks. What's your name?"

"Jess," I said. Then it was question after question. I stared in front of me looking for that bus. I nodded my head and shook it and once or twice said yes or no. I couldn't miss that bus. Up until that point this bus was the most important thing that I had ever waited for in my life. And because I had waited too many times for things that didn't happen, this bus had to. I silently begged this Becks to shut up and she wasn't doing that.

The bus arrived. A big white bus with a window at the front that went nearly all the way down to the wheels. It rolled into the stand and stopped right in front of me. On the top it said, *Milan.* This was my bus.

I refused to let my bag go into the hold. It couldn't be out of my sight. It was all I had now. The girls in the home would have divvied out anything I left behind very quickly. They would have all sussed by now that I'd gone. I didn't leave a note. Who would I address it to?

I got a seat next to the window about half way down the bus. Next minute there she was.

"Great," she said. "We can sit next to each other."

It didn't bother me too much. I was on the bus now. I could relax. I felt in my bag. Money, ticket, passport, map. I fingered them all as I had done a million times since setting off. Now I was on the bus I could look at the map. I had looked at it many times in the library and the library man had showed me on the computer a big image of the church where I was heading. The Pieta. Practically every stone and every bit of fancy work on the big wooden door was imprinted on my mind. I pulled the map out. I opened it up. As it unfolded on my lap it looked like it had the wings of an angel. The bus started up and moved backwards and then went forward. I went forward with it.

Chapter 2

Journey

Eventually my unwanted companion fell asleep and I watched the lights of unknown places flash past. I knew the journey off by heart. I had followed it on the map in the library. Night after night I had sat at the table, my finger tracing the journey to the Pieta, filling more space in my head. London, the sea, France Italy. When we got to the sea I knew we all had to get off and show our passports and then sit on the boat. Becks was all gab again but she did go and get some drinks at the bar. I didn't like the boat very much. I lost my focus. It was like I wasn't on my journey any more. People were moving around, talking, playing with their kids, smiling with excited looks on their faces. I didn't want to be part of this, I didn't want to be part of anything except my journey and my task.

Eventually the boat docked and I got off in France. So then I felt happy again. I had changed countries so then the boat thing did not seem so bad.

I continued to look out the window of the bus and watch the lights flash by. It was the middle of the night but I wasn't tired. I was used to staying up at night but I was also so alert there was no way I could sleep. Becks was asleep again. She knew where she was going so it was different for her. I had dreamt before of new beginnings and it had always gone wrong. The wrong people, the wrong place, the wrong decision. This was something I had decided for myself. It was my dream that I was living. I had something inside of me that nearly burst my gut in two when I thought of what I was doing. Something I hadn't ever felt before. A good feeling, I didn't know what. Now, when I sang in my head and watched the lights, that bursting feeling happened. I clenched my hands trying to hold back the excitement that was exploding inside of me. When I felt my eyes closing, I clasped my bag tight into my chest.

When I woke, the sun was a bright red ball low down in the sky and it was nearly light. The bus was flying along a busy road and there were farms and houses on the roadside that looked completely different to English ones. The cows looked the same. The grass looked the same but there was a different feel about what I saw. Not that I knew anything about the countryside. It was like the seaside. I didn't know what to do with it.

The sun was shining. I smiled at my reflection in the window of the bus. I was definitely doing this. Going to the Pieta. I felt in my bag. Passport. Tickets. Money. Map. That was all I needed. And my spirit. Now when I look back at my story, I realise how strong my spirit was. I didn't know what spirit was then. But I knew that the Angel of the North with her great big wings had wished me well on my journey. I latched onto the angel. The angel travelled with me.

The bus pulled into a garage. Lots of sleepy people with untidy looking hair got out and walked over to a big building behind the petrol pumps. Becks opened her eyes. "Where are we?" she said as she lifted her head and rubbed her face.

"Don't know," I answered. "In a petrol station."

"Let's go for a pee," she suggested. "And a cup of coffee. There's bound to be a café over there where all those people are."

I took my bag off the rack and followed Becks. Coffee seemed like a good idea. I stood in the queue in the ladies toilet and held my bag close to my chest.

"You can clean your teeth here, and wash your face," Becks said when she came out of the toilet.

I opened up the plastic bag that I had put my toothbrush and soap in. I didn't take my eyes off the bag. I didn't trust anybody. But it was good to feel the toothpaste in my mouth. And the water opened my eyes properly and when I dried my face on the paper towel, I felt that surge again in my gut. I was on day two of my journey. Maybe, today, I would reach my destination.

I walked into the café with Becks. I watched everything that she did. She lifted a pot and poured a coffee and then took a pastry thing off a glass shelf. I copied her.

"Oh my god, I forgot to change my money into Euros. Have you got some? Pay for me and I'll pay you back."

She turned and walked away carrying her tray. I pulled a few Euros out of my bag, counted them onto the counter and gave some to the cashier, who didn't smile or anything but that didn't worry me. I knew what it was like doing those jobs. It killed you. Specially in the night.

Everything was spanking clean in that café. Wooden tables had vases on the top with flowers in. Big glass windows led your eyes into a field full of poppies and big daisies and blue cornflowers. I had worked on the flower stall in the Grainger Market with my nan. I knew flower names. I had loved touching them. Nan would let me sell them to her customers. Roses and carnations. That didn't last very long because Nan would go off to the pub with the guy from the vegetable stall and get pissed and then somebody reported the whole thing to the social services about leaving a little girl on her own on the flower stall. So my social worker came and off I went to another foster home. I didn't mind what Nan did except that she should have been looking after me. But it was good in the Grainger Market. Kenny from the coffee and tea house used to make me lovely teas with flowers in and just now and then a cup of coffee which he said was the best. That's how I knew flowers and special cups of tea. And coffee that was the best.

This coffee tasted like Kenny's. Not the rubbish stuff we used to get in the home. The pastry was good too. All crispy. I put some jam on and gobbled it down and that made me feel good inside and excited about the rest of my journey. I smiled for the first time in ages and asked Becks questions about what she did and why she was going. I listened to her story of how she had met her guy in London and he travelled all over selling bags. And when she could she travelled to see him. I asked her if she wanted another cup of coffee.

"God, yes, great," she said. I bought the same again for both of us. She had to go for another pee then and we had to run back to the bus. It almost left without us and I felt sick then that my plan had nearly gone wrong. Focus, Jess, I said to myself. That's all. Focus.

She wanted to talk now she was full of coffee. I didn't tell her anything about me. I just told her I was going to Venice because I'd always wanted to go there. She asked if I spoke Italian. I said I had learnt some bits just to get by. Nights in the library and using up more space in my head. She said it must have been hard because of my weird accent.

"I'm a Geordie," I told her.

"Weird," she said. I thought her accent was weird too but I didn't say that. She said she would show me where to go once we got there and how to get to the main part. I thought that would be good, I'd get to where I wanted to go quicker. I fingered in my bag. Map, tickets, passport, money. The map with all the marks on to show me where to go. The tickets to get me there, and the money which was all I had in the world. I didn't know what I'd do when it was gone. I didn't care. No money was not as bad as having a knife in my face on Christmas day or standing on the high level bridge ready to throw myself into the river. But there was always a little glimmer that life might one day have something good for me. Perhaps the Angel of the

North saw me and knew there was something good. I hoped so, the bus, the journey and what was in front of me when I got off the bus. Mr Vivaldi and the Pieta. The bus moved on and after two more stops to go to the toilet, eventually pulled in to the side of the road in a big city.

"We're here. Milan. Come on. It's just a hop, skip and jump to the train station." Becks sat up straight and pulled out her bag from under her seat. I clutched my bag close to me. I was another step nearer to my goal.

Chapter 3

Arriving in Venice

She was right. It took only a few minutes to get to the railway station. It was full of cafés and people standing at bars talking. There was a big glass roof and lots of lights. I didn't look around as I was frightened I would lose sight of Becks, who ran forward to look for the train. I didn't say anything to her but I had never been on a train before. I didn't know what to do so I followed her. We stood in the ticket office and somebody stamped our tickets. She looked back at me. "There's one we can get down here. Quick."

I climbed some steps into the train and followed her into a compartment with lots of empty seats. There was a mix up with the man in the uniform because I didn't understand that my ticket didn't have a seat number on but it got sorted. Besides, there were loads of spare seats. It was very late by the time we got on the train. Another journey in the dark night.

I liked the space on the train. You could get up and move around and that was better than the bus. Other people in the compartment fell asleep straight away but I wasn't tired. Even though I had been travelling now for two days and one night. Becks closed her eyes. I didn't. No way. I tucked my bag in between my legs and watched the lights go by and the early dawn sky come up in front of my eyes. The train was warm. I pulled off my fleece and sat there in just a tee shirt and jeans. For the first time since I started my journey I felt dirty but I didn't want to change my clothes till I got to my destination. I didn't doubt that I would get there. I never had. Or that anybody would stop me. I hummed a little piece from the Requiem that was the last piece that I had learnt in the cathedral choir before I left. I was a crack shot at remembering the notes and the words. Better than anybody said the choir master. I told him it was because I didn't know much so there was lots of room for all that new stuff. The library man said that I was obviously bright as a button as I had learned so much in such a short time. He didn't understand that the window of opportunity that he kept talking about was non existent in the life that I'd had. Learning was about avoiding everything that I was now leaving behind. What I had left behind. Now my new learning was singing and there was room for a lot more. I smiled to my reflection in the window on that train. Good luck, the library man had said. Well it had got me this far. That and the angel waving me on as the bus had passed by her wings.

After a screeching of brakes and a huge shudder it stopped. I knew I was there. I had arrived in Venice.

I didn't expect that I would start shaking. Great shakes ripping through my body. I remember as a little girl, when I was frightened, I would start to shake. I would try to hide the shaking in case it made things worse which, generally it did. But I wasn't frightened. I tried to stand and my legs wouldn't hold my body up. I started to breathe quickly and had to sit back down. Becks had jumped off the train and was standing on the platform. I couldn't speak. Nothing came out of my mouth except these silly gulping breathing sounds. I had to get off the train. I had to make my body move and get it down on to that platform.

"What's the matter with you?" Becks kept shouting through the compartment door. "Come on." Then she jumped back on and hauled me up on to my feet and pushed me out of the compartment and down the high step onto the platform. Clutching my bag, somehow I managed to stay upright and then the doors closed behind me.

On the platform the shaking slowed down a bit. I tried to take deep breaths through my nose and that seemed to work. Eventually my legs started to work again and we walked along the platform. Nearly there, nearly there I said to myself in between the breaths. Perhaps I had been holding on too tight. Slowly I started to feel normal again. I lifted my bag on to my back.

"We'll grab a coffee," said Becks as she walked in front of me down the platform. "Maybe you'll feel better then."

The platform was emptying. I looked back at the train, the steam, the glass roof over the platforms, it was all dark and dingy. Becks pushed open a door and we walked into a big room with a curved bar down one side. All I could hear was the hiss of coffee machines and the smell was overwhelming. My body was holding up now and coffee seemed like the best thing. Becks ordered some and picked up two cheese sandwiches and a couple of glasses of water. She held out her hand for some money muttering that she still hadn't changed hers into Euros, and she would pay me back as soon as we got to where her bloke was. I put my hand into my ruck sack and took out another Euro note.

"Oh and I forgot, we'll need some for the boat fare." Away she went to a table. Forgot, I thought. She's good at forgetting. I knew she wouldn't pay me back, but she had got me off that train. So I paid the cashier and walked over to a table. I needed to eat. I knew that. I drank the glass of water in one and chewed on the sandwich like I'd never eaten before. It worked. I felt my energy surge. Becks picked up her bag and said she needed to get the boat tickets. She went forward without me after I had handed over another note. My little pile of notes was getting smaller.

I pushed open a big glass door and walked outside. What was in front of me now was all the light in the world. The early morning sun. Water full of boats and colour falling out of buildings onto it. People were sitting on the great steps leading down to the water. Staring, smiling, talking, laughing. Maybe I had been in the darkness for ever.

My brain started to work again. This was the Grand Canal. This is what the library man had showed me on the map. He had said I would go right down to the bottom before I would get to the Pieta. All the way down were palaces, he said. I could see that now. And I could see that this was my place in the world. Standing on the steps of Santa Lucia Station, gazing ahead of me down the Grand Canal, I knew that for sure. Gold and yellow and pink and blue winked and glinted at me.

Wooden jetties bobbed on the canal, secured to a palace by ropes. Gondolas were tethered to the wooden railings on the jetties. It was just like I had read but it was different. There was beauty in everything I saw. I soaked in the steps, the bridges, the windows, the shapes of stone walls with water lapping up.

"Hurry up, here's a number one, that's the one we'll get," Becks shouted loudly from the bottom of the steps. I caught her up. "Here's your ticket." She handed me a slip and I stood beside her on the side of the canal. The jetty we were standing on wobbled as the boat banged against the side and someone pulled a rail back and tied a rope to a big pole. I pushed on with the others in the queue and stood back whilst the rail was pulled back again. I made sure my bag was tight against my back and then I held the rail as the boat pulled out into the canal. From side to side it went. Stopping, banging, starting, avoiding smaller boats and hooting at bigger ones. We passed palace after palace. Went around a curve and there was the bridge with windows that the library man had said we would go under. Onwards we went down the canal. I felt a little breeze in my hair, could see an opening at the bottom, we were going into the sea.

"Three more stops," said Becks.

We must be going in the right direction if that is what she thought. Three more stops. Two more stops. One more stop. We were there. The boat pulled up in front of even bigger palaces, but I couldn't look at that now. I must get off and work out where I am. The sea was to my right. The buildings to my left. I must then turn right according to my instructions. When I got off the ferry I had to cross three bridges and take about thirty steps, the library man had said.

Becks went on ahead. "There he is," she shouted. She ran forward to a man selling bags from the ground. He put his arm around her and they walked away together. She didn't even look back at me. She disappeared through the crowd with my change from the ticket money and never thinking what she owed me. But she had pulled me off the train and here I was. Three bridges and thirty steps away. Bridge one, bridge two, bridge three. Twenty eight, twenty nine, thirty. He was right. There was the door. There were the patterns on the stone.

No more stops. No more steps. I wanted to bang on the door. I wanted someone to open it and say "Is that you Jess? Come on in." But of course nobody did. That didn't matter. I pushed open the door and I walked inside the Pieta.

It wasn't easy to see but the outline was there. An angel hovered on the edge of the ceiling. The railings, they were there. Right up high. Iron railings. I recognised them. There they sang, those abandoned little girls. Cared for and taught something that would be good for them. My heart went up there because I knew abandoned. A broken little girl, left. With sweeties to eat and whiskey to drink. How long did I stand there staring? I don't know. Still clasping my bag tight against me. I don't know if I thought about what would happen next. I had done a big thing. I had arrived. And this moment was so precious. This moment was to last for ever. Then I realised that there were other people moving around me. Walking up and down, looking at the angel. Pointing fingers at the treasures. My treasures. I moved up towards the altar. I wanted to kneel. I had never kneeled before. Even in the cathedral when other people did it. Now I understood why. When that first precious moment was over a panic set in. What would I do next? The church would close. I hadn't thought beyond this point.

I walked back to the door and stood at the desk. There were postcards on the desk. There was a picture of the ceiling. I picked one up. The woman at the desk, who had long dark hair and glasses, looked up and smiled at me. She spoke. I tried not to look confused.

"English," I said hoping she understood me.

"One Euro for the card please. You like stamp?"

"I would," I answered. I opened up my bag and took out two coins that I knew were one Euro each and handed them over. She put the stamp on the card and took my money. I put the card into my bag. I couldn't believe what I said next. Not when I thought about it. Was it me that said it? I asked her if she knew of somewhere I could stay.

It was even harder to believe what she said back to me, although there were lots of things about this whole situation that were unbelievable for a girl called Jess from the backside of Newcastle.

"Okay," she said and opened a drawer. She pulled out a leaflet. "Here, at the back of the Pieta we have a hostel for travellers or pilgrims. I am sure there may be a room there." She paused. "It is around the corner from here and if you like I could ring to see if there is a room." She pushed the leaflet across the table.

"How much for a room?" I said. She told me. I walked away and sat down and opened up my bag. I took out my money and counted how much I had left. There was enough for seven nights. I would stay.

I went back to the desk. "Yes please." She picked up her phone and made a call.

"Yes, they can give you a room. You must go now and check in with them. Please take this leaflet. You go out of the door and turn left and then there is a large door. You must push open this door and go up the stairs. There you will find reception. Good luck."

"Can I come back here?" I needed to know that this was not the only time I would be here.

"Of course. We are closed between one and three and then shut the doors for the night at six o'clock. And in the morning we are open for prayers at eight and then again at ten for visitors."

Reassured that I could return to the Pieta, I went off to look for the door. I walked out of the church and turned left straight away. I found the door and pushed it open. I went up the stairs and in front of me was a desk with a woman standing behind. She beckoned me in. I asked if she understood my English.

"Si, of course. Your passport please." I wasn't ready for this. Money, map, passport, tickets. I couldn't separate them. They were my life now.

I must have looked confused.

"I need the number," she said. She took a piece of yellow paper and showed me that she needed to fill it in. I took out my passport and gave it to her. This was a terrible moment for me because I didn't understand what was happening. She wrote lots of things from my passport on the yellow form and then said, "Sign here". I did and grabbed my passport back and put it into my bag.

"Can I stay for seven nights?" I asked. I couldn't believe the words were coming out of my mouth. She took out a calculator and added up seven nights and then showed me the figure. Cool as a cucumber, I took out my money pile and counted out the right money. I handed it over.

"Thank you. Breakfast is at eight till ten and I shall show you where it is."

I didn't expect this. Did I have to pay for breakfast? If so, how much?

I asked her how much was breakfast? She replied that it was all included with the room.

"Now come." She led me out of the hall and up a stairway. We went into a big room with chairs. There were doors down each side. She took a key from her trouser pocket and opened door number three and led me into a tiny little room with a bed in it. I noticed a chair as well and a little table and a curtain. There was a small sink.

"If you have any problems, please ask. I shall be downstairs. Here is your key. Please hand it in to reception if you go out of the building." The woman turned and went out of the door.

Can you imagine how I felt? Can you really imagine? Me. Here. In this room. I walked over to the window and pulled back the net curtain. There were wooden shutting things over the glass. I pushed them open and there was my view. I could see a canal. And a little square surrounded by a wall with a tree in it. A wooden chair was underneath the tree. I could see a blue sky. I put my bag down. I walked out of the room and into the sitting area. I pushed open the door into the bathroom. There was a shower and a toilet. I had a pee and then went back to the room. I suddenly felt really thirsty, so I went back to the desk and asked the woman if I could buy water. She pulled out a little trolley from behind the desk. There were bottles of water and biscuits. I bought the water and a packet of biscuits. I was starting to feel in control of the situation I was now in. I went back to my room and opened my bag. I laid out some clean clothes on the bed. I went into the shower room carrying my bag with my important things tucked inside and the crispy white towel that was on a rack beside the sink. There was also a little soap wrapped in paper and a plastic bottle of shampoo. I stood under the spray of the shower and scrubbed my body. I was washing off more than all the grime of the journey.

I drank the water, I ate the biscuits. Then I thought maybe I would go back to the Pieta and sit there again. I lay on the bed and put my feet in under the bed clothes. I had one important thing to do. I took out my pen and the postcard from my bag. I carefully copied an address written on the back of the map. I had promised I would let him know and I kept my promises. Except some of the bad ones that I'd made, like I promise I'll get you for this. I had to put his proper name on the card but to me he would always be the library man. I wasn't sure what to write on the postcard. I'd never written one before. There wasn't much space.

"I am here and it is all very well. Thank you. Jess."

I didn't need to do anything more in my life now. Except maybe I could sing in the Pieta. I didn't know how I would get to sing there, but, like lying here on this bed, you just never knew. My feet found their way to the bottom of the bed and I slept nearly for ever.

When I woke I was sweating. I rubbed my hand across my face and into my hair. Everything felt wet. I had been dreaming. I was in a strange house. Great cracks had appeared in the ceiling, water had poured in. The room was filling up and I was drowning in the water. I was screaming for help and got to the door. The door was locked. I pulled but it would not open. Then I woke. I was groggy, confused. Was I in the house drowning or somewhere else? I was somewhere else. I was in my little room. Relief poured into my body and I pushed back the damp sheets. I put my feet on the tiled floor. It was cool. I put my head in my hands. What was wrong with me? I stood up and walked to the wash hand basin, turned on the tap and splashed my face. Then I pulled back the net curtain and opened the window wide. I couldn't work out what time it was. I pulled on my jeans and a tee shirt. Unsure of myself, I opened the door and peeped out into the sitting area. There was a clock on the wall that said six o'clock. I stared at it hoping that eventually it would tell me whether it was six am or six pm. I looked out of the window and decided because I could see nobody outside or hear anybody inside, that it was six in the morning. That meant I had slept half of yesterday and all of the night. No wonder I was groggy and hot. I went back into my room and picked up my towel and soap and quietly went into the bathroom. Again, I showered for a very long time. This time washing off an unwanted dream.

Back in my room I laid out on the table my possessions. A small pile of underwear, tee shirts and trousers. One short denim skirt. One bracelet which I had found in a second hand shop and a pair of silver loop earrings. One map, one passport, one wallet with money and a used up bus ticket which could now be thrown away. I didn't need the ticket any more. I put my hand back into my bag and pulled out a notebook. The library man had told me it would be useful and was a present for my journey. It had a leather cover and a piece of elastic around that kept it closed. I pulled back the elastic and opened it up. Blank sheets of paper stared back at me. I took my pen out of the bag. I pulled back the chair from the table and moved the clothes onto the bed. I neatly placed the passport and the map at the back of the table. Put the wallet back into the bag and pushed that underneath the bed. Then I sat at the chair and looked at the open notebook. I took the pen in my hand and wrote at the top of the page. *Venice*. I had to think very hard what the date was. I reached into the bin and took out the screwed up bus ticket. Twenty second of September was the date on the ticket. The day I left Newcastle. One night, two nights, another day and another night. It was now the twenty sixth of September. I wrote that. What could I write now? My mind went a blank. But my hand moved across the page. There appeared on the page the image of the Angel of the North. I put a hand out towards it. That was my hand waving goodbye. Then I turned the page over and I drew another angel. This time it was the one I saw on the ceiling of the Pieta. Another hand waved. Hello.

I had got all the way from that angel to this angel. I thought about this for a long time. I believed what the library man said. That I had a brain, that I was clever, that I could work things out for myself. So that is exactly what I would try to do. This was all good. One thing I didn't want to think about was what I left behind. That would not go in my book. Nothing good there. My dream told me that. It was a dream of my life. Always drowning. Always trying to escape.

I have arrived at the Pieta, I wrote. *I am hungry and longing to go for breakfast which is not served until eight o'clock. Then I will choose what to do with my day and when I write again in this book I'll tell what it was.* I chose my words carefully. I wanted to be precise.

I peeked out into the big room again. The clock said seven forty five. Nearly breakfast time. I sat on the bed to wait. I wasn't lost. Neither was I confused. I just wanted to get it right. Not rush at anything or do something without thinking. This was a Jess who had taken a great journey. Made a big physical space between her old life and now. Now is what matters. So I must learn about now. Be slow. I knew that my defences had to be in place. There were hundreds of miles between me and there, but there might still be people who weren't good. That was how I thought and it wasn't all wrong. With that in mind I opened my bedroom door and put my bag on my back. I walked through the big square room and through a door with net curtains on. Everything in the breakfast room was so neat. Cups turned upside down on saucers. Knives placed across plates. Little paper napkins were folded into triangles which stood upright on the table beside the plates. Knobs of butter lay in a glass dish and there were tiny plastic pots with jam in. At the side of the tables was a long bench with a white table cloth neatly spread across. On the table stood bowls of fruit, pots of yoghurt, jars with cereal. There was a dish of boiled eggs. One basket with sliced bread and one with white rolls that smelled hot.

"Good morning Madam," said a woman who stood behind a counter. "Would you like tea or coffee?"

"Don't know," I answered. That must have seemed very rude. I didn't have to be rude any more. But I really didn't know. I didn't know what to do with all this food. With all the neatness and the care in presenting it to me. Calling me Madam. Me. Because this was mine. I had paid for it with my money.

The woman carried on filling pots with hot water and wiping down the coffee machine. I still didn't know. Didn't know anything about this sort of life. I had to say something otherwise she would think I was just plain daft. So I smiled my best smile. The smile that had found its way through all the massive defence system in place in my head when the library man had said "I think I know what programme you mean, just wait a moment." I remember the words. So that smile came back again.

"Please could I have a cup of tea?"

"You can take from here what you want," said the woman as she placed a teapot next to a cup on a table that was set for two people. I tried very hard not to grab everything I could see. I made sure that I walked very slowly over to the bench and then just as slowly picked up a yoghurt and put some cereal into a dish. I sat down again at my table. I ate the yoghurt. Poured tea into a cup after I quietly turned it over, put some milk in and took a sip. Then I started to eat the cereal which tasted better than any other cereal I'd had. It had raisins and nuts in. I went back to the table and took a boiled egg and a slice of bread. I ate that. Then I got a roll and put some butter on and opened a little pot of jam and spread that over the bread. Then I poured another cup of tea. I ate the warm roll. The butter had melted into the dough. The jam was sweet and had real strawberries popping up through the sticky liquid. I hoped that the woman had not noticed how much I had eaten in case it was too much. I wanted another roll. I sat on at the table. I poured more tea. The woman was taken up with serving other people so, after I sipped the tea a bit, I went back up to the table and took another roll. I opened a fresh pot of jam, this time it was yellow. It was thick and gooey not runny like the last one. I looked at the label. Apricot it said on the top. I had eaten apricots in the Grainger market. The man from the fruit stall gave me one once. My nan seemed to think that me having an apricot was a good excuse for her to go to the pub again and leave me.

The apricot jam mixed in well with the butter. I was gaining confidence and nobody was watching me. I drank another cup of tea and finished off my bread roll. I picked up my napkin and wiped my face and hands. I had watched someone do that. Where I came from that's what you blew you nose on. Other people ate quickly. They just had a roll and a cup of something. Then they wiped their face and hands and left. I couldn't leave the table. I sat there until all of the tables were empty. It was precious being at that table. Better than anything ever in my life so far. Because after this I knew I could go back to the Pieta. So it was the best. The best ever. I went back to my room. I pulled the postcard out of my bag. I added underneath my name. *I have had a lovely breakfast.* Who else could I tell of the best thing ever? Then I picked up my notebook and I wrote all about my breakfast and that I couldn't wait for tomorrow morning to do it all again. Had I ever felt like this before? Never. To celebrate, I put my elbows onto the window ledge, stuck my head outside and started to sing. The sun was shining into the yard down below. Today, this was my world.

Chapter 4

Life at the Pieta

I went back to the table and sat down. I picked up my pen and opened the notebook again. The day ahead of me was empty. But not empty like other days. Not empty like waiting for something to happen that would make me frightened or want to run. Not empty like waiting for a care worker or foster mother or my own mother. They were really empty days. Empty of what I felt now. Today, the day ahead was empty but waiting to be filled with goodness knows what. I couldn't imagine. Whatever it was I knew it would be different.

I could choose. I wrote in my book the things I could choose to do. *I could choose to go back into that bed and lie with my arms under my head and watch the curtains suck in and out of the open window. I could choose to sit at the table and write the story of the bus. I could choose to walk down the stairs and out of the door and down the lane. Sit in the Pieta and look at the railings and the ceiling. I could choose to wash my dirty clothes.* And that's what I did. I used the soap in the paper packet to rub my dirty travelling clothes clean in the water in the basin. I squeezed them out as much as I could and then hung them over the sink and the chair and hoped they would dry quickly, so that nobody would see them.

Then I chose to do something very important. I would post the card I had written to the library man. I wouldn't be here if it wasn't for him. Maybe I would have found another way but it would have been a lot harder. I wouldn't have all that stuff in my head if it wasn't for the library man. It was a good card for him. A picture of the ceiling in the Pieta, by somebody called G B Tiepolo. The library man would know who that was.

Did they have post boxes here? How would I know? I would have to ask. I brushed my hair and put my bag on my back. Passport, money, no tickets needed. I walked out of my room and along to the desk. The same woman was sitting there, going through forms. She smiled as I walked towards her. That gave me enough courage to open my mouth.

"Is there a post box here?" I asked her and then I added the word please. My new world meant that I would try to be polite and learn to smile at people when I spoke, because these people did not want to send me back to the care home, or refuse a reasonable request or persuade me that it might be a good thing to return to where I came from, or tell me that I wasn't worth anything.

"Of course," she replied. "If you go out of the door and turn right and left on to the Riva delgi Schiavoni and then walk to St. Mark's Square, there is a post box just beside the Campanile. Here, I can show it on the map." She lifted a map from a pile on the table, unfolded it and put some pencil marks on it. She handed me the map.

"Thank you very much," I said carefully to her and walked to the lift. I pressed the button and went down to the old door and out into the street.

I went back over the bridges that had, the day before, brought me to the Pieta. I held my postcard in my hand. I soon moved into the crowds at the quayside where I had got off the boat. I reached the turning into the square that was marked on the map and there was the post box. I walked over and let the card go into the slot. I heard it drop. That was it. My promise was kept. My hand lay on the opening to the post box. I had released the post card and it had disappeared. Something moved inside my head as I stood staring at the post box. Bad memories and bad people in my life didn't live up there at the top any more. There was space up there for a new beginning. I had to believe that something, somebody, maybe even angels, would help me to carry on.

I turned. Now I could look. Now I could see. Because I was here and nothing bad had happened. I released my hold on the post box and walked into the square. It took my breath away. Like on the steps at the station. This was St Mark's Square. I had looked at it many times on the computer in the library. There's the church with big gold horses on the roof. I knew where I was. But I was overpowered. There were too many people. Again my legs went funny. I wobbled. I took deep breaths until I could turn around and away from the square. I walked back past the quayside and the markets stalls where my travelling companion had met her bloke and didn't even say goodbye. So what I thought? Does it matter? Not really. Not now. Over bridges. Counting steps till I pushed open the great door of the Pieta and there was the same friendly woman at the table. I smiled.

"Hello again," I said. I wasn't sure if she remembered me so I didn't say anything else. I walked forward and sat on a bench and looked at the railings and the ceiling and the angel. A word came into my head. A word I had never used before. Homage. Maybe I had heard it in the choir in Newcastle. I don't know. But there it was in my head. Homage. It sounded right. I said it aloud. I looked at the angel. What did it mean? I didn't know. But it didn't matter. I would write it in my notebook.

I sat there looking until a hand touched me on the shoulder and the woman from the table said that they were closing and if I liked I could come back at three o'clock.

"Oh right," I said and rushed out of the door. Fear bubbled up inside me. Had I done something wrong? If so, what? And then I thought I hadn't. She was just telling me it was time to close. Nothing else.

I went back into my room. I turned the key in the door and lay on the bed. I still wasn't hungry after all the food I had eaten at breakfast. But I finished off the water. I didn't want to move from here. I didn't want to go out and explore. I didn't want to go to that lovely church in the square and find the gold horses. It was all enough for the moment. I could rest. That was a strange word. Rest. I don't think I had ever rested. Some kind foster mother had often said to me, try and get some rest. How could you rest when every moment of your life had been to watch for the next action? Hand, cup, raised, flying, spit, burn.

Not now please, I asked the angel from the ceiling in the Pieta. Never again.

Resting was hard so I sat up on the bed. I would write a story of what I had done. Just in case the library man ever came and I bumped into him accidentally. Who else would I tell my story to? I didn't have any friends to tell. My family? That's a joke. But the library man would want to know.

So that is what I chose to do. It was easy to write about the bus and the station and the water bus. It was hard to write about the things that came into my head. Feelings and stuff. But I wrote down what I could and thought about the words very carefully in a way that I hadn't thought before. I thought this was good. There were lots of words to think about. Lots of words to write in the notebook. I wrote so many words that when I looked at the clock in the room outside it said four thirty. I decided to have another shower. In the bathroom I looked in the mirror. I'd always had short hair because new girls coming into the home always had nits. It was thick short hair. Long at the neck and short on the top. It was dark and shiny. A bit punky, I suppose, and it would be rough looking if I had that type of face. But I didn't. I had a face that was pretty on the outside. Being pretty never helped. China cheeks, I would get called. Lippy, they'd say about my big fleshy lips. Black eyed Suzy was a nickname I once had. "She's a stunner," someone once said at the police station. Never helped. Probably made things worse.

 In the shower I rubbed soapy bubbles over my eyes and lips. I pushed my fingers through my hair and into my scalp. Shampoo dripped over my forehead and off the end of my nose. Everything was changing in my head. When I was rubbing myself with my hands, I didn't try to scrub myself away.

 I dried myself with the crispy clean towel that had replaced yesterday's towel. Maybe I will get a clean towel every day. Maybe I won't get surprised any more when things like that happen. I put the towel over the back of the chair and put it near to the window to dry in the heat that was blowing in through the window. I ran some water into the little wash hand basin and washed all the clothes that had not been washed. I rubbed soap into them and squeezed and rinsed till I thought they were clean. I let them drip in the sink until the clothes I had washed that morning were properly dry. Satisfied with my cleaning activities I sat down again with my notebook. *I am clean now*, I wrote, *everything that I have has been washed with water from the Pieta.*

I felt I ought to write down what I needed to do. What did I need to do? Everything had happened as it was supposed to. I was here. So I wrote that. But nothing had just happened. I had made it all happen. I had worked hard in the choir. I had spent night after night at the library. I had taken the bus. I had turned my back on a life that I did not want to think about any more. And now here I was writing in a notebook.

Smiling was something I needed to learn.

"That's a pretty smile, little girl." Pain. No more smiling. Now, I wasn't a little girl. I was eighteen, a young woman who had to learn to smile again. That would be a start for things to do. I wrote it down. Smile Jess, smile.

I practised smiling when I stood at the desk and asked if I could buy a bottle of water. Good result.

"Did you know there is a little terrace upstairs where you can take your biscuits and water," said the woman sitting at the table.

"I didn't," I replied. "Can I go there?"

"Of course. If you like I can bring you a coffee up there too. Would you like a coffee with your biscuit? We have many biscuit types. This one is very much from this part of Italy," she pointed to a packet on the trolley behind her. I said I would like that. I didn't say it might not be good for my budget.

There was a leaflet on the desk and I asked if I could read it.

"Of course. Here is an English one." She handed me a leaflet and I went off in the direction she pointed out, up a little staircase that went round and round till I reached a glass door which was wide open. I could see tables and chairs neatly arranged on wooden boards. I stepped out onto the roof. The sun glinted in my eye and I couldn't see very well. Then when I turned, I could see all around me. Roof tops, water boats, little people, shapes up and down, red and brown towers and islands glistening in the blue sea which went way beyond where I could see. I sat on a chair because I could have fallen down with what I saw. The woman from the desk appeared with a tray. There was a pretty tissue on the tray, some biscuits, a cup of coffee and a big glass of water. I didn't care about my budget, just for a little while.

Crispy clean towels and a tray. A chair on a roof top. Sun glistening on water. Red rooftops. Today, budgets were for tomorrow.

"Thank you," I said. And then I smiled. "And thank you for the leaflet." I smiled again. I was learning fast.

"Si. Your name is Jess?"

"Yes, my name is Jess," and I smiled again. She smiled back. It was safe to smile.

I had to make the biscuits last till tomorrow morning. Slowly Jess. I tasted the biscuit. They were nutty and sweet. I drank some coffee. The froth stuck on my top lip and I picked up the tissue and wiped it. Then I picked up the leaflet and opened it up. It was about here, where I was staying. I read carefully. *Provencal Institute For The Care of Childrens, Maria Della Pieta. The Institute on the occasion of Jubilee 2000 has set aside a large area to accommodate pilgrims in the Jubilee year.* I am a pilgrim. *The Institute's activities include caring for abandoned children.* I am a pilgrim.

I wrote in my notebook. *Pilgrim. Homage.* I was satisfied with my progress. Maybe it was time to explore a little more outside of my pilgrim paradise.

I walked down the street where I now lived. For today, tomorrow and more. Down the Calla della Pieta. This time I turned left. It was less crowded. Over a bridge. Over another. My legs wanted to go. Like singing, they had always worked for me. Got me out of a scrape and away from danger. I could move pretty fast if I wanted to and sometimes I had to. They had been an important part of my survival. Moving me quickly. I stopped on the top of a bridge. How do I slow down? How could I send another message to my legs? Stop them being nervous. I looked back. Back to the Pieta and beyond what I had watched night after night on the computer, the place of Mr Vivaldi and the women who sang in his choir. I looked out to the water. There was noise in the mass of water that I was looking at. Chugging noise, engines, big boats, little boats. Bus boats that had brought me all the way down the canal to here. There were no cars, no real buses, no motorbikes. Just boats and people. A dog ran over the bridge and cocked its leg at the bottom of the step and then ran on along the waterside. It ran without danger. I could do the same. Walk without danger. Willing legs walking without fear.

This time there was no panic attack as I walked into unknown territory. I could start, stop and look. The heat of the sun on my face slowed me. My eyes stopped darting around. My shoulders dropped. I was walking without purpose, discovering a Jess that had been buried under a pile of a bad start to life. It may not last like this. But it could for the next six days. I had a bed and I had food. I had paid for that with my own money. When had I ever known what was front of me anyway? Why worry about it now? Now when I could walk without fear.

I walked over another bridge. A long straight street, an ordinary street, was on my left. Tables and chairs were all over the street. People were standing talking with cups of coffee in one hand and a cigarette in another. Women with dogs on leads walked and stopped and talked and then walked on. Men with dark glasses shook hands as they passed. Sometimes, when the sun was shining in Newcastle, Northumberland Street looked a bit like this. People talking and relaxing and listening to the bands playing outside Fenwick's. I walked on till I came to a canal with paths down either side and bridges leading into little alleyways with steep houses on either side. Washing hung across the alleyways between the windows. I saw little bridges leading into the dark doorways. I wouldn't go there. I turned back into the street shaded on both sides with a great streak of sun going down the centre. Lighting up the talk. I turned again to look at the little bridges and the narrow pavements on either side. A boat was tethered next to the pavement. There were apples and oranges and boxes of salad things in shapes and colours that I couldn't put a name to. If you can't get a lorry through these streets to the shops, then I suppose that is the only way. On a boat. I like that. The man on the boat was whistling and moving boxes. He looked happy. I watched his big brown arms lift the boxes onto the side of the pavement. He shouted something to a man in a shop who shouted back at him through the open door. The man on the boat saw me watching him. He winked at me. Then he smiled. Then he turned away and lifted up another box. I quickly turned away and walked back down the middle of the street. I moved in and out between the people talking in the street till I got to the bottom. I stopped again at a shop with a sign outside that said English Guide Books. Underneath the sign was a pile of books. I picked one up and opened the front cover. The writing said that it had essential phrases for the tourist. I wasn't a tourist, I was a pilgrim, but essential phrases were still important to know for the pilgrim. If I bought the book it would mean that I would be spending money. But I could learn to ask for things. Thinking about my need for that book made me think about my future and I felt a bit scared. For the first time I thought about what I was doing here. My happy feeling in the sun had faded. What was I doing?

Was it enough to be good at surviving? I put my hand into my bag and took out my money. I picked up the book. I held it out towards the woman behind the counter. She said something I didn't understand. She said it again and then clicked her cash machine and pointed to the number that came up on the screen. I handed over a five Euro note. She took it from my hand, put it into the till and handed me some coins. I thanked her very carefully and put the book into my bag. There was real purpose in what I had just done. If I came into this shop again, maybe I would be able to understand her words. I looked at the name of the street. Via Garibaldi. I would remember that.

When I got back to my room I opened my bag and took out the book. Then I picked up my notebook and sat down at the little table. I started to write.

I am sitting at my desk. Today I bought a book. It is a history of Venice with important phrases for tourists. I am not a tourist. I am a pilgrim. Even though I am not sure yet what a pilgrim is. I bought it on the street called Via Garibaldi which was a straight street with tables and chairs and lots of people talking. There was a long boat which I think is called a barge with piles of fruit and vegetables on the top. A man winked at me. I left pretty quickly when that happened.

I closed my notebook and opened up the book I had bought. The words were written with how to pronounce them next to the words. Buon giorno, I repeated over and over again till it was in a place in my head. I learnt to say thank you. I said it over and over again till it had found a place in my head where I could remember. Next word. Excuse me. That's a good one, Imagine how many of those I have had in my life. Excuse me while I totally diss your life which is already a miserable pile of horrible events. No, not many words like excuse me around there.

I had perfected three words. I now spoke three Venetian words. Good morning, thank you and excuse me. These words were not common in my other life. I stood up, opened the window wide into the air space. I practised my words to the world outside. Bells were ringing and mingled with my new words. I listened to the bells and hummed with them their tone and their tune.

The clock in the sitting room said three thirty. I could go back to see the angel and the railings in the Pieta. This would always be in me. The longing to belong there. For the first time in my life I had a place to go where I felt received.

The church was full of people, all talking. The same woman at the table near the door smiled at me as though she recognised me. "Buon giorno," I said.

"Buona sera," she said back. Then she said something I didn't understand. She smiled. I smiled back and said "Mi scusi."

"Very good," she said. "You are learning."

Me learning. I have learnt. This pleased me so I didn't mind that there were people filling up all the space in the Pieta. I went forward and sat down on a bench and looked around. There were the railings. There was the angel. I put my arms down by my side and watched the angel. Up in the ceiling flying amongst the blue sky and the clouds. How did they paint that onto the ceiling? What could I know about a painting on a ceiling? Only that it was beautiful.

There were more paintings on either side of the huge marble altar. I sat down on a bench. Light flooded in through the top of a dome in the roof. I practised my words as I looked around. As well as the railings and the angel painting and the altar and the light from the dome there were stone poles and tiles on the floor in diamond shapes. Then just as I was taking it all in the people who had been standing around in the aisles started to form themselves into groups on either side of the altar. A man at the front of the group started handing out sheets of paper. Then it clicked. I recognised what was happening here. These people were going to sing. What a time to come. It took a long time for them to organise themselves but I didn't mind, where else had I to go? Where else could I be? I was in the Pieta that was the only place I had to be.

Gloria, Gloria. I knew it off by heart. Gloria, Gloria. I sang away in my head. I couldn't help it, Gloria, Gloria came out of my mouth. I could sing my own part quite happily sitting on the bench.

How much better can it get? I was singing in the Pieta. Amen, Amen, Amen I sang. I knew it all. A few people watched me singing and at one point the conductor looked around. I sat there for what must have been nearly two hours. Listening, humming, chanting, trying not to rush up there and join in with the choir. There were men in the choir so it wasn't like it used to be. Not like with Mr Vivaldi up there waving his baton and guiding the young women and the little girls into beautiful sound.

Dear God, whoever you are and dear angel above me please can I be here for ever and ever? That was the first prayer that I ever made up. The church emptied slowly but I just kept sitting there. The conductor passed my bench. He nodded to me. Like he approved. I closed my eyes and a host of figures appeared in my head and my ears were full of sounds.

Gloria, Gloria. Gold and orange dresses, green cloaks, white hats floating between the pews and gathering behind the railings. Es Spirito, I sang. Es Spirito. The noise got louder and louder until I felt my ears were going to burst open. The feeling swept right over me, I was there. Jess from the dark side of Newcastle, her voice floating with the angels and all the women of the Pieta.

"Mi Scusi, we are closing now." My eyes shot open. Had I been singing or done anything silly? The smile of the woman from the desk said I hadn't done anything wrong. "Of course you can always stay for prayers if you so wish."

"No, thank you," I managed to say. I stood up and walked quickly down the middle of the church out of the open door and down the steps. I walked to the water's edge. I stood till the heat of the sun made me feel normal again. Till my tee shirt started to stick to my body, till the cold shivers inside stopped. I sat down at the water's edge and watched the boats and the barges. I listened to the lapping of the water just beneath my feet. Then I was okay. I got back up onto my feet and turned down the alleyway and back to my room. I opened out my notebook to the next blank page. *It was like they were with me. The women. Singing and holding the hands of the little ones, protecting from harm and menace, raising their voices in wonderful sound. Bright colour floating on air. One word. Magnificent.*

I remembered that my nan once said that I was lucky I came out of it all alive. Lucky because you were born to satisfy someone's nasty ways of going on. Is that lucky? Now, sitting at the table in the room remembering the singing and the ceiling, walking to the water's edge and looking at the boats, feeling the sun on my face, I felt lucky, more lucky than anybody else in the whole world. That feeling was so big. I had nothing in the world except the knowing that I could stay in this room and sit at this table and sleep in that bed for another five nights. And for five more mornings I could choose cereal and warm bread and jam and ask for tea or coffee and have it served in a little pot at my table. For me, that was unbelievably lucky.

I closed my eyes and let lucky swim over me. I am lucky. It was luck that made me flick that telly, luck that got me to the right library man, the one who listened. Luck got me to the cathedral, then to the bus and it was real luck that got me here in this place for pilgrims to stay just behind the Pieta.

How lucky was that? For someone who hadn't started with anything like luck in her life it was certainly pouring in now. You might think it's not a lot of luck, not knowing what might happen next. If you had my life you didn't worry what happened next, you just ran because you knew. So then I wondered if I could make more luck happen, did it just come upon you or did you make it happen? I couldn't answer that question. When I really thought about it, I thought that it was lucky to have seen the television programme. But then after that what happened? I moved. I moved pretty quick. I had one voice in my head. Mr Vivaldi and the abandoned little girls. Somehow that voice led me on.

I got more luck.

Chapter 5

Meeting Angelo

I could sing for money. It was a good way to get enough to live on. I'd done it before. Sung on the street and outside the pubs down on the Quayside in Newcastle. If you didn't mind being sworn at or occasionally being spat on and if you were quick enough to get out of the way, when two men fell out the door of the pub flying at each other with their fists, then you could make some money. I didn't think that would ever happen here, all that nasty stuff. I had seen people busking on the little walks I had taken around the squares. I didn't go far. I knew from the map that there was a lot more squares and canals that I could walk to. I was happy here, on the roof with my notebook, watching the boats and the sun shining on the shapes of all the different roof tops and towers. I was happy in the church looking at the angel and imagining Mr Vivaldi teaching his choir. I was happy walking at the water side between St Mark's Square and Via Garibaldi. But if I wanted money I had to be brave and find somewhere to sing. I was thinking about my future and I had to think lucky. I would try it for about an hour. That way, I reckoned, if I didn't get greedy I wouldn't get caught.

Working out where to be was important. Catching the right crowd at the right time. So I stood around a bit and watched. I walked right through St Mark's Square, into the alleyways and past smart shops with leather bags and brightly coloured shoes. I was focussed on what I needed to do to survive. I watched and I walked. This bit was too busy, this bit was too quiet. Over there was too narrow. I went up dark cavernous tunnels and into bright squares. Eventually, I found myself in a big open space. I looked at the name. Campo San Stefano. There were cafés and a well in this square. I turned left and walked past a big gate. On the side of the gate there were two people busking and round the corner some people selling jewellery and bags. A wooden bridge went over the canal. I'd never been to the other side of the canal. Loads of people were walking over the bridge towards me. I turned around and followed them. Most of them walked off in the direction I had come from. I followed the others as they went straight on. Along an alleyway full of shops. There were lots of stands with postcards. They didn't look like my Pieta postcard, but that was special.

I came out of the busy alleyway and walked over a bridge and into the sunshine. I'd found a square with no buskers, not too big, full of light. There was a café and a well. I stopped walking outside a big red building that looked like a palace. There were lots of posters on the wall with singers and musicians in the pictures. I looked at the name of the square. Campo S. Angelo. This was it. The angel square. I hoped that my angel would be here, helping.

I didn't hang about because I didn't want to get noticed before I started singing. I put down my cap outside the red building. There was a tree beside me and an alleyway just behind it. Good hiding places if I needed to hide. The space in front of me was empty. I used my diva voice to sing old popular songs that I had rehearsed in the cathedral choir for a special concert. I only needed to sing three or four songs because I was sure that people would only listen for a while and then pass on.

I sang. Not many people came through that square but they listened and some put money in the hat before they walked over the bridge. I stopped for a while and moved around the square. And then went back to the tree and sang again. It didn't take long to get enough money for my food and my bed for another night. So far so good. One person even clapped and said, "bravo". I smiled and thanked them..

I went back into Campo San Stefano and sat down on a pavement table. A waiter came to my table. I asked for a coffee. When he brought my cup of coffee I said, "Grazie". It was getting easier to say. He nodded and smiled as he turned away. Children played around the well. Men walked by with suits on, talking and carrying bags. Groups of people stood looking at maps and pointing to one corner after another. I didn't feel like any of those people, I felt different. I felt better about myself. I didn't feel angry. That was different. I didn't feel like everybody thought I was bad even though I wasn't. I'd had to learn quickly how to defend myself. I could see how people would think that was badness. I didn't feel bad here. That was different.

I had learnt how to sing for my living. That was different. I had my own little room and I paid for that. That was different. My life had moved on. Drinking that coffee was memorable and a happy feeling came over me. I wanted to smile and say hello to the people who passed by me at the table. That was different. I shall never forget that coffee. I didn't know what was going to happen to me in the future. I didn't mind. This was a great moment for my memory to remember.

I decided to sing one more time and then find my way back to the Pieta. I picked up my cap and went back. The square was peaceful in the hot, afternoon sun. There were shadows around the square. It was lovely. That was different, to think in my mind that something in my life is lovely.

I laid my cap down and waited for the next group to come through. I sang. A man was standing on the other side of the square. He turned when he heard my voice. He looked like the men who stand on the canals talking to each other beside their gondolas. He leant against the wall and listened to my song. He made me feel a bit nervous because he was watching me so hard. He walked over, dropped a note into my cap and smiled.

"Grazie," he said and walked away.

I watched him disappear down an alleyway. His smile was nice, but I knew not to be taken in by a nice smile. Then I recognised the smile. It was the man on the boat with the apples and oranges who had smiled when I walked to the bottom of Via Garibaldi.

I picked up my cap, put the money in my pocket and left the Angel Square. I found my way back to St. Mark's Square and turned left onto the Riva. I knew where I was now. I walked into the Pieta and said hello to the friendly woman who sat at the door taking the money for the cards. I did what I had done every day since I arrived. I looked at the angel on the ceiling and thanked her for being here. I felt she flapped her wings when I talked to her. It was good to believe that.

Happily I lay on my bed and wrote in my notebook. Then I went up to the roof for a coffee and a biscuit. I had earned enough for a treat. That night I lay in my bed remembering the day. I tried to push away any thoughts of what next. Where next? I knew I couldn't stay here forever. That thought didn't push away my happy thoughts of my day.

After my special breakfast, I went back to the angel square next morning. There were more people standing in the square than there had been the day before. I was a bit nervous about putting down my cap and singing. But I did it anyway.

It wasn't long before he was there again. The smiling man from yesterday. Watching me. He smiled and waved. I started on my second song. His lips started to move. He started singing my song. I didn't know what to do. He came over and stood beside me and sang along with me. I froze. The words didn't come. I was ready to pick up my cap and run. But he looked at me and something in that look said it was okay. Okay to smile back. Okay to follow him when he beckoned. Okay to sit down at the cafe table and accept the coffee that had been ordered.

"Ciao Giorgio," said the waiter in the café to the stranger I was sitting with. I drank and watched his face. He said something I didn't understand.

"English," I said.

"Hello, English singing girl," he said. I laughed. That was a nice name.

"Come," he said when the coffees were nearly finished. We walked through an alleyway, into another square and then he turned down a narrow street.

He pointed to a building with a staircase on the outside. "Bovolo," he said. He paid some money to the person on a desk near to the staircase and beckoned to me to follow him up the staircase. Round and round we went up the marble staircase till we got to the top. We stood in a little tower and looked over the red rooftops of

Venice. Blue sky peeped through the spaces in the tower. It was beautiful. Then he led me back down the stairs. Out into the hot day.

"Come," he said again. I followed him back into the angel square and we walked back to where I sang.

"Ciao, little English singing girl," he said.

"Bye," I said. At the end of the square he turned and waved. I lifted my hand and waved back.

I called him Angelo.

He called me little English singing girl.

I grew up thinking my real name was little silly cow. The words were always accompanied by something nasty.

But he called me little English singing girl. And he held my hand and kissed it gently with his lips. That was on the third day.

On the fourth day I followed him to a canal near the street called Via Garibaldi. He led me over a plank and onto the old barge where I seen him for the first time. The top of the boat was covered with a tarpaulin. He pulled it back and underneath there were apples and oranges and masses of vegetables. Down some stairs at the bottom of the boat there was a little room with a stove and two chairs and an old gas cooker and a small wooden table. Underneath the window was an old china sink. Through a little door there was another room, a big one with a shiny wooden floor with a pink rug in the middle. There was an old bed with iron railings and cupboards built in on either side. There was another table and two chairs. At the other end was a little room with a funny toilet in and a sort of shower thing.

Everything in the room was spotlessly clean. There were flowers painted on the walls in bright colours. The windows were low down and round. I sat quietly at the little table in the kitchen as he put the kettle on the gas stove without saying a word.

When I went back to the Pieta. I knew from the quick beating of my heart that something had happened. I looked at the angel on the ceiling. I told her that I didn't feel bad about this. That I would know if it was bad. She fluttered her wings. She didn't think it was bad either. That's how I knew.

On the fifth day of singing in the square, I went to live on the barge. We didn't need to say the words even if we could. It was sad to leave my safe little room in the Pieta hostel for travellers and pilgrims. I took one last look out of the window, down into the little garden with the table and two chairs underneath the tree, before I packed my bag. I shook hands with the woman at the desk and I said thank you for having me to stay with them there. I left that room well. I left with a thank you. That felt good to me.

"Why you call me Angelo?" he said as he lifted my bag down the stairs and put it onto the little kitchen floor. "My name Giorgio."

I don't think he understood a word of what I said. I told him that ever since I had started on my journey there had been angels and that I met him in Campo San Angelo. My angel square.

"I knew you were another angel," I said.

He was.

It all happened like it needed to. He was sure and he was right. I was small so I fitted into the little cabin spaces easily. I had nothing to add, I didn't come with possessions. I just put my bag into one of the cupboards and folded up my jeans and tee shirts and put them onto a shelf in the cupboard and I was complete. I ate the food he prepared and then we sat up on the top of the barge and he moved it down the canal and into the open water. We rocked with the waves caused by other boats passing us faster than we could go. Sometimes, there would be a shout, Hey Giorgio. Angelo would shout and smile. Then he stopped the boat. There were lights everywhere on the water bobbing around. The Riva was lit all the way along to the end. I could see the outline of the Pieta from where I sat.

Did I feel like a princess? I don't know. I might have thought that this wasn't possible. But when you know how possible really bad things are then you have got to know that it's possible for really good things. It just makes sense.

I sang. Angelo sang too. In a fine way. And that's the way it was. We were fine together. What luck.

Every day we would go to the market. He would start the engine on the old boat and we would go up the Grand Canal past the palaces till we got to the bridge with the windows in. Underneath there was a big market and Angelo would buy vegetables and fruit and then he would get on and off the boat carrying boxes. He would take them into this hotel and that hotel. When that was finished, he would steer the barge into narrow canals and park it at some steps near busy neighbourhoods and people would come and buy the vegetables. I could eat apples and plums and oranges all day long if I wanted. Angelo didn't mind. He didn't mind anything.

We didn't talk much, we didn't know each other's language. At first we just looked at each other and for me it was a like a deep knowing. I watched him and he watched me. I was shy. I moved slowly around my new place. Learning new ways. I had to find my way around when the boat was moving and sit on the edge of the hold whilst he loaded up and talked all the time to people who were always patting him on the back and shouting at him with laughter in their voice. I don't know if they asked him who I was. I don't know what he told them about me, but I trusted Angelo. Because everything in my life had been about not trusting, I was expert on who not to trust. I hadn't trusted that Becks on the bus. I'd been right on that one. But I had trusted the library man. And I trusted Angelo. I could see no bad in him. And I wanted to fit in to that so much. Because I had not done anything bad either. Just got put into a bad place.

Angelo would cook for us but as I got less shy I would shop a little with the money that he put on the table. I bought coffee and cereal and teas and coffee. Every morning very early we would have breakfast. I set the little table and put out bowls and cereal and a yoghurt and then at least three different kinds of fruit. Lucky breakfasts every morning. I found a little shop that sold tea with flowers in. He liked that. If the barge wasn't there when I came back from shopping I would sit on the side of the canal. He always came back for me.

I realised that I was living in a city full of treasures. At first I didn't know that. I had found my treasure in the Pieta. And then I had found Angelo, or maybe he found me. All these thousands and thousands of people who piled off the great ships at the Riva did not come to Venice to look at the Pieta or to buy a banana off a boat. They piled into the big Square to look at the church with the golden horses. They stood on the bridge with the windows. They climbed into those funny boats called Gondolas. I got to know this slowly. I read the phrase book on sunny mornings sitting on the front of the boat. I learnt more words and said them to Angelo. "Quanta tempo rimane?" I would say. He would smile patiently and answer. There was no frustration between us. I got to know the routes and recognised the people we sold vegetables to. Some would shout to me and I would smile and wave. In the café at night Angelo talked to his friends and I sat and watched him talk. I listened, trying to understand the words, sometimes I did. He never made me feel as though I shouldn't be there. With him. We walked back to the barge through little streets away from the crowds. We'd stop at tables on the pavement as he greeted people. He always held my hand.

I still went to the Pieta nearly every day. When Angelo finished selling from the boat and lay on the bed for a rest, I would walk along the Riva to the Pieta, open the door and look at the angel. I dreamt I would sing there some day.

I used my phrase book and pointed to words that would help Angelo to understand what I wanted to do. Eventually he did and one day he came with me to the Pieta and spoke to the woman at the desk. They spoke for a long time. Then Angelo said, "Grazie", and took my hand. "Is okay."

Maria smiled at me and said that if I came back at six I could talk to someone about the choir. We did exactly that and a woman sorting out music sheets told us to go behind the door. Which we did and a funny looking little man with long grey hair and a beard was there humming and waving his arms in the air. Angelo spoke to him.

Lots of words passed between them. Angelo kept pointing to me.

The man turned round and pointed his finger at me. "Sing," he said in English.

"What?" I said. I hadn't expected this.

"Anything you want to. Just sing." He continued humming and waving his arms about. I pushed down my old attitude. The man asked me to sing. So he was going to listen to me even if he did not watch me. I thought for a while. Remembering words. Remembering tunes. I sang. He stopped sorting and humming and started to watch me.

"Come," he said. We went back into the main part of the church. "Come, stand," he said again and we went up some steps near the altar.

I was looking right down the church. I could see the railings from where I stood and I could see the angel. The angel watched me. I held on to a big wooden chair near the altar. I was dizzy. Could I sing. Yes, I would sing to the angel.

"Sing," the man said again. I held on tight. Then I sang. And it happened all over again. Women singing everywhere around me. The same greens and oranges and reds. Dresses of bright colour. Black and white veils. Sound. It was my sound. My voice. I was singing in the Pieta.

"Yes, good. I like very much," said the man who then turned to Angelo and spoke very quickly. Angelo said something back and waved his arms. The man turned back to me.

"I see. I explain. You come to choir practice here on Friday at six thirty. We see how it goes. Your voice is good. It needs training. We'll see."

That's how I got to sing in the Pieta. That is how I knew I could trust Angelo. He made my best dreams come true. All that night till bed time I smiled at Angelo and picked up his hand and kissed it so gently.

"Good Jess, little English singing girl," he said "Good."

I wasn't that person without a friend in the world any more. I had Angelo, I had lucky and I had the angels.

The tiny mirror in the space where we slept showed a woman with big black eyes. With short curly hair, now a bit wild without a cut for a long time. It showed a woman with large lips and high cheekbones. The eyes were the same eyes but with no black circles. The lips were no longer tightly drawn over teeth. The lips could move wide in a smile and it didn't feel strange any more to do that. Skin was brown with sun and wind and sea. I looked at my arms, tanned and strong with lifting boxes on and off the boat. Body still thin. I touched my throat. Would it get me through the next test on my journey? When I started the journey I didn't care what happened as long as I got to the Pieta. Now, I cared that I sang in the Pieta. I cared that I could stay here with Angelo on the barge. I knew now that life could be different. Memories could be pushed away. I could sing away the past. I could sink into Angelo's goodness and believe the past was all make believe. That's what I thought as I stared at Jess in Venice. Brown and bright eyed for the first time and longing for more.

On Friday at six thirty I entered the door of the Pieta. I could feel the smiles inside of me as I walked past the table with the postcards. Smiles bursting onto my face. Angelo blew a kiss through the open door as he stood on the steps. I gave a little wave and walked up the aisle towards the altar where the choir was standing. They were already singing. I stopped smiling. I was late. What did I do now? Run Jess, run. I'd got it wrong, wrong. I stood still. People looked at me as they sang. The choir master didn't turn and look. I stood and waited with my face burning. I was on fire. Bubbles of sweat burst out on my forehead. Run Jess, run. I knew this feeling. Fear.

The baton went down and the choir master turned. "Come. What is your name girlie?"

"Jess," I answered.

"And I am Mr Frandetti and this is my choir." He turned away from me to face the choir. "Here is Jess and she may join us. Let us see where you fit. Sing girl. Sing."

I wiped the beads of sweat off my forehead, but my hand was wet anyway so it just made my face more wet. I wiped my hands down the sides of my jeans and wiped my forehead again. I stood alone in front of the altar and at least twenty people stared at me with blank faces. I couldn't remember what I was going to sing. But sing I had to or it would be over. I might never get a second chance. I looked at the railings, I imagined that I was there with the strong women of the Pieta holding the hand of the new abandoned girl, Holding her hand. I looked at the ceiling. There was the angel. Coaxing me to go on. And in front of me was Mr Vivaldi, pleased with his new student and wanting her to show him that she was worth the saving.

I took a deep breath and opened my mouth and hoped that something would come out. "I feel pretty, I feel pretty, I feel pretty and witty and gay," I sang. My hands went into the air higher and higher and my voice went higher. I stopped. And then all the people behind me clapped and shouted. Some came forward and clapped me on the back. The choir master said good, good and pushed me in between two women on the right and that was how I got my place in the Pieta choir.

Unbelievably lucky.

I smiled at the angel as I took the music sheet into my hand. I smiled at the women on either side of me as they moved a little way to make room for me. I fitted in well. I sang as well as I could. Mr Frandetti kept coming to me to give me advice. I didn't always understand but I just kept trying. Then choir practice was over and somebody wrote down on a piece of paper when I should be there next. There was going to be a next time.

Angelo was there on the steps when I came out the door. I gave him the piece of paper and one of the women talked to him. I didn't understand but Angelo smiled and took my hand. He looked proud of me. I shivered inside.

Proud of you. Your mother will be proud of you, the teacher had said as she put a tick on the little book I was to take home. The book was thrown down. The man in the corner sniggered as he drank the white stuff out of the bottle. I crawled away into the room with the heap of coats on the floor that was my bed. I made sure I didn't make anyone proud after that. Not till now.

Chapter 6

Christmas Time

How did the time pass so quickly? Did good time always pass quickly? Why did bad time pass slowly? That was another thing that I learnt. Good time passes quickly.

I wasn't in bad time and it was almost Christmas. Angelo steered the barge backwards and forwards to the market. All the hotels wanted more fruit and vegetables and the customers who came to the barge to buy were ordering like mad. He sat at the little table night after night working out his orders. I couldn't help with that because I didn't understand, but I could sort out the fruit and vegetables for him, make sure there wasn't any bad stuff in the boxes. He appreciated what I did and put his arm around me and said that Christmas would be a happy time for him and me.

Christmas. The word sent shivers down my spine. Not a present in sight. More bottles than ever. More lonely than ever. I remembered when I was in the hospital ward and this creature came up to my bed with a present for me. Shouting and carrying on. There was such a commotion in the ward and I lay in the bed and stared. My arm was in a plaster and the creature said that he was so sorry for me because I couldn't be with my mummy and daddy. I stared some more. Mummy and daddy wouldn't care where I was. Christmas was not about presents for their little girl. Then all the nurses came in and sang about baby Jesus being born. I wanted to sing. That was the only nice bit. I tried to sing but then I was worried that someone might put the other arm in plaster if I did.

This wasn't that Christmas. This was a Christmas of preparation without threat. Angelo excited, willing to share it with me. The choir were preparing for Christmas in the Pieta and I was practising every night. I was used now to all the crossing and bowing and waving incense about and there would be even more because it was Christmas time but it was the singing that made it for me. I loved singing the Christmas songs and a group of us were to sing a special song behind the railings. Just by ourselves. That's why we had to practise so much. We weren't allowed up there till we sang because it's so precious. I understood that. I couldn't wait for Christmas in the Pieta.

But there was still a dark shadow over other things about Christmas. I think Angelo knew that there was something wrong about Christmas for me. I had never told him anything about what had happened to me. He didn't push me to tell him. Maybe he understood that it had never been right. He asked me if we would go to his mother's on Christmas Eve. To see all the family. I couldn't say no. How could I? It was his family and I don't think that he got a black eye from an empty bottle on Christmas day instead of a present.

There was something else to think about. Angelo told me in his way and I looked words up in the dictionary and then I understood. On Christmas Eve there would be a great big wave coming in to Venice and we must move the boat to somewhere else. He made telephone calls and looked at maps till at last he told me it was okay. The boat would be safe on a canal further into the city. I was glad about that but I was worried about the Pieta. Would the service be cancelled? I wouldn't be able to bear the disappointment.

I tried to imagine what a big wave would be like coming in to the city, right over the Riva and into the hotels and cafés and even into my Pieta. Maria, on the desk in the Pieta, told me in her very good English that I shouldn't worry, that it happened in Venice every now and again. But she did say that this was a big tide and that lots of precious treasures would have to be moved just in case.

Another preparation I did was to buy Angelo some presents. I bought a brown wooden box from one of the guys selling bags and jewellery on the Riva. I thought I would put the music sheets from my concert in the Pieta inside as a special gift. Then I noticed a tee shirt with a big yellow sun on the front on a stall in the market. I thought that was perfect. Angelo loved chocolate, so I got little slivers of orange covered in thick dark chocolate and had them specially wrapped in a bag with pretty purple ribbon which curled at the end. It took a lot of walking backwards and forwards past the shop before I had the nerve to go in, because it was so classy. I had often stopped outside and stared through the window. There wasn't a bar of chocolate in sight. Not a packet of biscuits anywhere. Glass cases showed off chocolates like they were as precious as diamond rings. Each one with a different little squirt on top. Some had stripes and some had carvings on the outside. Little cakes with chocolate fans on top and pastry cakes with cream and fruit bulging over the sides, were displayed along the front counter. I got over my feeling of not being good enough to go into the shop and chose my chocolates for Angelo. The woman behind the counter spoke perfect English and was so polite to me that I said thank you far too many times and she had to say you're welcome too many times, and then she laughed.

So I laughed and never felt nervous again about going into the shop.

On Christmas Eve, Angelo took me to the Pieta and told me to stay there until he came for me. He was going to move the boat now and I wouldn't know where it was. Then we would go to his mother's for food to celebrate Christmas. I was glad I was going to sing because I knew about that. I didn't know about celebrating anything.

The Pieta was lit with hundreds of candles. All flickering in the dark church. That meant I couldn't see the angel but I didn't mind because I knew she hadn't gone anywhere. Not tonight, not when I was going to sing behind the railings. She wouldn't miss it for the world, would she?

The choir members were all talking together and the ones who could speak English talked to me as well. I put on my choir robe and within no time at all, Constantine called me over to say it was time for us to go up to the railings so we would have plenty of time to organise ourselves before we sang. Up we went. Up the stairs and along the passageway.

Then we were there, standing behind the railings, looking down on the candles, fluttering with people breathing. Could anyone have imagined that I would be here singing on Christmas Eve? I knew the choir master thought he was lucky to have me. He told Maria and she told me. He told her that my voice was special and though I sometimes made mistakes with the way I said the words, I made up for it with my ability to blend in well with all the other singers. Ability. That's a word I shall write in my notebook. Ability. Pilgrim. Homage. Now I had three special words. I made my words into a sentence while I waited for the choir master to give us a nod. I am a pilgrim, paying homage, with ability. I am a pilgrim with ability, paying homage. That sounded great for me, standing behind the railings. I was the real thing. I was the abandoned little girl who would have been rescued by Mr Vivaldi had I been a little girl in Venice, instead of a little girl in Newcastle.

The choir master nodded. The choir below started to sing. Then silence. Behind the railings we started to sing, The people below looked up in surprise. I had a one line solo. My heart just burst open and my voice flew right up into angel territory. Then it was over. The congregation clapped. We bowed. And then we filed back down into the choir area and the service went on.

Everybody kissed and clapped each other on the back. I suppose this was the start of it. Merry Christmas. I had to try. Cut the thread to that part of my past. The Christmas story. I wished Angelo would come.

There was a flurry at the door. The wave had arrived and was pushing against the steps. It flowed into the church and onto the beautiful tiled floors. People waded through the water holding onto each other as they moved towards the door. I couldn't leave till Angelo came because I didn't know where to go.

Maria wanted to lock the door. I huddled into the wood, holding onto the stone. How high would the water come? My only thought was, please come Angelo. Please don't let it be Christmas.

"Jess, Jessie," I could hear him shout. "I come Jess." Was I imagining it? No, I could see the outline of Angelo running along the boards, carrying a bundle in his arms. I couldn't move from the doorway. "It's okay Jess, is okay." I was shivering and remembering and wanted to feel him now, his realness. Feel his rescue.

"Here Jess, put on feet." The great angel had brought long rubber boots for me so I could walk through the water. I pulled on the boots and put my shoes in the bag he was carrying, which he then slung over his shoulder. He took my hand and led me through the water and along into St Mark's which I had never seen empty before. It looked strange without people in every corner talking and standing, feeding the pigeons or gazing up at the cathedral. There were no lights in the cafés, everywhere had been boarded up. Walking boards had been placed all round the square, but not a single person was walking except me and Angelo. I was still shaking and hung onto Angelo's hand as tight as I could. It was spooky in here in the dark, like a dream, with water lapping around under my feet and the buildings with no lights and not another soul in sight. We walked on the boards, then we had to get off and walk through the water, but Angelo picked me up and carried me over the worst bit. The water was still pushing in. It was the biggest wave in twenty years somebody in the choir had said. We went further into the city away from the water's edge, till we got to the square with the hospital. I could see our boat bobbing in the canal which ran past the entrance to the hospital. It was all lit up with fairy lights blinking on and off. Angelo picked me up again and carried me onto the boat. Inside our little kitchen there was a Christmas tree.

Just a plain Christmas tree. Underneath the tree were some little parcels.

"For you, Jess," he said, smiling at me. I sat down at our tiny wooden table and looked at the tree and the parcels. For me. They were for me. I had been rescued and I had Christmas presents.

"Santa Lucia tonight. We go to Mama's. And eat."

I am glad that I had bought the little presents for Angelo. I had put them at the back of the cupboard. I kissed the music sheet before I folded it up and put it in the box. I tied a piece of ribbon around the box, a little bit I had saved when I wrapped the other parcels. I took my little pile of presents into the kitchen and put them under the tree.

At last it was like it should be. A tree. Hiding parcels. Parcels under the tree. Pretty lights. I could be a little girl now, just for a moment, and gaze at my Christmas.

There wasn't a bottle in sight in our Christmas. There were no strange people lying around on the floor swearing. Nobody was drunk in the street. There were no strangers at the door.

I could hardly bear to leave our Christmas and go to his mama's. But I would do it for Angelo. We walked away from the lights and through narrow alleyways till we arrived at a door. There were lights and music coming through the window. We walked through the door and into the crowd. This was his family and there was his mama. She caught me up and kissed me first on one cheek and then on the other. She talked and talked and pulled me into the room and said, in words I couldn't understand, that this was so and so and that was so and so, Then she put her hands to her mouth and pointed to a table that was bursting with food. Ham and sausages and salads and great pans of pasta with different sauces. Cakes, bread, chocolates. Everything that was wonderful to eat was on that table. People laughed and talked as they dipped into the goodies. I was in unknown territory. What should I do? I didn't have to worry because Angelo's mama pointed to me and said some words. I walked towards the table. But Angelo touched my elbow and whispered close to my ear.

"You sing Jess. Sing for Mama." I didn't know if I could sing in front of these people who were all Angelo's friends and relations. I could sing by myself in churches and cathedrals. But this was different.

"You like to sing for Mama, Jess?"

I owed him some sense. Not silliness like this, being too embarrassed.

"Ssh Ssh," said his mama. I sang. Amazing Grace, like I had learnt in the choir. And when I finished everybody clapped and Angelo rushed up and kissed me on the cheek and took my hand. His mother shouted "Bella. Bella."

They want more. So I sang a very popular song in the Pieta. Ave Maria.

Mama wept. "Magnifico," she cried as she blew her nose.

I filled my plate and sat down to eat the delicious food from the table. I looked down at my feet. I still had on the rubber boots Angelo had brought me. Everybody else had smart shoes on. So I tried to take them off and my plate wobbled and some salad fell off onto the floor. You can take the girl out of Newcastle, but you can't take Newcastle out of the girl, I thought as I tried to pick it up.

"It's okay," said a woman with a tight short skirt on and a low top. She had dark hair pulled tight into a pony tail. This was Angelo's sister. She smiled with thick red lips. She took a paper tissue and put the bits of food off the floor into it. I hadn't done anything wrong after all. I watched his family being happy together. Laughing and hugging and kissing. It glowed. Happy Christmas glowed. When it was time to leave everybody kissed me and said, Buon Natale.

The rain pounded down on us walking back to our boat. We didn't care and we didn't rush. I was so happy having a happy Christmas. I think I had made Angelo's Christmas happy too. Seemed that way. Our arms were wrapped around each other. Back in our fairy light boat we sat on the floor beside the tree and opened our presents. For me there was a notebook with a cover that had beautiful swirls of colour on. I had seen them in a shop near Campo San Luca. Inside a little parcel there was a bracelet made of glass. Every piece was a different colour; pink, green, blue, yellow, red. There was a pretty blouse which was pink with red buttons down the front. They were lovely presents. Angelo opened his and said they were the best ever. That night I gave Angelo all the love in the world.

Christmas can be happy and life can be different and love is a great thing to do, like when I sing, or when I opened up Angelo's presents. Still, deep in my mind were the memories that came over me in the doorway at the Pieta, when the water was coming and there was no one there. On Christmas Eve.

The next day was Christmas day and there was nothing for Angelo to do. No going to the market, no selling of fruit and vegetables. We had our breakfast with a different view from the boat. There was this great statue of a man on a horse. The horse was rising up on its back feet. It was green and blue coloured. Angelo said it was a very famous statue. I could see the hospital and the church in the square. A café was opening its doors. Small groups of people were going into the church.

The wave had gone and we were going to move the barge back down to our usual mooring place. Angelo started the engine and off we went down this canal and that canal. We kept the coloured lights on as we toured. Friends of Angelo's called as we passed saying Buon Natale, and other words I couldn't understand, because everyone wanted to talk about the wave that had flowed into the city the night before. The sky was grey, but our fairy lights made people smile. The nearer we got to our landing place the more we could see the effects of the wave. Puddles were everywhere and the only noise apart from the roar of the engine on the barge was the swoosh, swoosh of brush strokes as we passed people sweeping the water out of the dark, gloomy cellars.

Once we were back moored in our usual place, Angelo said we should go walking and as we set off along the Riva, the morning light was changing. The sky was lifting and bits of blue appeared over the lagoon. Even in the poshest hotels they were sweeping out water. Angelo talked to everybody about what had happened the night before and waiters with brushes pointed out to him how high the water had gone. We walked through St. Mark's Square. It was eerie and quiet. There were no visitors.

"Bad snow," said one of the waiters to me. "No planes and no trains."

I lived in my little world on the barge with my Angelo. There were other things happening outside of my world. Bad snow was falling and making life very difficult for people. I was safe from all of that.

We walked over the Grand Canal on the wooden bridge and past the huge art gallery where there were always queues to get in. Today it was closed and the small alleyways were empty. We walked on and stopped at a little café full of gondoliers. They had no work because there were no tourists. But they looked happy as they sat at the table with water under their feet. There were still puddles on the floor.

"Ciao Giorgio, Buon Natale," they said as they slapped his back and kissed me on both cheeks. I held tight onto his hand, proud to be with him. He knew everybody did Angelo. He was born with these people, worked with them, went to school with them, all the history of his life was around him. I was part of that. Not the snow in the world outside. That world was fast becoming a stranger to me.

Now the light was brighter. We walked onto another waterfront. I liked this best. The Zattere.

"There Guidecca," said Angelo pointing to the island across the lagoon where we delivered vegetables on a Tuesday and a Friday. Swoosh, swoosh, the brushes went as people called to each other on Christmas day. In a big square near the Zattere, the cafés were all open. Aqua, aqua, were the words that people were saying to each other. We joined in the talk standing at the bar of a café.

Aqua, aqua. I knew that meant water. Familiar words. Like Guidecca. I belonged to the words. There was excitement in the voices as they told their story. I was part of that story. Of the great wave on Christmas Eve. That was my Christmas story. At last I had one.

Chapter 7

Meeting Jude

For days after Christmas the sun shone. No more tidal surges. We travelled to the market every morning, picked up the fruit and vegetables and delivered them to the customers.

I couldn't have predicted what happened next or what the outcome would be.

I had washed and ironed my choir cassock and was returning it to the Pieta. Maria did not warn me as I headed down the aisle.

I didn't know what it was and I didn't like it either. There was a sort of scaffolding thing right at the end of the aisle. On top of the thing there was a platform.

I stood at the end of the aisle and stared. This was wrong. This wasn't how it should be. I walked towards the scaffolding. Then I heard this voice. Somebody was singing up there. I looked up. I saw a woman on top of the platform and she was messing with my angel.

"What you doing up there, what you doing to my angel?" I called up the platform not having the sense to ask Maria what this was all about.

"I'm touching her up," this posh English voice shouted back. "Oh and I like the accent."

"You taking the piss and have you got permission to be up there?" I shouted up the platform. I'd reverted to type. The type of person I had been in Newcastle. On the defensive. But I couldn't help it.

"No and yes. Hang on. I'm coming down."

She appeared at the bottom of the scaffolding. Great bunches of dark curly hair stuck on the top of her head. Dangly earrings hung down to her shoulders. She had on a flowery blouse and a pair of navy blue dungarees. She looked English. And a bit mad.

I folded my arms and leant against the scaffolding, determined to challenge this usurper into my church and messer with my angel. The scaffolding, which was on wheels, moved backwards and I nearly fell over.

"Whoops," said the curly hair and she reached out and steadied the moving contraption. Silly cow, I said to myself as I tried to regain my stand. I'd lost my cool.

"Hi. I'm Jude." A hand covered in blobs of paint came out towards me. I couldn't do anything else but put out mine.

"Jess," I replied, not very friendly.

"I recognise that accent. You're from Newcastle." She rubbed her hands down the front of her overalls and pushed her posh smile into my face at the same time.

"Yes and so what?" I replied. "You're daubing paint all over my angel."

"Well, that's what I do. I'm an art historian and I also restore paintings that have become rather dull. So because she is a little dull, I'm giving her a makeover. I'm not changing anything, just making her a little brighter. So you can see her better. Also it preserves her, so she'll last a little longer. My nan was from near Newcastle. Ashington. My grandad worked down the pit."

Now where I came from working down the pit was considered posh. My uncle used to work down the pit. He always gave us money when he visited. Then he stopped when he saw what it was spent on. So I didn't feel as though we had anything in common.

"Oh right," I said. I felt a bit daft now and didn't know what to say next.

"You on holiday?" said the curly hair called Jude.

"No, I live here."

Now she lost her cool a bit and looked surprised. I could tell that. She was thinking what's a Geordie like you doing living here?

So then she said "Oh right," while she thought about this. So I asked her if she lived in Newcastle.

"Near there. I live in my nan's little house. I didn't move there until after my nan died. I grew up in London. I love it being up north. So how come you live here?"

Nosy thing. What was it to her? Then I thought that's the old Jess talking, I was learning to be different.

"It's a long story." Then I made a big effort and smiled. "I'm glad you are looking after my angel. I like to think she looks after me."

"Great. Well that's that. Better get on." She turned and walked back towards the platform. Then she turned back round and shouted out "I say, do you fancy a coffee?"

"Can do," I said. I fancied speaking to somebody without having to think so hard about what I was saying and looking in the dictionary all the time.

"Do you know a good place? Away from the tourists?"

I was on home ground now. My only home ground ever. "Follow me."

I led her out of the church and onto the Riva. A boat had just arrived and tourists flocked onto the waterside and started taking photographs straight away. They clicked away at the stalls selling flags and cards and masks. The frenzy of people started to come towards us.

"We are going in the opposite direction. Don't worry." I said as we turned away from the crowd.

"They seem to have no free will these tourists off the boat. So many treasures to see and they never get beyond the Rialto," she said as we walked over the bridges to Garibaldi. By the time we got over the second bridge the crowds had gone.

"Well, they have to walk over all these bridges and then they arrive up here and it's not very grand. Except there," I pointed to the gates of the Arsenale. "Lots of people go there, and there is an art thing on there every couple of years. But I expect you know that."

"Yes, I've been. It's called the Biennale. Pretty popular kind of gig. When I was married, my husband and I came every time it was on. We needed to look for new blood."

"You are not married any more?"

"No, not any more. My husband was a serial adulterer, only I was the last to know. Then he went off with this very glamorous older woman who suited his image much better than I did. They are very happy together. Only problem I have now is that my daughter has to spend time with her when she visits her dad. That's where she is now.

And of course Lulu adores her because she takes her to all the designer toy shops in London. I gave all that up when I left London and I don't particularly want her to be influenced by that lifestyle, but she loves her dad and he is great with her. So I have to let it happen." She stood on top of the last bridge and looked out to sea. I stood still till she finished her story.

"But mostly," she continued as we went down the wide steps, "she is with me and we go to the beach and make do with buckets and spades and a little four wheeled bicycle. She does go to a school which is paid for by her father. I had to make that concession when we left London. But I don't think it will make her into too much of a snob."

I led her into Garibaldi and we left the waterfront behind. It was market day so the street was all bustle and groups of people standing talking. Dogs ran backwards and forwards in between the groups and cocked their legs up against the railings leading into the park.

"I've never been up here before. It's like a real street."

"It's a local area." My local area, I was going to add but I didn't want to give too much away. Just because she came from Newcastle didn't make us best buddies.

We walked down the street. It was busy. Colourful. Washing hung across balconies, blowing like the flags that drape across streets when it's festival time. Women with bright red hair, dark glasses, short skirts and high heels walked up the street talking on their mobiles. Men stood together shaking hands and slapping each other and laughing while they drank their espresso. Old women pushed trolleys from stall to stall buying as they went. Old men leaned against the walls and smoked as they talked. I turned into a café halfway down the street. She followed me.

I leant against the counter.

"Ciao Jessie, Ciao piccolo Jessie," Guiseppe leant over the counter and kissed me on the cheek.

"Ciao Guiseppe." I looked at Jude. "Cappuccino?" She nodded. "Grab a seat outside and I'll get them." I ordered our coffees and two amaretto biscuits and went to sit beside her.

"You must have lived here a long time when you know everybody," she looked at me. There was curiosity on her face. Nice curiosity.

"For a little while." I didn't want to tell her too much. I didn't know her very well. Then I thought, well she is making my angel better. So I told her that I lived on a barge. That my bloke sold fruit and vegetables. And every morning we went to the market. And at night we often came here to have a coffee and sometimes to eat.

"So how did you make the shift from Newcastle to Venice? That's a strange combination." I looked away from the question. Then I did something I never do. I blushed. I went bright red. I could feel heat creeping up my cheeks and into my hair until it all felt tingly. I could feel her watching the blush. I felt cornered. I looked at my cup, took the handle and lifted it to my lips. I drank. I don't know why I felt embarrassed, I hadn't done anything wrong. Or maybe I thought that she thought I had. Old stuff back again. I looked away and smiled over the top of my cup at Guiseppe who was clearing the next table. He winked. I was back in my place.

"I don't think you'll believe me if I tell you, and as for Newcastle, well you don't want to know." I sipped my coffee again. "And I don't want to tell." I looked straight at her. Old Jess back again, warning. Back off.

She got the message. "Why the Pieta then? Do you like going there?"

"Yes, I like it and I sing there, in the choir".

"No! How incredible!"

"Not really. Don't you know the story?"

"No, tell me."

Just then a loud voice bellowed over from the other side of the street. "Jess, what you doing?"

There he was. My lovely Angelo. Broad and dark with curly hair that touched the collar of his open necked shirt. Wide smile.

"Ciao Bella. Who this?"

I explained as best I could who Jude was. But I needn't have bothered because she could speak Italian and she told him exactly who she was and what she was doing. I drank my coffee and tried not to scowl. What was she saying? Why did I feel so threatened? I tried not to think in the old way. This was not a father ignoring me. This was not a new person in the flat who would end up noisy and drunk. That nobody would think about me till I couldn't stand it any more and I went out into the cold night and they didn't even realise that I wasn't there any more. Then some person would feel sorry for me and give me a sweetie and tell me to go home and I would believe that it would be better by the time I pushed open the front door and walked into the room. Usually there was nobody there. So I would put myself to bed and maybe in the morning somebody would be there. It was not like that now but sometimes, something would remind me what it used to be like, and I would go back off into that past. I hated that, I hated being reminded.

Then Angelo turned and caught hold of my hand and told me that he would pick me up after choir practice and he would cook some tea. This was all said slowly and with hands pointing at clocks and the bottom of the street and fingers going to his lips. Our being together was all gestures and trying to understand each other but it didn't matter. He kissed the top of my head and walked off down the street shouting at this one and that one and raising his arm and laughing. Then he turned round and threw me a kiss with his hand.

I don't know why. I started to cry. I rubbed my hands across my eyes and face. What had this Jude done, making me blush and cry?

"Gosh I'm sorry. Did I say something?" Jude stretched out her hand and touched my shoulder.

"No it's alright. I'll pay for this and we'll get back. I don't want to be late for choir practice." I longed to be back in the Pieta, singing. Just to be me, the Pieta, Angelo and song. I didn't want memories or people who made me remember.

Next time I went to the Pieta she was there again. Up the scaffolding. Daubing away on the angel and singing away to herself.

I shouted hello. "Oh hi," she shouted back with this loud posh like anything voice. "I'll be down in a minute. Just have to finish off the edge of the wing and then she's all done. Pretty as a picture."

I chatted to Maria. It was my turn to arrange the music lecterns for choir practice that night. I moved the wooden boards around. There were quite a few visitors in the church that day. I felt very important being up there in front of the altar doing my job. I was always very particular that I did this properly. It was a special duty and I took it very seriously. I placed all the music sheets for the practice that night on the lecterns. Mr Frandetti always fussed if it wasn't right and some of the other members of the choir did it in a rush and didn't always get it right. I always got it right and Mr Frandetti would tell me that I had done well and how good it was he could rely on me. My pride would swell in my chest. What a feeling. I never had that feeling before I came to the Pieta. No running away with shame and failure here. I know Mr Frandetti liked to have me in the choir and only saw me and heard my sound. Not the bad girl who ran. I fussed with the sheets of music and then there she was by my side.

"All done?" I said.

"She's done. I would die for a coffee now. Do you fancy one? God, I've been at it for hours."

Jude rubbed her paint covered hands down the front of her dungarees.

"You can come to my place for a coffee." I couldn't believe I said that.

"Really. Is it far?"

"Ten minutes." What had I done? It just came out. I couldn't believe that I had invited her to our home. That was something that other people did. I'd never done anything like that in my life. I had never had anywhere to take somebody for coffee. I didn't think Angelo would mind. He would be pleased that I was bringing a friend for coffee. I'd said it now. No going back.

We chatted as we walked. I told her about choir practice in the Pieta that night. She told me she was here for another week and then she was going home and then coming back again for a week at Easter. I told her how I discovered Mr Vivaldi and the Pieta and the little girls. I even knew some of the names of the women who became famous in the choir. She was full of questions. Her huge mass of bouncing curls went this way and that as we walked quickly. I was surprised at how much I talked. Telling her things about our life and where we ate and where we walked on a Sunday. I wasn't used to talking much. I had never talked much. Angelo and I didn't talk much. We didn't need to. I was learning more words and we spent a long time looking for words in the dictionary, but we didn't chat on. Not like I was now. Chattering away.

We walked down Garibaldi. I led her through alleyways into the opening of the wide canal in front of the little island of San Pietro. I pointed to the barge and we walked along the waterside. Angelo was busy moving empty boxes out of the barge hold. He pulled the barge in when he saw us coming.

"Ciao Jess." He pulled the walkway onto the jetty. "I just leave. Boxes go." He talked to Jude. She blabbered away to him. I didn't understand what they were saying to each other.

"How fabby," said Jude. "A cruise. Apparently he needs to take all the boxes to that island over there." She followed me down the wooden steps which led into our kitchen.

I pointed to a chair she could sit on and put a match to the gas stove. I filled the kettle from the white plastic bottle which Angelo always kept filled for the kettle and cooking, and then reached into the cupboard above the sink for the little cups that we drank our coffee out of. I filled the coffee pot with water from the kettle. Then I put the coffee in the pot and put it on the stove. I reached for a little tin that had our biscuits in. I did all this with much efficiency as well as staying completely cool. I didn't want her to think she was the first person I had ever made coffee for apart from Angelo. I am a late learner, but I am learning at a great rate. I held out the biscuit tin. She was watching me. She was wondering.

"Do you live like this all the time?" she asked.

"I do," I answered.

"It's wonderfully simple," she said. I didn't know what she meant. I never thought about it that way. To me it wasn't simple. To me it was where I started to live in peace with the love of Angelo and where I began my singing life in the Pieta. I didn't tell her that. There was a low rumble and slowly there was that feeling of movement underneath my feet. A little shudder and we were away. Heading out into the lagoon making waves through the water. Going past the Goldoni Park and navigating between big boats and little boats. A proud barge that carries apples and potatoes, sweet smelling basil and thyme, heady sage and courgettes. Simple, I don't think so.

She looked puzzled. I could tell by the way she's staring at me with this look on her face that said she was stuck. And I could tell by looking at her that she wasn't the sort of person who got stuck. And then it came, the question.

"How on earth did you land up here?" It was the way she said 'you' in her posh like anything accent. I stopped looking out the window. I put down my cup. Up until that point I had been okay about having her here. I hadn't felt threatened Old Jess was back.

"What do you mean you? Like I couldn't. Like I'm not good enough or brainy enough or posh enough to be living here. And for your information, I wouldn't walk into your house even if it was a back toilet or a bloody castle and say it's simple. I might have been dragged up, no not even dragged up, by some hopeless case druggies in the back streets of Newcastle but I would not walk into your house and say it's simple. I think it's time you left."

"I don't think I can. We're in the middle of the ocean."

"Well, we'll soon be at the Guidecca and you can get off there. Then you can get the vaporetta back."

I picked up my coffee cup again, and looked out of the window. Off I went again.

"This is my home. This is my life. This is the only life that I ever want. So please don't use that tone of voice with me because I know that what I have here in this simple cabin kitchen is very special. I don't think about it. I don't question it. I never wonder how. But I know and I accept and I take every day and know it's the best. I sing. I count onions, clean carrots, sort out apples, I could do that anywhere in the world but it happens to be here with this man and that church. So please never say to me how did you land here just because of who I am and just because you think in your arty farty ways you know who should be here and who shouldn't."

"I didn't mean anything like that Jess, honestly. I was just wondering. Probably if the truth was known I'm green with envy. I mean who wouldn't want to live like this. And for the record, I live neither in a back toilet or a castle. I do live in a simple little house near Newcastle. Nothing posh. Where my mother was born and where my grandmother lived. Her dad was on the Jarrow March and because it was so important to her, for the last years of her life, she talked about nothing else. So I know all about the back streets and what happens there."

I looked at her. "You know nothing."

The boat shuddered and then there was a little bump and I knew we were at the island where Angelo dropped off his boxes.

"I have to help Angelo." I ran up the stairs. I would never have anybody back for coffee again. It didn't work.

She followed. "Can I help?"

Then she spoke to Angelo and started to unload the boxes. Of course she stayed on the boat and came back all the way back. Chatting away to Angelo like I wasn't there and making me feel paranoid.

"Great you have friend Jess," Angelo said with that great big smile on his face.

"It's okay," I said. Now I felt guilty. I had been horrible to her. And Angelo was so pleased about her. I was mixed up.

I asked Jude if she wanted to walk back with me to the Pieta. It was time to go to choir practice. She said she had to finish off her work and put her paints away. I nodded and we set off towards Garibaldi.

I calmed down. "I'm sorry I got like that. You don't know what my life was like before I came here. It wasn't good. I was in care. Sometimes I lived on the streets. I never found anybody to like except the library man. He helped me. Not the social workers or the police or the doctors. Only the library man."

"What about your parents?"

"They hated me. They acted like they did. So I hated them. When I was sent back to them it only lasted days. They weren't parents. They weren't a mam and dad like other people had. They were useless."

"Why?"

"You don't want to know and I don't want to tell. It's over. I got here. It's where I am. It's not simple. It's beautiful."

She walked beside me. She tucked her arm into mine. I didn't like that. Too close. So I pretended that I wanted to look at a shop window on Garibaldi and broke away from her hold.

"I didn't mean anything bad Jess. I'm sorry I pushed you about where you came from. I love my family connection there. My nan. My mother and father are great. They have always loved and supported me."

"You were lucky."

"Anyway here we are. I'll see you again at Easter. Perhaps we can have coffee together again?"

"Perhaps," I answered.

I didn't know whether I wanted to see her again. Something inside of me didn't like the gap she opened up into my past. I walked into the Pieta and went into the choir stalls. I said hello to my choir friends. I watched her up on the scaffolding putting her paints away. She waved. I was glad she was going. This was my place and that was my angel. She could have Newcastle. It was hers if she wanted it. This was mine. Then I was singing and the gap closed up again.

Chapter 8

Jane Eyre

Pungent, cavillers, lamentable. I didn't understand the words.

Angelo walked backwards and forwards with his order book in his hand. "It's good Jess, yes?"

I tried not to let my frustration show. I told him that I was sure that it was a good book but some of the words were difficult for me. I hadn't even got past the first page. I felt bad.

The night before, Angelo had come back from his deliveries at one of the hotels. "English book for you Jess." He had handed me a paperback book. I sat at the little table with my book. I had two reading books on the table, my new book and my guide book and two notebooks, two pencils and one pen.

On the front of the book was a picture of a woman. She had on a grey dress which came down to her ankles and a green shawl over her shoulders. She was not a woman of my time. She was of a time past. She looked as though she had sadness in her.

Angelo put some wood on the stove and it crackled and spat. The light was poor in the cabin. There was no light outside to help. I struggled to read the words. Up and down the page my eyes went. I tried to make Angelo understand that I didn't understand the words. He stood for a while and then picked up his coat and told me that he would be back soon. I might have given up on that book if Angelo hadn't been so proud of his gift. I might have thought I was not clever enough for such a book. I might have just kept it on the table as a mark of respect and never known the story. But Angelo, being the man that he was, came back with an English dictionary.

"From Mr Andreotti at Franchetti. Very good customer," he said. He handed me the dictionary with the brown leather cover. The words inside were so small I had to move closer to the lamp. I looked for the words I couldn't understand. I couldn't even pronounce some of them. I found caviller. Petty objection it meant. Slowly I started to understand.

I turned to page two and then three. There was a word I did understand. Bully. The story was starting to make sense. I struggled on. I knew that little girl who took those awful blows, who got blamed for being who she was. She read her book for the same reason I sang. Then she got more blows for hiding with her book, like I used to when I sang to block out the pain.

Abuse. The word I had heard so many times. Now I couldn't stop reading. What did pungent mean? I couldn't stop to find out. I didn't know whether Angelo was there or not. I was inside the life of the little girl who was being treated badly. I wanted to turn the pages, hurry past the pain, but I slowly read every word. She fought back. She is blamed. She is punished. She is locked away.

The heat in the cabin was overpowering. My hands were sticky. I kept on turning the pages. Injustice after injustice on every page. She had been abandoned. There it was on the page. My word and the word of the little girls in the Pieta. Abandoned. We were all one. She felt bad feelings in her breast. How I knew those feelings. I couldn't take another blow. I closed the book. Poor Jane, poor little Jane Eyre.

"It's good?" said Angelo. I jumped at the sound of his voice. He was lying on the bed with his arms under his head. He had watched my frantic efforts moving backwards and forwards between pages, peering into the dictionary.

"It's very good. But it's very sad too." He knew nothing of my life, he knew nothing about Jane Eyre. He didn't know that the word abandoned had brought me here. By now my skin was brown with the sun and wind. I ate apples and oranges and grapes and peaches and peppers and tomatoes. My hair shone. My eyes were bright. I smiled. Sometimes I laughed. I didn't look like Jane Eyre. I didn't feel like Jane Eyre. But I knew her. She was my past and I wanted to run up the steps to the deck and throw the book into the water so that Angelo couldn't see what I never wanted him to know.

I piled my books into the corner; my guide, my dictionary and Jane Eyre. I placed my notebooks on top.

"I love my book," I said to him as I lay down. That was the only time I ever told Angelo a lie. I felt a bad pain in my chest.

I didn't throw Jane Eyre into the lagoon. Next day, when Angelo steered the barge around to the market, I got out of bed and picked her up again. I sat at our breakfast table and looked at the picture as I ate my muesli and drank coffee. The mornings were dark. Angelo would not let me help in the dark, I think he was frightened in case I hurt myself or slipped off the edge of the barge. Early in the mornings I often cleaned down in the cabin or sat watching the lights bobbing across the lagoon. On this morning I went back to our bed. I pulled the covers up and even though the light was very poor I started reading again. I didn't worry about the words I didn't know. I had got the thread of the story, so I kept reading slowly and turned page after page. When Angelo came down his face burst into a smile when he saw what I was doing.

"You love book, Jess?"

I gave him a kiss and smiled. I didn't love the book but I couldn't stop reading the book. Sometimes the words didn't make sense to me. The way they were put together. It wasn't the way I spoke and what did I know about books like this? It wasn't like my school books but they didn't count for much. It wasn't like the books the library man had given me to plan my trip.

I read on till my eyes were so strained I couldn't see the writing on the page any more. Then I went into our little shower and by the time I was finished, the daylight had come and I could go up on to the deck and start to help with the day's work. It was a cold morning and I wrapped myself up in the new fleece I had got from the market. I tied one of Angelo's big scarves around my neck and pulled a baseball cap onto my head. He thought it was too cold for me. I said it wasn't as cold as where I came from. I didn't tell him it wasn't as cold as the nights I spent in a freezing flat with just coats for bed clothes. Or when I didn't even have a freezing cold flat to protect me. I wasn't as cold as Jane Eyre in her school. The scarf was a luxury. I didn't have to fight for it or hide it. All I had to do was snuggle my nose into it.

For one whole week I went back to bed and read the book. The mornings got darker and my reading spells longer. I could have stayed there all day reading. Now I took the dictionary with me because I worked out that the language I knew was not enough to understand the book. Dark mornings meant more time to look up every word I didn't understand. I might not do it straight away. I just marked the page and went back. This way I was learning. Filling more space in my head.

One morning, after market time, Angelo came down the steps and into the cabin.

"Up Jess, we visit." It was very unlike Angelo to be bossy, so I thought it must be something important. The morning was well on. I pulled on the fleece over my jumper and wrapped the scarf around my neck. I had a wardrobe of clothes now. At the end of every week Angelo gave me some money for the work that I did. I could buy what I needed with that money. I only ever got what I needed. The rest I put in my ruck sack. There was always more than what I needed which meant that there was a little pile that could be called savings. Tee shirts and jeans had expanded into fleece, two jumpers, socks, boots, warm trousers, one blouse and three pretty cotton vests with low necks and lace around the edges. I kept them folded neatly in the cupboard and washed it all by hand in the little sink in the kitchen. I hung them on a line which straddled across the barge. I always had something clean to wear from the neat little pile in the cupboard.

I pulled on my boots and went up to the deck. The barge was moored near to the wooden bridge which went from one side of the grand canal to the other. There were always crowds on this bridge. We walked onto the jetty, up a little alleyway and came out in the big square where we had our first coffee together. Campo San Stefano. Since that coffee a lot had changed in my life. I was clean and wore warm boots. I was together with him. I had three books.

"Come Jess." We walked through some iron gates into a garden. In front of us was a very grand building. A palace. There was a lion in the garden. Not as grand as the one on the Riva. Or the ones at the gates to the park in Garibaldi.

"We say thank you to Signor Andreotti," said Angelo as he pushed open a glass door. He walked straight up to the man behind the desk and shook hands. I hung back. Inside this building was just like being at the steps at the station. When I couldn't believe what I saw. Angelo took hold of my hand and led me up the staircase. I was walking on shiny white marble stairs and there were carvings of figures in marble holding pens and strange instruments all the way up.

For me, there was nothing in this world more beautiful than the Pieta and there never would be. But I could tell this was another special building. Light was pouring down the wide marble steps from the windows at the top I climbed on, holding Angelo's hand. I knew he was used to being in palaces with his deliveries. But now, I was going to visit somebody in a palace. We walked past rooms with beautiful wallpaper and paintings on the walls and great curtains hanging for miles from the ceiling to the ground.

We stopped at a dark wooden door and Angelo knocked. We walked in and a little man with white hair jumped up from a chair and rushed over.

"Buon giorno, Giorgio." He turned to me. "Signora, welcome to Palazzo Franchetti." He held out his hand. I knew about this now. It was the custom. I held out my hand and shook his. I tried to smile.

"You are English, my friend?" he said. I nodded. Speechless. "Come sit down. Now where are you from?"

I said I was from Newcastle. It was such a stammer I don't know how he understood but he did.

"Ah, there is a very fine university there. I have visited it on occasion." He sat down again. "And tell me now, how is the dictionary?"

"Fine thank you very much. It was very kind of you," I answered trying to find the right words to say.

"Angelo says you are reading a book, may I enquire what it is?" Mr Andreotti's eyes fixed onto me.

"Jane Eyre," I replied.

"Ah, Jane Eyre. One of the finest of the English classics. This book is a wonderful book. It has been translated into many languages. There have been many films made of this book. How do you find it?"

"Well, actually, I think it is a bit sad."

"Oh very sad too, but she triumphs in the end."

Does she now? I looked around the room. There were rows and rows of books. Some in brown leather, some with a red cover, some were even gold. The desk where he sat was huge. It had a green velvet cover over half of it and there were papers scattered from one end to the other. Not like my little old wooden table with its three books and two notebooks neatly stacked at one end.

"Could I borrow the dictionary some more?" I asked.

Mr Andreotti looked at me. "Some more." He repeated my words. He stopped talking. Now he knows, I thought. I've said it wrong. He knows that I'm not clever. That I shouldn't have a dictionary.

What's a little rubbish like me doing with a dictionary? What's she doing reading a great book like Jane Eyre?

Then he smiled. A very nice smile. "Of course you can borrow the dictionary some more. You can keep the dictionary. I have many more. Look at all my books. Far too many. You can borrow another one if you like. I have a fine collection of English books. And now I must get on and pay Giorgio for the lovely vegetables he delivers to me. I liked especially the potatoes. They were English, I have a little soft spot for them I think you say in English. I hope to see you again."

He took out his wallet and handed over some notes to Angelo. They shook hands and then Mr Andreotti turned to me and shook my hand. We left the room and went back down the shiny marble stairs. I had now been up two palace staircases. The first one went round and round on the outside and now this one with carved ladies carrying books and musical instruments.

I sat on the deck of the barge staring at the building with its white balcony and long narrow windows with strange circles round the edges. Angelo handed me a leaflet that he had picked up from the desk in reception. It was in English. The Institute of Science, Arts and Letters, it said on the front. Whatever it was, whatever all that meant, that's the palace where my dictionary came from. My brown leather dictionary.

"Okay Jess?" said Angelo.

"Very okay. Thank you," I replied perched in my usual spot watching the other boats, looking at the palaces that we went past, one after the other, till we reached the lagoon and turned left for home.

But one thing troubled me. That night it troubled me a lot. I sat at the table pondering on my troubled mind. Angelo was playing his guitar. Sometimes he liked to play and sing alone because that was what he did before I came. I was writing in my notebook about the Franchetti Palace and Mr Andreotti's words. He said that she triumphs in the end. There was no triumph for me so far. The book is over one hundred and fifty years old. It has been made into a film. Millions of people have read the story. Tell me please, how is it a triumph that if so many people have read the story of Jane Eyre, that little girls still get abused, bullied and abandoned? How can that be?

I was glad that choir practice started again that night. It had been a long break after Christmas. Although I went to the Pieta nearly every day, just to say hello to the angel and touch base as they say, I was glad to be back singing, saying hello to all the choir people and ready to learn some new songs. Our choir master, usually very slow and sometimes a bit forgetful, was very excited. His hands were waving around and he kept kissing different members of the choir on their cheeks. I stood there waiting for him to translate to me what he was telling everybody else. He was always very good at doing this. Even though he lost his music sheets and forgot which piece we were going to do next, he always remembered to translate his instructions for me. I never knew what words to use back to him but I always understood the music. So after he told everybody what was happening, why he was excited, he turned to me and said that this year our church had been selected to sing the Easter concert. He said he had not decided on the programme yet, but was working his way through all his music to find something that would show what a wonderful choir we were.

We practised our pieces for that week and I moved away from the troubles of Jane Eyre. I opened myself right up when I was singing that night. I got that feeling again. That the women were all around me, singing in their fine frocks that were nothing like my jeans and hoody fleece. I felt I could sing all their parts. The choir master clapped and kissed me on both cheeks. "Bella Jess, good, good," he kept saying.

I smiled all the way back along the Riva. Bella, Jess. Good Jess. I wonder if you can imagine how deep into my body the smile went. Nearly to the scars. One day a smile would be so deep inside of me that the scars would be wiped out of my body and maybe I wouldn't remember any more. That's what I thought that night as I walked along the Riva, over the bridges, smiling. Smiling in the café where Angelo was waiting for me. Smiling, drinking my coffee that tasted especially good. I smiled as we walked back to the boat, and at the little kitchen table eating the squiggly pasta that Angelo had cooked. How good to smile. I wouldn't read Jane Eyre that night. Not when I was smiling so much. Not when I didn't want the scars to come above the smile.

Imagine how big the smile was on the next choir practice night. Mr Frandetti had chosen the music for the Easter concert and there were two solo parts. One went to Mario, who didn't speak very much but always sang louder than anybody in the whole choir and the second part went to me.

"You will sing with Mario at first," he said. "Then you will sing by yourself up behind the railings where nobody can see you and you will be like a hidden voice coming through the darkness when only candles light up the church."

Yes, the smile was big. But they didn't reach the scars. The scars came back to the front because I was full of fear. Yes, I was frightened of singing on my own, but bigger than that was the fear that it may not happen. That all the excitement would lead to nothing. I could always get myself to my choir practice and I could keep my day good because I didn't think about doing anything other than being with Angelo, helping with our life together. I didn't go looking for anything else. Things happened, like Mr Andreotti and the Franchetti Palace and the brown dictionary. But this, singing by myself in the Pieta. What if I got it wrong and it didn't happen? In the past I got it wrong and bad things happened. But that was then.

I looked up at the angel. Help me not to be frightened, I kept saying over and over again. Help me to do this, I asked all the invisible women in the Pieta. How frightened they must have been too. Help me.

Angelo hugged and kissed me when I told him what was to happen at the Easter concert. It took a lot of explaining. He lifted my body off the ground and swung me around right in the middle of Garibaldi. He told Guiseppe in the café who came round from behind the bar right in the middle of frothing up some milk and he shook my hand and said loads of things that I couldn't understand and poured some wine into glasses and held it up.

"Such a clever girl," he said in English. I think it was the only English he knew because I had never heard him say a whole sentence before. There were great celebrations in Guiseppe's that night and then Angelo took out his phone and said "Ciao Mama" and told her all about it. I was a singer in the Pieta. I smiled but my heart beat very fast in my chest. What if it didn't happen? Nobody here thought it wasn't going to happen. They were already celebrating it happening. Only I thought of the fear of good things to happen.

The days got brighter and I sang. The evenings were lighter and I sang.

In and out of the Pieta I went with my music sheet. Mr Frandetti praised me sometimes. Other times he would say, "No, no, no Jess. You are not trying hard enough. Up up, down down. Good. Better. Again. Once again."

I never ran. Not even when he said, "You are very bad girl for not listening to me now again."

I never ran from the Pieta when Mr Frandetti told me I was a bad girl. I knew he was trying to help me get it right. I knew that bad girl did not mean some kind of punishment. It meant just words and then next time it was good girl and I would try harder and it would be very good, very good Jess. Once he said, "Ah, that my dear child, is just perfect."

So I didn't have to run because after bad came good and after good came perfect and he clapped his hands and I could smile again.

One morning Angelo pulled out a bundle of money. He said I needed to buy some new clothes for the concert. He said that we wouldn't go to the market for the new clothes. We would go to the shops and buy something beautiful. Something beautiful. What did that mean? It was a new idea for me. Something beautiful. Something more beautiful than Angelo's scarf that I snuggled into.

We walked through the back streets, past Campo Sant' Anna, where the old woman who shouted all day, was out shouting. This time at her son. Her long black skirt was trailing on the ground. The black scarf tied around her head was wonky. She waved her stick in the air, her shrieks pierced my ears. When we walked past she stopped screaming. She looked at Angelo and then at me. Her stick came down on to the ground.

"Ciao Mama Monique," said Angelo. She stepped up to him and touched his face and said things I didn't understand very quickly, that's what happened with this Angelo who was going to buy me some beautiful clothes. People liked to see him. Even Mama Monique who screamed at everyone else. As soon as we had passed the screeching started again. The stick banged on the ground and Mama Monique's son rushed past us muttering.

We walked on round the back of the Arsenale. This was all new to me now. Walking on new bridges, past more palaces and down streets with washing hanging between the windows. On into the square called Campo Santi Giovanni and Paolo. I recognised this campo. It was where Angelo had brought the barge on the night of the big wave. We passed the flower seller who carried all his flowers on his back in a big basket. He was so small it was hard to imagine how he could carry all that on his back. Angelo said that he had done it all his life, since he was a little boy. He had a horn that he hooted as he went past the cafés and when he turned into the campos. We walked down the side of the canal. On and on for beautiful clothes. We arrived on a shopping street. Not a shopping street like Garibaldi. This street had windows with beautiful cakes balanced on glass plates and lots of clothes shops.

Look," said Angelo. I looked. Then I looked away. I looked up at him. Could I have these clothes? Were they for me? Smart clothes. Like in the windows on Northumberland Street. But I had never bought smart clothes before. Second hand tat. That was all I had till I met Angelo. Just tat that I needed to cover me up.

We stopped at a shop door. It was open.

"Ciao Maria," said Angelo to the person who stood inside the shop doorway. Angelo spoke quickly to her and then stood back.

"Come in Jess. Giorgio my cousin. Ah good. Let me see." She whisked me in to the back of the shop and pulled some dresses off the rails.

"Let us see Jess. Come." I didn't have time to think. Yellow, blue, green. On and off the dresses went. Long ones, short ones. In the end I chose my own.

The dress I chose was pink silk.

"All silk," said Maria.

It had a round neck, very plain. The skirt was straight and went as far as my knees. Around the waist was a dark pink band in layers. It pulled in neat at my waist. There was a pink scarf that matched the pink band. Maria wrapped it around my head and I thought that it would look daft, but it didn't.

"Beautiful, beautiful," Maria said. And then she went back into the shop and came back with a pair of pink sandals with a bow on that matched the scarf and the band of the dress. I put them on my feet. They felt perfect. Maria tweaked at the scarf and tugged at bits of my hair. Turned me round. Moved her hands down my body. I stood still. I didn't know what to do. I couldn't say a word. I don't think she would have listened to anything I said anyway. She turned me around again. She disappeared through the curtain. I didn't move. She swished back in through the curtains.

"Face up," she said. I obeyed. Out of a little blue make up bag came some lipstick which was brushed across my lips. Some beige stuff was put across my cheeks. Black lines were drawn around my eyes.

"Okay, you can look. Look." She put her arms on my shoulders and pushed me out of the little cubicle. She then spun me round to a mirror. I could only feel happy at the person who stood in the mirror. Jess who made a journey with a purpose. The purpose had happened and now what had happened from the journey was staring back at me from the mirror. The change of the journey.

Maria called Angelo back who had been standing outside in the street.

"Si Giorgio, she beautiful, look at her."

I was still looking in the mirror. Angelo put his arm around me. Me, all pink and silk. Then the outfit was wrapped up in creamy, fine tissue paper and we left the shop with lots of kissing from Maria.

I insisted on carrying my bags. Shiny with ribbon and big names across the front. We walked down to the palace called the House of Gold and that was just exactly the right place for me to get the vaporetta back to our home. I clutched my bags on the boat. Angelo stood talking to the boat driver and kept looking at me and waving. I held on tight to the handles of my bag as I climbed on to the barge. I went down into our room and opened the cupboard door. Maria had put a hanger into the bag. I hung my dress on the hanger. My beautiful dress. I wrapped the scarf around the top of the hanger. Then I looked at the shoes and then put them back into the box. I hung the dress inside the cupboard and put the shoe box underneath. I closed the doors. Then I opened them again and looked at my new clothes. Beautiful dress. Beautiful scarf. Beautiful. Nobody to rip it. Nobody to steal it. Nobody to make fun of it. I knew what I looked like in that dress. Beautiful.

The days passed. The sun shone from early morning now. The darkness had passed. I spent my time practising in the Pieta whenever I could. When the crowds weren't there. I sat on the boat and went over my music till I knew every word off by heart. I was going crazy with practising.

The other thing I did was look at my dress. Not only did I look at it but I would touch it. Feel it. It felt different to the scarf that I snuggled into on cold mornings. It felt like something you should always have in your life, something special. Something that should always be there to touch, to feel when you needed it. If I absolutely knew that my hands were spotlessly clean then I would cup the skirt of the dress in the palms of my hands and hold it to my face, like I was smelling it. But I wasn't. I was looking at the pictures. The dress made roses and rainbows and smiling angels holding out their arms inside of my head. I thought they were probably very childish pictures. Pictures that you should have in your head when you are a child. I didn't know. But now I knew the scent of beautiful and when you smell beautiful it makes pictures in your head.

When I touched Angelo I never felt frightened. Like a child clinging to the person who is there to look after them. When I had food on a plate it was mine to eat. In peace. I could walk and sing and eat and read Jane Eyre. I could take a peach, an apple or a pear. I could smile. That's what my beautiful dress told me when I cupped it in my hands and held it to my face. Childish things. Things that Jane Eyre and I could never do when we were children. We both had to wait.

Chapter 9

Solo Singing

Easter day arrived. My last practice had gone really well. I was confident. My dress was ready.

I spent a long time in the little shower room. The water was hot and I sprayed and sprayed, scrubbed and scrubbed some more. Then I put lovely sweet smelling oil all over my body. The little shower room was steamy. That made it smell gorgeous and all that gorgeousness steamed into me. Inside my steamy, gorgeous smelling body was a voice. That voice was going to give me more than what I ever thought I would have in my life. It was going to give me more than a dream. How could I ever have dreamt of this? It was going to give me more than pleasure, more than people clapping for me. That voice was going to give me a place with Mr Vivaldi's abandoned little girls. Singing behind the railings. Saved.

"Bella," said Angelo when I stepped into our kitchen with my pink dress on. I had made sure that the oil on my body was dry before I had lifted it over my head and smoothed it over me. The scarf was successfully wrapped around my short curls. The pink slippers glided onto my feet. I was satisfied.

"You beautiful Jess," said Angelo as he presented me with little pearl studs to go into my ears. I thanked him over and over again for giving me so much and kissed him ten times at least. All the joy in the world was in me in that moment. Nothing but joy. He took my hand and we walked along the Riva to the Pieta. I knew he was full of pride walking beside me. He looked strong as he guided me over the bridges. Smiling at everybody. When we got to the Pieta, he kissed me and left.

"I go for Mama," he said. I walked up the aisle feeling like a bride must feel as she walks to her love.

All my choir friends looked surprised when they saw me in my beautiful dress. You very pretty said a couple of them to me. Yes, I'm very pretty, I thought. But I'm more than that today. I imagined what the library man would have thought if he had seen me there in my dress with my voice ready. Would he know me? Did he ever think that the Jess who stood in that library, begging to know the way to the Pieta would be this Jess, standing singing in that very building for such a special performance?

The choir assembled. Everyone took their place in front of Mr Frandetti. The seats filled up. The aisles filled up. The Pieta was bursting with people. I looked out over the sea of faces and there he was. Angelo. Watching me.

Silence. Mr Frandetti raised the baton. The organ began. We began. Slowly sound filled every nook and cranny in the empty space between people and stone. First the baritones, then the basses. Next came the tenors. Then I joined in with the sopranos. Pages turned. The baton signalled. This was my cue. Silently I slipped away from the singing mass. Up the curling iron staircase. Through the little wooden door. Tip toeing along the narrow passage way. Fingers steady me as they grasp the iron railings. It seemed an age that I stood there. I didn't think of anything. I was waiting for my sign. Silence. The lights are dimmed except around the ceiling. Hundreds of candles flicker below me. I raised my eyes to the angel. The organ heralds my cue.

The angel raised her wings, the ghostly shrouds swirled in the dome. Pink, blue, golden, green. Weaving around the angelic guardian and holding out their arms. They were my example and they came to listen. I sang to them with all the gratitude that I could feel in my body. To them. And there tucked away behind the angel was Mr Vivaldi, the champion of people like me. Lost and hurting.

Gloria, gloria. The glory was all mine. I pledged it for every other little girl who hurt. Every Jane Eyre who walked on this earth. Glory to them and to me.

Chapter 10

Betrayed

It sounded like a great roar going right up into the beams. Clapping and shouting. I left my lone spot behind the railings and walked along the passageway and down the stairs. I took my place back in the choir. There was still a roar. Mr Frandetti smiled and winked at me as he swung the baton in front of the singing choir. It was over.

The clapping noise was overpowering. I jumped nervously as people on each side of me took my arm and guided me to the front of the choir and left me there alone. Mr Frandetti bowed to the audience and then he waved his hand towards me. So I bowed. I didn't know I was going to do this but somehow it just came naturally. Down I went and the clapping got louder and louder. Down I went again till I could see my beautiful pink shoes in front of my eyes. Then Mr Frandetti took my hand in his and waved his arm to the choir and I stepped back into my place.

The audience filed out of the church. I stood in my moment. Blushing, smiling, shaking hands. Taking kisses on each cheek.

"Perfect," said Mr Frandetti. "You were all perfect. And you Jess were magnificent. Magnificent." The rest of the choir paid me great compliments as well.

I wanted to say I wasn't alone up there behind the railings but they probably wouldn't understand. Besides they were all getting ready to leave. I didn't want to leave that moment. But I had to. Angelo was there in front of me. So proud of his Jess. His mama kissed me. He guided me down the church.

"Look who here Jess," he pointed his finger to the last pew. There she was. I had forgotten about her. The toucher up of angels. Jude.

"Hi," she shouted. "God you were fantastic. What a voice. It was amazing. Wasn't it lucky I was back here in time?"

"Yes," I answered clinging to Angelo's hand, who announced that we were all going to Guiseppe's to celebrate. Jude as well. I stepped out on to the Riva. I was the diva. Strangers looked at me. Angelo spoke to unknown voices congratulating me.

"Hooray," shouted Jude. Hands went up and down, saluting. We walked over the bridges, past the Arsenale, and turned into Garibaldi and stopped at Guiseppe's. The noise started again as the café heard of my triumph in the Pieta. I didn't understand a word. There were more kisses on the cheeks and a big pop as the champagne bottle was opened. A table was cleared and we all sat down. It wasn't long before Angelo was up again, talking, laughing, cheering, calling to someone else. So happy. That was all that mattered now. I'd had my moment. It had happened and now it was his moment. I didn't need any more. His mama smiled and drank her champagne and held up her glass to everyone who came into the café. I didn't like the champagne but I managed to take some sips. Jude spoke to Angelo's mama.

"Friend," said his mama to me. "She nice your friend." I nodded and sipped.

I didn't know about friends. I had angels and happy ghosts and Angelo. I didn't know what friends were about. I watched Jude go up to the bar and stand next to Angelo. He put his arm around her in his happy way. They talked. I could see him listening and listening more. And the more he listened the more she talked. Then he looked at me and I didn't like that look. It had something in it. I didn't know what.

More cheering, more champagne. I was on edge. Maybe it was just those sips of champagne. It smelt like something in my past.

It was. Angelo walked over to me. "Why you no tell me Jess?"

"What?"

"You mama and papa not kind."

I froze. I looked at Jude. She smiled and waved, talking away to Mercudio who drove the vaporetta. He laughed and patted her on the back.

"I'm just telling Mercudio about the angel. He thinks it's really funny." She shouted across the room.

I went over to her. "I don't think it's funny," I said.

Then she said "Oh don't go into that again Jess. Being like that."

"Being like what?" I said.

"Touchy," she said.

"What did you say to Angelo?" I asked.

"I just told him you'd had a really crap time, just what you told me, rubbish parents and living on the streets."

I stared at her. Just stood staring in my beautiful pink dress. My mind went crazy.

I ran. Out of the café in front of everybody. I ran down the canal side, into Sant' Anna and stood there in the little square. Nobody, not even Mama Monique was there. I stood there and I cried. Now he knew. All his pride would be gone. He would never look at me again with love. I could never cover my shame now that he knew. I would have to go. How could he want me now? Now that he knew.

I ran to the boat. The door was open and he was there. So was she.

"Why did you tell him?" I screamed. "Why did you bring that here? I never wanted it here."

"Jess, Jess," said Angelo. "Is okay. Tell me truth."

"Honestly Jess, he really doesn't mind. He knew something must have happened because you never talked about where you came from or your family."

"What the fuck has it got to do with you?" I screamed.

Angelo held his hands up. "Jess, I never see you like this before."

I ran downstairs. I had to get my dress off. I had to put it away. I had to hang it on the hanger. That I could save. But not myself. I couldn't stay. It was here now on my beautiful boat. That life. Not in a book. Not a secret. Right here. The words had been said to Angelo. The words were there on the boat, in the Garibaldi, out on the lagoon. Shame.

Chapter 11

Run Jess, Run

The bus stopped in Mestre. Where now? I walked down street after street not knowing which way to turn. Where could I go? There was nowhere. Did it matter?

Cars screeched, the air stank of petrol fumes. People walked quickly down the pavements and rushed across the roads taking no notice. I felt my heart breaking for a smile, the feel of the water underneath my feet and an angel above my head. Gone, gone, gone.

Eventually I walked into a bus station and looked at the headings on the tops of the buses. Destination anywhere. North, south, east, west. I couldn't care less. I would get on and then get off. Somewhere. I was running away. Not running to like when I left Newcastle. I didn't fiddle in my bag. Passport, money, map, ticket. If they were there or not I couldn't care. The bus said, Genoa. I climbed aboard. Paid for my ticket. Sat down at the front and went to Genoa. It was that simple. Easy. No looking, no seeing. No heat, no cold. No hunger, no thirst. Nothing.

Then I walked. I just took a road. It didn't matter. Any road. Because I didn't know where I was going the road was not important. Not running now, walking away. Into an unknown land. I walked all day down the road. I stopped at a café and bought biscuits, milk and cheese. I ate these without interest. It was just a necessity. I kept on walking until my legs wouldn't carry me any further. It was cold. I pulled a fleece out of my bag. I went into a field and lay under a tree behind a hedge where I couldn't be seen. I stared at the sky. No angels up there now. Only a few stars. I could feel the earth seeping damp and cold into my body. I put my head on my bag and closed my eyes. I didn't think about Angelo or the barge or the Pieta or the friend that I took into my life who then ruined it. I just thought, back to base Jess, this is where you belong. Not quite in the gutter but heading towards it. Where you were told you would always end up.

When morning came I stood up. My clothes were damp. The sun was starting to shine so I put on the dry ones I had in my bag. I hung the damp ones on the tree. I sat for a long time. I had slept a little bit. But mostly I had thought of all the bad things that had happened in my life and that took up a lot of time.

I wrote in my notebook. I wrote that I didn't know where I was or where I was going. I wrote that I was like Jane Eyre wandering around the countryside. Cold, wet and hungry. Betrayed when everything seemed so fine. Cast back into the past. All I could feel was the past. I couldn't think of the treasure in between.

I only had a few pages left in my notebook. Maybe it was enough. Soon, there might be nothing more to write about. I packed my bag and hung the fleece from the straps on the back so that it would dry. The sun was hot now and I started to walk again. I went back to the road and my legs started to move quickly. I ignored any hoots that sounded and cars that slowed down as though they were going to stop. I wanted to keep going on that road. But the cars kept hooting at me and one or two stopped and men looked at me as though they were expecting something. I knew the look off by heart. So I left the road and went up rocky banks and a steep hill and just kept walking over all this rough ground. There were animals around. Some I knew were cows and sheep but there were others that I didn't know. I still didn't know about country and fields. It went on and on into the distance and I kept walking into the distance. There was a stream running fast down the hillside. The water looked clean. I knelt down and washed my face. I took out my toothbrush and cleaned my teeth. I still had some biscuits and a piece of cheese. I ate. I took off my boots and put on sandals. The air and sun on my feet eased the aching tiredness of my body. My boots hung from my bag and jostled against my back as I went further and further up over the rocks, following tracks.

Another stream, another biscuit, another piece of cheese. I soaked my feet as I ate. I wrote more words in my book. Mostly about what I saw. I could see for miles and miles. Hills and mountains and little fields with animals at the bottom of where I was. There was not another person in sight. I had not seen anybody apart from in the cars for that whole day. And now as I walked I realised that it was getting dark again. I would have to find a new place to sleep. I found a little hut with no windows in. But it had a wooden roof on and some straw on the ground. By now I was thinking. That would stop me getting damp. But I didn't know that the higher you climbed the colder it got at night. I put everything in my bag over my body. It wasn't a lot and it did not keep out the cold. Bitter cold.

The sun came up again that day and warmed me through, but my biscuits ran out and my cheese was finished. I was on the last page of my notebook. I had to find a road again. I went down the hill on the faint narrow tracks. I pushed past high rocks onto steep drops. I turned back up the track to find another way down. This went on for a whole day until I finally found a road. But I was too tired to go on. I lay down in a wood. It wasn't cold but the damp was back again. I couldn't tell what state my body was in now after sleeping out all night for I didn't know how many nights. Or how much food I had eaten. I had drank from each stream I passed. Washed my face and body and cleaned my teeth. Took care of myself in some way. I dried my clothes in the sun. That was the most sensible thing I did in all of this. I rubbed my sore feet.

Next morning, when the sun was starting to make some heat, I made for the road I had seen the night before and walked along it. I came to a village. There was a little shop. I bought milk, biscuits, cheese, chocolate and most importantly, I found a notebook. I paid for all of these things and ignored the funny looks from the gathering of people talking in the shop. I understood a little of what they said. I knew then I was still in Italy. Not that it mattered. I took my tattered body out of the village and started to walk again. I found a place to sit down to eat the biscuits and cheese. It helped. But I knew I wasn't feeling too good. Usually, I never got sick. But there'd been too much cold. Too much damp. I sat down on the side of the road. I wanted to sleep. Then I wanted to fade away.

I don't know how long I was sitting there before this van screeched up beside me. I opened my eyes, held on to my bag, ready to run.

"Hya," said this woman's voice. "You all right? Can I give you a lift?"

I didn't know what the accent was. "Where are you going?" I managed to say.

"Yeah, I'm going to Spain. Right through France and into Spain. Does that help you. You don't look too good. You okay?"

"I'm going to Spain. Can I come with you?"

"Well you can honey. but it's a long old slog and I kind of sleep in this thing, but I suppose you could sleep in the cab. Won't be very comfortable."

"That's okay," I said. I took my bag off my back and opened the door and got in. It was that simple. I was going to Spain with god knows who, but what did it matter?

I tried to pretend I knew how to put the seat belt on when she told me to. It was a fiddle and eventually she leant over and clicked it into place. I felt shivery and my throat hurt but I sat up in the seat and tried to talk. I wanted to be friendly, polite. It was an effort.

She asked me where I'd come from. I said I was just travelling around. So was she apparently. She'd been to places like Rome and Florence to look at some pictures but she hadn't made it to Venice which she had really wanted to. She talked on and on. I watched the road. I was trying not to be sick. Then she asked me if I had my passport because we were going through a border check. I fiddled in my bag and found that. We stopped at a barrier and men in uniform stood at the window and inspected the passports. And when they waved, we drove on again.

"There now, we are in France," she said with a huge smile on her face. "Great place for food so we'll find a place to eat. Is that okay?"

I nodded. Did it matter? I didn't think so. It wasn't long before she pulled into a café on the side of the road. I thought that if I had hot food I might not get sick. I asked for soup. It was hot and spicy and full of tomatoes. The woman asked me if it was good.

"Very good," I said. But it made me remember. Lovely soup made with Angelo's vegetables. Chunks of bread and lots of parmesan. That took away the pleasure of eating it.

I asked her where she came from and she said originally, she was from America but she had kind of travelled around a lot and now she lived in Spain. She wanted coffee because she wanted to drive a bit longer and that would wake her up. So I had a coffee too. That made me remember as well. My little kitchen with the coffee pot on the old cooker. And the tiny table with the cloth on which I kept spotlessly clean. Two cups and a coffee pot. I forced the coffee down over my sore throat till I nearly choked. Choking from remembering or from my throat. I don't know.

I knew that she was starting to wonder who I was. I said I was going to meet a friend but I'd forgotten where till I looked at the map. She didn't ask again. She either thought there was something weird going on with me or she believed me. I hope she didn't think I was weird like I would do something awful.

When we stopped again it was on a camp site. It was dark. I lay across the seats of the van and pulled the blanket around me.

I slept till the woman opened the door and called out loud. "Hey sleepy head, time to get going." She talked like a movie star. I felt rough but my throat wasn't hurting any more and I was stronger. Strong enough to go on to wherever I was going. Now I had to think about where I was going, because eventually I was going to get somewhere and something would have to change. It wasn't long before she stopped again for breakfast. More coffee and bread. I needed it all. This time she paid for everything and said it was her treat.

Then she talked about paintings and living in America and Spain. She had a daughter who lived in Spain and she was excited about seeing her because she hadn't seen her for two whole weeks. She asked me if I missed my mom.

"Not really," I said. I didn't say two weeks wasn't even a second in not seeing my mother.

I think I must have fallen asleep again because next thing we were up in some mountains.

"Not long now," she said. I felt groggy and dirty. But she stopped the van up a mountain road and there was a stream. I took myself to the water with my bag and washed my face. I sat cross legged and cleaned my teeth then splashed my face again. The water was icy cold but it brought me round.

"You've done that before honey, I can tell. You're a natural." She watched my movements.

I didn't say that was how I lived my life now. There wasn't another one I could think of.

Another border control. I was in Spain. Italy, France, Spain. Well travelled.

The woman told me she was nearly at her destination. I said she could drop me off in the next town and I would find a café and send a message to my friends. I didn't really want to tell a lie, but I'm sure she was glad not to have the responsibility of me.

Before I got out of the cab she asked me if I was okay.

"Course I am," I lied again. "Thank you very much."

She told me that if I was her daughter she would have wanted someone to pick me up and make sure I was safe. I told her I had felt safe and thanked her again. I walked down the village street until I was out of the town. I took a track up a hill. I wasn't numb any more. I wasn't feeling nothing. I was feeling so lonely and so missing my Angelo and my angel and my Pieta. And feeling safe with them. But now I was so far away I would never be able to get back. Never.

I walked as far as I could, then I lay on the ground and decided that I couldn't get up again. I was hurting all over my body. I was thirsty. My eyes were sore. Did it matter? Not really. Not now I was feeling again. Feeling the silk dress on my face. Feeling the wind in my hair as Angelo took the barge out into the lagoon. Feeling the taste of peaches and oranges. Feeling the smile of Maria in the Pieta when I walked in through the door. Feeling so happy to be going to choir practice. All my feelings came back to me. I felt everything. I stood up and forced myself to walk on. I couldn't bear the feelings. The sun was up and I needed to go. Then I stopped feeling my lovely life. It was gone.

I lay sick on the ground. I groaned and cried for help. I couldn't move. Wet clothes sticking to my body. Helpless. Poor Jane Eyre. Poor little Jane Eyre. Abandoned. Abused. Punished. Shame. Shame on you Jess. To be abandoned, abused, punished. To feel the shame of Angelo knowing that you are not worth anything.

Poor little Jane Eyre.

Chapter 12

Sanctuary

My eyes opened. Have they been closed? Don't know. My eyes looked around. What's this? There's a circle of women all around me. I'm dreaming. My eyes closed. I felt heat and softness. Something soft lying over me. Soft and furry. It's still. Very still. My eyes opened. The women are silent.

"Poor little Jane Eyre," I say. I'm in a tent. A round tent. Light pours in through some windows in the top. My eyes scan the circle.

"Poor little Jane Eyre," I say again. Nobody moves. It's like being in a church only the walls are soft and the ceiling low and floppy. Sacred. Like music. A sacred tent. That was enough looking. I didn't want to look any more. Eyes closed back into the dream. Back into the pain of me and Jane Eyre. Too hungry. Better to sleep.

Next time my eyes opened, the circle is still there. One woman is standing up and waving her hands in front of her. Dancing. Smoke curled from her hands. There's a smell. A strong smell. Yes, pungent. Sage. I knew that smell well enough.

I wasn't bothered by this strange woman dancing around me. What did I care? The sage smell stuck in my nostrils. Pungent. My brown leather dictionary.

"Poor little Jane Eyre," I shouted. Silence in the circle. I shouted louder and louder. "Pungent, smell. Take it away." Eyes closed.

They opened again. There was a fire in the sacred tent. Little figures danced in the fire. Flickered and floated in the red embers. Angels. They looked like angels. Happy little angels. Dancing. I didn't wonder why I'm here in the circle watching angels in the fire. Whatever it was, it didn't matter. Of that much I was sure.

Next time I opened up my eyes it was dark. There were no more embers in the fire with dancing angels. In the corner of the sacred tent a figure bent over a book. A woman. She was reading by candlelight. Long hair flowed down the sides of her face. She had a blanket wrapped around her. "I need a pee," I said to her.

"Oh, sweetheart, you're awake." She stood up and put the blanket down. Gently she moved over to me.

"Can you stand?" She pulled back the soft furry thing and knelt in front of me. I moved my legs off a mattress I was lying on. There was nothing in me to make me move. My body shivered then froze. Was I dead?

I asked the woman. "Am I dead?"

"No sweetheart, not dead. But you are ill and you have been sleeping. Can you stand? I'll hold you."

She held me under my arms. "Easy does it. That's it. Forward with me. Good girl. Step by step. You're getting there." She pulled back a flap and we went out into the night. She held me and guided me into a tent toilet. I sat on a funny bowl. She held out some paper to me. She was taking great care that I didn't fall down. I didn't care that she saw me pee. After all this must be a dream.

Then she held me till I lay again on the mattress and she covered me with soft fur.

"What's your name honey?"

"Jane Eyre." I understood about Jane. I didn't understand about Jess. I thought Jess had died.

"Would you like a drink of water, Jane?"

"Yes," I answered and then she walked away. She came back with a cup and held it to my lips. Water dripped down my chin. I put my hand up and wiped it away.

"More," I said. She held the cup up again. I drank. Then I waved my hand and she took the cup away. I lay my head back down again. My hand stroked the furry soft thing covering my body. My name is Jane Eyre. Poor little Jane Eyre. I drifted away.

Next time I woke the circle was back again.

"Who are you?" I said.

Then one of them said, "My name is Virginia. And who are you?"

"Jane Eyre." That's what I said every time they asked. They asked more than once. Like they didn't believe me. I didn't care. It didn't matter. Why didn't it matter? I tried to remember why it didn't matter. Because Jess had gone. The only good bit of Jess wasn't there any more so I didn't want Jess. Jane Eyre triumphed in the end. Why did I think that? I struggled to remember. Somebody told me. So I would be Jane. Then I will triumph.

One of them sat beside me with a bowl of rice in her hand. "Can you try to eat?" I could. I did. It was sweet. Sweet with honey. It slid down my throat. Honey is good for you. Who said that? Enough. I waved the spoon away. Now I must go. On with my journey. Where? I couldn't remember. I tried to stand.

"Sweetheart you must rest some more." A voice gently spoke.

I lay down again. Then there was sound. Singing. They were singing. I am Jess again. Singing in the Pieta. That's where Jess is. She hasn't died. She's in the Pieta singing. I sit up. And I open my mouth and try to sing. But I didn't have the strength.

"Shut up," I said. But they didn't. The song went on and on. Till I lay back again and listened. I didn't have to sing. I could listen instead. I knew the song. I always knew the song. The songs were always in me.

Then I knew the women. I'd got it. Mr Vivaldi must be here too. We were all together. Singing. The circle of women disappeared behind iron railings and rapturous sound filled my ears. "Where is Mr Vivaldi?"

The singing stopped. "Mr Vivaldi?" One of the women said.

"He must be here. Abandoned, punished. Poor little Jane Eyre. Mr Vivaldi knew all about that."

They didn't understand. So they weren't Mr Vivaldi's women. I decided to sleep again. Each time I woke somebody gave me water and food. I went back to the tent toilet sometimes.

I don't know how many days and nights passed before I felt as though there was some life in my body. And in my mind. I started to take notice. There was always somebody in the sacred tent. Reading or just sitting watching. One day a woman sat down wrapped in a blanket. She had long hair hanging over her shoulder. She held a violin up to her shoulder. I recognised the first notes. I knew the words. Gloria, gloria. She played on. I hummed till I couldn't hold my head up any longer. It fell back down onto the pillow and then I remembered.

"Stop," I screamed. "Stop. Stop. Stop." Over and over again the word came out of my mouth. Stop. I couldn't make sense of it all. "Poor little Jane Eyre."

I got up onto my feet without any help. The circle was back and one of the women wrapped a blanket around me and led me in to the circle.

"Would you like to sit with us?" I nodded. I sat in a space between two of the women.

I looked around the circle. Each woman looked a lot older than me. Some had really grey hair and lines on their faces. They all wore different clothes. The one next to me had a long skirt on. She wore a loose blouse. Her grey hair was tied up in a bow on the top of her head. Out of a face full of lines and wrinkles were eyes that were the brightest I have ever seen. The woman stared at me. In a nice way. She didn't smile. She sat cross legged on the floor and was very still. I didn't remember that she had given me any water or food. Or taken me to the tent toilet.

"My name is Freya," she said. So what I thought.

The one that said her name was Virginia, who was really thin and had long blonde hair that came down over her shoulders, wore jeans and a tee shirt that was low at the neck and the lines from her forehead went right down over her neck to where her tee shirt started. Her skin was like the brown leather cover on my dictionary.

Another one wore spotty trousers. Real baggy things. She had on a tee shirt with thin straps and I didn't think she had a bra on. She wore a very thin scarf around her hair with a bow at the front. It was spotty like her trousers. Her eyes were covered with thick black lines. I'd never seen so much stuff around anybody's eyes. She also had red stuff on her cheeks.

"I'm Willa," she said. So what, I thought.

The one next to her was younger than the others. She wore a floppy hat. Her hair came to just below her ears. It was curly. She had freckles all over her face and down to her throat. She wore a frock which came half way down her legs. Her feet were bare. When her mouth, which had huge lips, smiled it made all the freckles run into each other and her eyes wrinkled so much they looked like laughing eyes. She waved her hand.

"And I'm Alice," she said. Again I thought, so what. I didn't wave back.

There was one who wore a scarf around her head so you couldn't see her hair. But it didn't matter. She was beautiful. She looked like somebody from a magazine. Big eyes, little nose. All perfect. And she had a sun tan and one or two lines round her eyes. She wore a white dress that flowed straight down to her ankles and red sandals on her feet.

She smiled at me. "I'm called Cora," she said. So what. I couldn't care.

Then there was one really serious one with black glasses on. She wore a long scarf wrapped around her ears and the sides of her hair. Short spiky bits of hair stuck out the top. She wore baggy trousers and a long cotton top. She didn't look at me.

"Charlotte," she said quietly. So what Charlotte, I thought.

There was another one who had given me water and tried to talk to me. She sat on a chair and had a walking stick across her knee. She wore crazy colours all over, pinks, oranges, yellows. She had a red scarf tied around her head but it didn't hold in all the bits of hair that stuck out on either side.

"I'm Kate dear, and I'm glad you are getting better." She smiled at me.

I thought am I mad or are they? Were they from the circus? Had I lost it?

"What am I doing here?" I didn't say this to any one of them in particular. I wouldn't know which one to say it to. They were all staring at me. You could have heard a pin drop in that sacred tent.

"Where am I then? Why won't you talk to me?"

Not a word. They were mad. All of them. This was starting to get spooky. Had I been captured or something? Were they some kind of crazy old women's gang? Bandits. Was I a hostage? Little in it for them if I was. Nothing in fact. Should I tell them?

"You'll get no money for me I can tell you that now." Still nothing.

Then after a while someone spoke. "How do you feel now, Jane?"

I frowned. Stared. "I'm Jess. My name's Jess. I'm not Jane."

"Oh I am sorry Jess. Just you told us your name was Jane."

"I never did." Why would I tell them that my name was Jane?

The woman who was talking sat back into the silent circle. Staring.

Then I lost it. "I don't know why I am sitting here. Will nobody tell me? My name is Jess and I think I might have gone a bit mad but looking at all of you, I'm not the only one."

"Actually sweetheart, I think we might just have saved your life," said the serious one with the black glasses.

"We found you up on the mountain. You'd fainted." said the one with the walking stick. "We brought you here. You were exhausted and delirious. You have been very ill. But now you seem to be on the mend. You were lucky. It's very cold up the mountain at night. You could have died."

"Well that wouldn't have mattered," my reply was short and rude.

"Maybe not," said the serious one. "But we didn't know that did we? So we brought you here and nursed you and here you are. We probably need to talk about what happens next. Were you going somewhere? Can we ring somebody for you?"

"Don't know. No and no," I looked down at my feet. I felt the old stuff crashing in. Being got at. Doctors, nurses, social workers, teachers, foster parents, judges, policemen, care workers. Trying to sort me out. Like it was me that needed sorting out and not the shit life that I was born into. Shame on you Jess. Back to square one. Being got at. This time by a bunch of mad old women with crazy clothes sitting round in a circle. So what if they saved my life? What was there to save? I suppose they didn't know that it wasn't worth saving. I hope they didn't feel good about it.

Then the really old one who said her name was Freya spoke. "I think it is time to stop talking for now. We will leave you in peace." Then she bowed her head. They all got up and left. I watched them leave. They didn't look at me. I knew why that was. Because they saw me as I was and had been. Hopeless. Worthless.

This was the first time I had been left completely on my own. I searched for my bag. I saw it on the floor beside the mattress that I slept on. I reached over for it. Unzipped it. Put my hand into the bottom. My fingers grabbed hold of my notebook. I pulled it out, held it to my chest. A leaflet fell out. Institution Provinciale Per L'infanzia Santa Maria della Pieta Venezia, it said on the front. My place. My Angel. My Angelo. All gone. That's all I wrote. Gone.

I lay down. It felt weird in this tent thing without anybody else here. I wasn't ill any more. I was thinking again. My head was clear. I didn't know where I was, who I was with, how I had got here. I tried to check back to my last point of remembering. A stream. A climb. Hunger. Tired, totally tired. That's the last thing I remembered.

I didn't remember being ill. I didn't remember being brought here. Now what did I do? I stood up and walked out of the tent into bright sunlight. For the first time I looked around beyond the toilet tent. This wasn't the only big round tent. There was a whole circle of tents. They all had chimneys in the centre of the roofs. Flowers grew everywhere. There was a strong smell of herbs; mint, sage, basil. I could see them growing all around. I walked towards the toilet tent. I decided to go in there because I didn't know what else to do. When I came out, one of the women was coming out of one of the big tents. "We will be having supper in about an hour. I think you should eat with us tonight. How do you feel about that?"

"Okay," I answered.

She pointed her finger. "We eat over there. Behind that yurt with the flowers painted on it."

I nodded. I wanted to get back to my mattress and my notebook. I pulled the curtain back and went into the circle tent. I was better in there. I wasn't ready for the light. It hurt my eyes but it also reminded me that you lived life in the light and I didn't particularly want much of that. I sat on the mattress and covered my eyes. Pictures came. Pictures I didn't want. I pushed my fists into my eyes to try and make them go away. One stayed. The angel. She got bigger and bigger till she was a huge painting filling the whole of my head. "Angel," I cried, "please come. Please."

I don't know how long I lay there looking at the angel in my head and asking, begging for her to come to me. She didn't come, but one of the women did. Asking me if I was ready to join them for supper. I wasn't, but I was hungry and so I stood up and followed her out of the tent. The light hurt my eyes and I didn't want to leave my own space but seeing as I wasn't dead I had to do something. Deep down I felt as though I should be grateful for what these funny women had done for me, so I would eat and that meant following the woman. My legs were weak, they couldn't carry me anywhere away from here. I wouldn't know where to go and I couldn't remember where I thought I was going when I collapsed, or whatever it was that happened to me.

Behind the tent in front of me was a large grassy area with lots of trees around. A great big table was in the middle and there were chairs all around it. There sat the women. Talking and lifting up dishes and passing them around. I found it really hard to take the last few steps to the empty chair and sit down. I felt clumsy and dirty. Unwashed. They looked so fresh these women with their funny hairstyles and bright laughing faces full of lines.

"Welcome to the table Jess," one of them said. I sat down not knowing what to say.

"I sing in the Pieta in Venice. Do you know about the Pieta?" I asked them. They didn't. So I thought, well they don't know anything so why should I be bothered. They probably didn't believe me anyway. But they gave me lovely food. Vegetables and fruit that reminded me of my boat kitchen. I could only eat a little bit but it tasted good. I put my knife and fork down. Then surprise. It turned out they did believe me. Because they asked me to sing. So I was sorry that I had boasted about my singing.

I didn't know if I could sing and I didn't know what to sing. I looked around. I decided that they were all Abba age so I would sing an Abba song.

The one Mr Frandetti used to tell me was a perfect song for me when I didn't have to be a diva. I croaked a bit but once I got going I could hit the notes.

That shut them up. I gave it everything that I could considering I'd been so sick. Only trouble was that I wasn't being clever because I cried at the end. I'd sung for my life. And it made me want to live again. I sat down. The women clapped. There were looks of surprise on all their faces, except for the really old one who was called Freya.

She didn't clap. Or smile. I looked at her eyes.

"My child, I am so sorry," she said and then continued to eat her meal.

Somebody passed me a dish with some cake on. I struggled to eat it. The tears rolled down my cheeks. It didn't make sense now, running away like that. Away from Angelo. He would have understood. He never would now. The cake stuck in my throat. I never wanted to sing again if it brought all that back. If I couldn't sing in the Pieta, I didn't want to sing anywhere. What did she mean she was sorry? She didn't look at me again.

The women started to gather up the plates and dishes. They chatted away to each other. I didn't know what to do. I sat for a while watching all the clearing up. Then I stood up and thanked them. I walked back to the circle tent and crawled onto the mattress and pushed my face into the pillow.

Chapter 13

Learning About Love and Other Things

I kept up old Jess for quite a long time. Not very nice Jess. Jess believing that nothing is going to work so why bother. I didn't even try to make friends. I was grateful and thankful that I had a bed and food but every bit of my body was waiting for that moment. The one that would happen because it always did. That I had to go. That I didn't fit in. That they needed my bed for someone else. That my attitude didn't suit. I didn't blame them. They were trying to be nice and I wasn't.

    I sat at the big table and ate with them. I stood under the shower in the washing tent. I washed my clothes and hung them on the line. I changed the sheets on the bed when they asked me to. I slept a lot. Sleeping was a way of hiding. I don't know why they put up with me.

Time went on and they didn't ask me to leave. Every morning they arrived into the tent where I slept and sat in a circle. They would quietly talk about who would clean the kitchen and the toilet. Who would be cooking the food, who would be washing the dishes and who would go to the shops. It was all very civilised. More than that. It was gentle talk. Nobody spoke when somebody else was speaking. Eventually I spoke. I said I would clear the dinner table at night and wash the dishes.

"Would you be happy doing that Jess?" said Kate, the one who needed a walking stick and who seemed to do most of the cooking and spend a lot of time in the kitchen tent.

"It's okay," I answered. Happy didn't come into it, but I wanted somehow to show that I was grateful.

Freya nodded. Freya nodded a lot. When people finished speaking Freya nodded. Sometimes if somebody was talking for a long time, Freya nodded whilst they were speaking.

Watching with her deep, looking eyes. She rarely spoke. I think she listened the way she looked. Deeply. She had never said anything to me again since she had told me she was sorry. I still wondered what she was sorry about, but she wasn't the sort of person you could ask.

Now that I had offered to do something I felt better. Truthfully, I had nothing else to do and nowhere else to go. So why not hang around here for a while? More truthfully, I would get a terrible panic feeling in me if I thought they were going to ask me to leave. I was rude and uncooperative, resentful even, but that was because I was frightened. Fright made me behave like that. I didn't have a goal any more. I didn't belong to the Pieta. I didn't have an old wooden table, a cupboard with a beautiful dress, an angel to take me out into the lagoon on an old barge. But I'd had it. There was too much old stuff up there in front of me that didn't look nice when I didn't have the Pieta and the barge and my Angelo. Old Jess, new Jess, now Jess. I didn't know who to be. I was all muddled in my head. I couldn't be new Jess because new Jess things had gone. It was easy to be old Jess, angry and on the defensive. If I was new Jess there would be hurt. But nobody seemed to want to hurt me here and nobody accused me of anything or asked me any questions except about eating and washing.

I knew that Freya had been watching me. She didn't join in the general chit chat around the table. She ate very slowly. She had long earrings that were made with very fine feathers that came right down to her shoulders. The feathers were held together by swirls of silver. They were beautiful. Just perfect. I watched her back. Not because I was paranoid about her watching me, but because I felt pulled into her deep gaze. I didn't feel it was bad, her watching. One night, when I was standing at the sink washing the dishes, a hand touched my shoulder. Old Jess would have clenched up. Jaw, hands, shoulders tightening. Anything that gave off a message. New Jess would have smiled. This Jess, who didn't know who she was, standing washing dishes, felt a tingle go right through her body. The routine clenching gave way to submission. My shoulders dropped, my hands fell open and I turned to look into Freya's eyes.

She took my hand into hers. "Child, would you like to come and sit with me for a while?" And that's exactly what I did. I sat with her. Not a word did she say. She sat on the floor with her legs crossed and I sat next to her. She closed her eyes and hummed. I didn't think about anything bad when I sat there with her. I didn't think there would be hurt or pain. I didn't think she was going to ask me to leave. I think she saw into me and saw all those mixed up things that were inside me. And when she told me I could go, I did. I walked away with a quietness in me that was new. That night in bed a little bell rang inside my head. I could go on. I could survive. There might be more in life for me.

The little bell was still ringing the next day. I sat at the table outside and ate bread and honey for breakfast, saying nothing as usual. I did a little washing of clothes and tidied up the space that was my bed. Then instead of sitting waiting for the circle to arrive, I went outside and started to wander around the tents. On each tent there was a sign with a name on. I stopped at the tent with the name Virginia written in big black letters above the opening. I stood outside looking at the letters. When the flap opened, I jumped back quickly and felt my face go red. Virginia looked surprised too. She pushed back her long blonde hair and her brown leather face broke into a smile.

"I'm off to the garden, would you like to come?" She was already moving off as she spoke so I turned and followed without replying. She walked quickly. Past the tents and the outside eating place. Through the trees and up to a wooden gate. I'd never been past the table. She opened the gate and beckoned me in.

I loved it at once. There were bright yellow marigolds everywhere. Herbs, lettuces, cornflowers and so many things I didn't know the names of. One big heap of lovely things all growing together.

"This is my potager garden," said Virginia.

"A what?" I said. I'd never heard the word. But then I didn't know about gardens so how could I know the word.

"Potager," she said slowly. "In other words, I grow what I like where I like and it works. Six different types of lettuce over there. Tomatoes in that corner. Courgettes in the frame over there. Peppers in that frame. Aubergines in the greenhouse. Dill, mint, thyme, basil, etc etc etc." Her finger pointed this way and that as we walked down a little path with slates on that kept disappearing under flowers and lettuces.

"I know it looks as though it's all out of control. But it's not. I know exactly what's what. I need some lettuce for lunch and some tomatoes. And some of that rocket. What about some fennel? Oh, better get some garlic."

She pulled out a big handful of lettuce and passed it back to me. "Hold onto that a minute please."

I bunched the lettuce into my hands. I held it up to my face. "Angelo," I said. I couldn't help it.

"Pardon Jess?" she said.

"Lollo Rossi," I said.

Virginia nodded. "Do you like it?"

"I love it," I answered. Loved it because it reminded me of my lovely Angelo. I didn't try to push the smell away. Or the image of him. His face, his arms, his hands holding out a bunch of green and red lettuce.

"Okay, that's it. Let's take them to the kitchen." I followed her out of the potager garden. Closed the gate behind me. Held on to the lettuce. The lettuce in my hand turned into memories of apples and oranges, bananas, boxes, a boat, a church and a choir. I sank to the ground with the memory.

"Oh dear, what have I done? What's happened now?" Virginia sat down on the ground beside me. "Have I said something?"

"I remember. That's all," I said.

"Do you Jess? You see we don't know. And we don't know because you don't tell us. What do you remember?" She touched my arm.

"New Jess. Jess who smiles. Singing. Safe. Silk. New shoes. So pretty," I pushed the lettuce back into my face. "Angelo".

"Who is Angelo Jess?" Virginia put her arm around me. "Can you tell me?"

I pulled away. "Nobody. He's nobody. I must get back." I pushed myself up with my free hand. I dropped the lettuce out of the other.

"Sorry, Sorry," I said. I took off past the trees and the dinner table. I ran back to my bed. I bowed my head. Shame again. Bad Jess. Not a nice Jess. Virginia was nice, I wasn't. I crawled into my bed. All was lost again. I heard somebody come in and whisper that there was some food and water there for me. But I didn't look to see who it was. I didn't even say thank you. Poor little Jane Eyre was all I said My mind blurred and raced till I could hardly bear it. When it was dark, I put my legs over the bed. I drank some water and ate the bread and cheese from the tray. I was back on a lonely hillside. Not caring where I was. Keeping alive with water and biscuits and cheese. I was on a boat with angels and love. Dark, horrible figures loomed in front of me. I pushed them away with my hands. But they kept coming threatening with their cruel faces. Jess, Jane, Jess Jane. Who was who? Who triumphs? I couldn't cry out. Nothing came out of my mouth. I sank back into bed exhausted. Please sleep. Sleep please. Sorry. I am sorry Angelo. The muddle went on until I did fall asleep and the muddle in my head turned into dreams.

When I woke Virginia was sitting in the chair close to my bed. She was reading a book. Just like when I first came. Watching over me.

"Can I go to the potager garden?" I asked.

Virginia looked at me. She came over to my bed and held out her hand. I shook my head. I didn't want to touch. I followed her out of the tent to the little gate leading into the garden. I picked a marigold. I held it out to her.

"I can't touch. Only Angelo."

"Of course," she answered. I sat on the path. Breathing in the soft smell of Jess on a boat. Basil. Breathe. Thyme. Breathe. Sage. Breathe.

Virginia took a book out of a bag she was carrying over her shoulder. It was a soft bag of pink velvet with flowers painted on the front. The book had the same flower painted on the cover. White with a yellow middle.

"My writing book," she said She opened the cover and flicked through the pages till she found a blank one. Her pencil started to move on the page.

"I write," she said.

"So do I," I said.

"Good," she answered. Her hand reached out and pulled the top off a little green plant and held it out to me. "Here," she said, "chamomile. It calms. Breathe it." I did.

We sat for a long time, she writing, me breathing. Should I say something to her about me? What would she want to know? When I told somebody about me last time it didn't work.

"Would you like some paper to write on?" Virginia lifted her head and looked at me.

I nodded. She reached into her soft, pink bag and brought out some blank pages of paper and a pencil. She smiled as she handed over the pages to me.

I sat with the pages on my knee. I didn't know what to write. I held the chamomile to my nose. I took a great, big breath and then I started to write.

"My name is Jess. I lived in Venice on a boat. With Angelo. I sang a solo in the Pieta. I sang in the Pieta choir. Just like Mr Vivaldi's abandoned little girls. Before that I lived in Newcastle. I was an abandoned little girl. Just like Jane Eyre."

Virginia looked up from her writing book and smiled at me again. She was always smiling. I handed over the sheet of paper to her.

She read my words. Then she passed the sheet back to me. No questions, no look of surprise. She turned a page in her notebook and started writing again. I watched a butterfly balance itself on a sage leaf. It was blue, pale blue, with black circles on its wings.

Virginia passed her notebook to me. *"My name is Virginia. I live here in Spain. I live with lots of other women and we all support each other. I write books. I used to live in London. I left because lots of things in my life made me unhappy. All the women here came because of some unhappiness in their life. One way and another. We built our community together although Cora was the first one to come."*

I looked at the butterfly again. Hovering. I started to write again. *"I loved my life on the boat. Something happened. Thank you for saving me."*

I watched her read the words. She picked up her pencil. Then she looked at the butterfly as well.

"I am sorry that something happened. Perhaps one day you can talk about it. I found it hard at first to talk about my problems and why I was unhappy. It helped a lot to talk. The butterfly is a symbol of transformation. It can happen. Believe me."

She passed the book back. I read her words. I looked at the butterfly. It's little wings fluttered as it moved to another plant. I think transformation means change. Change confused me. What could I change into? I thought I had. And then I hadn't.

"Can I stay here? Just for a little while. I have nowhere to go." I passed the paper back.

Virginia thought for a while. Then she spoke.

"I can't say yes. We decide everything together. I shall ask. But don't worry, everything is fine for now. Shall we pick some food for lunch?"

I wrote two more words on my page. "Thank you."

Next morning Virginia spoke at the breakfast table. "Jess asked me if she could stay here for a little while. I said that I would consult you all about it."

Freya nodded. There was a huge silence. Nobody spoke. Freya continued to nod. I felt sick in my stomach. What if they said no? Where would I go?

Freya spoke. "What can you bring to us Jess?"

What could I bring? Nothing. That was it. I would have to go. I stood up. "Nothing, I have nothing."

Freya nodded. "Please sit Jess. I asked what you could bring not what you have."

I did what she said and sat down again. I was dumbfounded. The word nothing kept going through my mind. I have nothing. I am nothing. A little nothing as a little girl. A big nothing now. Nothing. Then I felt a little nudge. Where did it come from. I looked around. Nothing there. But the words were.

"My voice." That was something. Not nothing. "And I can sort out vegetables and I can wash dishes and I can help Virginia in the garden if she'd let me." I was on a roll. "I can learn to do new things. There's lots of space in my head."

"So you could help in the garden?" For once Freya wasn't nodding.

"I could try. I'd like to learn about potaging," I said and watched to see what sort of reaction there was at the table. Freya nodded. There was general nodding all round. Eventually Virginia said she'd like me as a potaging assistant because she thought I understood what was going on in the potager garden. Freya continued to nod and then spoke to me.

"I think you could stay Jess. Till you figure things out. Maybe you can join in some of our ceremonies. We will be having a sweat lodge soon.

"Thank you." I didn't want to say that I didn't know what a sweat lodge was. But then I never knew what a yurt was or what a butterfly meant till I came here. It sounded like a good thing, like the yurt and like the butterfly.

Every day I washed dishes and then I followed Virginia to the potager garden and did exactly as she said. Not that she was bossy or anything. She was kind. And very gentle. My heart still broke with what had happened and sometimes feeling angry made me rude and unpleasant but the women seemed to know what that was all about. I often sat with them when they talked with each other. Discussing books, a trip to the shops, a letter or a piece of music. They were always comfortable with themselves and with each other. They didn't care too much what they looked like. Old fashioned, I would say with funny dresses on or over the top jewellery. They often wore hats or scarves around their heads. They hugged and gave each other kisses on the cheek. I didn't let that happen. I always sat a little bit away in case anybody thought it was okay to hug me. It wasn't. It made me clench if I thought it would happen. Tighten up. I know that somewhere in my mind I remembered why. But I didn't want to remember. Not now when I had found something to live for. Their chat. Their crazy clothes. The way they would stand up and do some mad dance to an old bit of rock and roll. A nice dinner together and lovely vegetables from the garden,

Each day had a rhythm. That's what Virginia said. A rhythm to the day was a good thing. She lent me a dictionary so I could look up what rhythm meant. I wrote it in my book along with my words from the Pieta. First came pilgrim, then homage, after that came transformation, then rhythm.

Sometimes at night I would sing. This was my bringing. They would join in and drum on the table or bang spoons together. They hummed and whistled and clapped and banged and taught me new songs from shows and old movies. It didn't make me feel happy. But it did make me feel wanted and a bit like I was giving these kind women something back.

I had walked the boundaries of the yurt village but I had never gone beyond them. There was a fence made of tightly woven willow all the way around the boundaries. The strips of willow were not even, they curved and swirled in pretty shapes. Sometimes they circled round a carved pole painted with brightly coloured faces and animal images like wolves and deer. Totem poles, Virginia called them. Alice made them, she said. On the ground were little figures made out of brown clay. They were dotted around the fence. Figures with funny heads and boobs hanging to the ground. They weren't pretty like the fence or colourful like the totem poles. They were quite scary.

"We make them," said Virginia. She told me that I could make one if I wanted. I wasn't sure about that. I couldn't see why I would want to make one of those funny things. Virginia said it was therapeutic. I asked her what therapeutic meant.

"Healing," she said. "It's good for healing."

I didn't understand healing and therapeutic. Virginia explained that we carried our wounds around with us and therapeutic meant helping those old wounds to get better. That made sense to me at last. Wounds. Not just my body which had been wounded horribly as a little girl. Wounds in my head. I knew they were there deep and unforgiving. I knew the wounds made me angry and rude. I knew the wounds made me want to run. Like I'd always done.

"Right," I said to Virginia. "I understand wounds."

I liked the fence. I liked to walk around it looking at the shapes of the weaving willow and the totem poles. To stare at the lines of the animals. Ears and tails stuck out. Red bodies and yellow paws. Dolphins circled the poles. With great eyes and sharp fins. My favourite pole had a great climbing bear carved into the wood. His strong body stood ready with paws forward from his chest, claws pointing downward. I would sit underneath this totem pole and pretend the bear was looking out for me.

"They are like guardians," said Virginia. I told her my guardians were the angels.

"Tell me about them," she said. So I told her about the first angel. The Angel of the North. "It has great big wings and stands over the city of Newcastle. If it had been built earlier it might have guarded over me there. But it wasn't. And I wasn't guarded." She didn't say anything.

"And then there was an angel on the ceiling of the Pieta. She used to flap her wings when I was singing."

Virginia didn't look at me as though I was saying daft things. She just smiled.

"Perhaps you need to make your own angel," she said. "Alice might help. Let's go and see her."

Virginia put down her writing book and walked to the garden gate.

I followed her to Alice's yurt. Virginia shouted at the door. Alice opened up the flap. "Come in," she said. "Welcome Jess." She opened the flap wider and stood back to allow enough space for us to walk in.

The first thing I noticed was a big bed with poles on every corner. The poles went right to the top of the canvas roof and were painted white. Every pole was carved with circles all joined together with squiggly hollow lines. The circles had little dots in the middle. On the other side of the yurt there was a large table with lots of tools on. An iron stove with a chimney going into the roof stood in the middle of the space. Silk scarves hung from wooden poles, pink, blue and purple. They floated into each other. A desk was in one corner. It was covered with papers and books. I felt a softness in this space. And I then I thought that this was an intelligent space. This is what intelligent looks like. Like Mr Andreotti's room in the Franchetti Palace.

Alice asked me to sit on one of the wooden chairs near the table. "This is my home and my workshop."

"It's a palace," I said. "Alice in her palace." What a thing to say. I don't know what made me say it.

But it didn't seem to upset Alice because both she and Virginia burst out laughing.

"So you are a poet as well as a writer Jess, well done. I like being Alice in a palace. Now what's this visit all about?"

Virginia told Alice that I had liked all the carvings on the willow fence and that I wanted to do a carving too. That I like angels. Could she help me?

"Are you free today Jess?" Alice asked. "You can sit with me and watch. Maybe you will feel you can have a go."

Virginia thanked Alice before she left the tent. I sat on the wooden chair not knowing what to say. I'd never spoken much to Alice before. She was always quiet at meal times. And she never spoke very much in the circle. She did like drumming though and always sang in a very loud voice when she was banging on her drum. The drum was hanging on a pole. It was round and had a black figure that looked like a deer drawn on it and feathers hanging from the bottom.

"I like your drum," I said. "And I love the bear climbing up the pole."

"He's a lovely old thing," said Alice. "The great sleeping winter bear wakes in spring. When he wakes up after his long winter sleep it signals the start of spring and rebirth. The time of the equinox. When life and the earth rejuvenate."

I didn't know what she was talking about. "What's the equinox, please?"

She told me it happened in the early spring, when the sun was in a certain position and night and day were equal and that meant that things would start growing again. "A time of transformation," she said. There it was again, that word. Transformation.

Alice pulled a stool up to the table with all the tools on. "Let's get going. What would you like to make?"

That was easy.

"An angel," I answered. I wanted to make my own angel. Not that it would take away from all my other angels. The opposite really. It would remind me all the time of those special angels in my life. The man, the square, the ceiling, the great wings flying over a city.

Alice picked up a tool. Then she took a piece of wood. She chipped away at the wood. I watched as close as I could. I could hardly breathe I was so engrossed in the way her hand held the tool and moved around the little piece of wood. After I don't know how long, I was concentrating so hard, she held up the piece of wood. She handed it to me. I closed my palm around it. It had transformed. It was a little bear. There were rough bits on it that dug into my palm. But it felt like something alive. It was like me, a rough piece of wood being transformed into something alive with spaces being filled with gardens and carving. There was a little glimmer of excitement inside of me. Nearly happiness.

"You can have that," Alice said to me.

A present. Presents are things that make you happy. I fingered the little bear again and then put it in my pocket. Just in case I forgot it and then Alice might forget that she had given it to me. Presents were treasure. I thanked her.

"Let's get down to business and get you carving." Alice picked up a new piece of wood. She handed it to me. She told me to feel the wood. Get to know it. Look to see which way the grain went. I did. I held it tight. I held it into my body. Next to my heart. I looked at the shape. I studied the way the lines went. I lifted it up and noticed the colour. I was learning. Alice was teaching me something and that felt good. Then she showed me how to hold the tool. How to hold the wood. Which direction to go in.

"It doesn't matter if you don't get it right," she said. "Just feel the wood in your hand. And when you are holding it, picture what it is you want to carve. It can be something very definite or something very abstract."

"Abstract, what's that?" I asked holding the tool in one hand and the piece of wood in the other and getting this really exciting sort of sensation in my body.

"Something like a shape or a pattern, let's just concentrate on the angel." She cupped her hand round mine and guided the tool. Magically, it smoothed away the wood.

"Right you're on your own Jess. You can do it. Just keep going and remember the image you have in your head."

I saw the angel clear as anything I had ever seen in my head. My hand smoothed and chipped. The tool seemed to have a life of its own. Alice watched for a while and then she wandered off. I knew she was somewhere in the tent, but I was thinking hard of the angel in my head and making my hand with the tool go in different directions. Then she came back and looked over my shoulder. Away she went again. All the time I'm looking inside of my head and my hand followed the tool. I never looked up the whole time I was carving. Slowly, slowly the figure emerged. She had wings and eyes. My tool gauged into the bottom of the wood till it shaped into a flowing robe. I chiselled hair. I pointed the wings. It was done. My angel. I held it up, triumphant.

"My God Jess, that's fantastic. Let's go and show the others." I think she was being really genuine when she said that. I could tell on her face. It was a wow look.

The time had passed so quickly that all the women were sitting around the table having lunch.

"Hey, look everybody. Look what Jess just made," Alice shouted as we got to our places at the table. I held up the angel high. There were hums and ha's and a little clap and general real appreciation of my carved angel. I sat down and took some bread. I put my angel next to my plate so that I could see her and so everybody around the table could see her as well. I looked up at the faces watching and I smiled. The smile was back. The real smile was back. The smile that first arrived when I was at the Pieta. When I had something to smile about. It reached right over my face and beamed onto my wooden angel.

After lunch I put the angel and the little bear that Alice had carved for me next to one of the funny dolls made of pottery, underneath the pole with the great bear. I would leave the bear there and let my angel be there just for the day then I would take her to the circle tent at night. Alice said it was nice that I wanted her to be with the other figures. Introduce her to the gang. Sort of a baptism. I didn't fully understand that at the time.

Later, Cora asked me if I wanted to go shopping with her. I was working in the potager garden. I looked at Virginia. She said she thought Cora would appreciate a bit of help to carry the shopping, that I didn't have to work in the garden all the time. But I could choose.

Virginia and I didn't talk much. She liked to think. Sometimes she thought all day and then she would sit down in the garden chair and take her writing book out of her pink velvet bag. She would sit for a couple of hours writing. I never disturbed her. I would carry on weeding the way she had taught me. I would weed all day if I could. Moving gently between the herbs and the plants nipping out the unwelcome intruders. The sun on my arms and legs. Willa had lent me a pair of shorts which were a bit long and flappy. Sometimes I put a straw hat on. There was a whole pile of them in the potting shed. Most of them had holes in the straw and coloured scarves tied around the brim with great bows at the front or back. My favourite was one with a huge brim and a pink ribbon weaving in and out of the straw. It was pretty. The pink ribbon reminded me of my dress and scarf. I could bear that now. And other things as well. Not too much, but a little bit. I could bear to think about the Pieta. One afternoon when Virginia and I were writing to each other, as we sometimes did, I wrote about my solo performance in the Pieta. She wrote back that it was a lovely story and I should write more stories about it. I wanted to write a story to her about my angel carving. I didn't want to go shopping with Cora. I didn't want to go outside of the willow fence. I had never been past the willow fence for I don't know how long now. There wasn't any reason to go past it. There was nothing on the other side for me. In here, I could weed and write a story, carve and wash dishes. Sing at the table at supper time. If I went on to the other side, perhaps they wouldn't let me back again. I think Virginia saw the fear written all over my face because the next thing she said was that I would be back before supper time and then we could do some more weeding together. Then it was alright to go. I knew I could come back.

I walked with Cora towards the fence. I looked back at the tents, the wood, the dining table and the little fence around the garden. Then it happened again. That knot in my stomach, my legs going funny, can't move forward, can't breathe. I held on to the gate and took some deep breaths. Cora looked at me. She understood. There were no sharp words. No looks of impatience. She held open the gate until I could walk through towards a bright yellow little car underneath an open shed. I was out in the world again and I didn't like it one bit. I got into the car and sat there, stiff as a board. We banged along a dusty road with rocks and hills on either side. Once in a while we passed a house with shutters over the windows, just like my window in the Pieta hostel. Cora waved to people standing on the roadside.

"You know everybody," I said.

"I've been here a long time," she answered. "Longer than anybody else. I was the first person to come here. I bought a piece of land and there was a little house on it. That meant there was water and drains but I didn't want to live in a house so I pulled it down and put up a yurt. Just one big one at first and a little one for the bathroom. And then Virginia came and then Freya. Freya was a lot older. Virginia and I had to help her a lot. But then she gives us back so much. She's kind of the mother of the community. Then Willa came and then Alice. After that Charlotte, then Kate. They all had to build their own yurts. Then, we built the kitchen and the big one that we share, where you sleep, between us. Virginia made the garden and finally we built the sweat lodge."

"What's a sweat lodge?" I asked. I was getting good at asking questions. The answers were more stuff for my head. Filling the space with things to know.

"You build a fire in the lodge and then you keep it hot with stones. Then, when it is really hot you all sit on the benches and sweat away and then all sorts of things can happen."

"Like what?" I asked.

"It's hard to say Jess. We are going to have one next week so you can come and find out."

I wasn't sure about that. Why would you want to go and all sweat together in a tent? Sounds a bit daft. I didn't say that, but I thought it. Instead I said that it must get very smelly.

Cora laughed out loud. "Well, we make it so you don't. There's lots of herbs and oils so that it smells really good."

We arrived at the town. Cora stopped the car in a narrow street with cobbles on the road. I imagined that we would be going to a supermarket to do our shopping but the shop we went into was dark and full of sacks and brown paper bags hanging from hooks. I wanted to cover my ears to block out the sound of the rock music playing. Two men with jeans and beards and long hair shouted at Cora from behind the wooden counter.

"Hi boys, "she shouted back in English. "How you doing?"

I hung back. Cora went up to the counter. Chatting and laughing with the men behind the counter. She started talking in Spanish so I didn't understand what she was saying. But then she turned and waved her arm towards me.

"This is Jess. She's staying with us for a while," she said in English.

"Hi Jess," they both said. "You okay?"

I nodded but I didn't say anything. I could see them eyeing me up and down. That made me jumpy. Angelo never looked me up and down. Not even when he first saw me singing in the Campo. He looked into my soul. And I looked into his. There was no confusion about this. I wasn't up for eyeing up and down. I went back outside of the shop again and stood on the street. The music blared from the shop onto the street. But I had no curiosity about it all. I was somewhere in the world, in a country that I knew nothing about, with a language that I didn't understand. I was only comfortable in that little land of yurts and a potager garden. With carvings and coloured poles and women who cared for me. I'd lost one little world and had found another. The bigger one, where I was now, didn't interest me. I didn't know it. I was glad to see Cora looking out of the shop to see where I was.

"Can you help me carry this stuff to the car?" I didn't want to be eyed again. So I didn't look at those blokes when I went back in. I picked up brown paper bags and carrier bags full of toilet rolls, bottles, candles, beans and rice. All of it went into the back of the car and then we drove away.

"Great shop," said Cora. "It's all organic. Just like the potager garden. No chemicals and horrible false colouring."

"That's good," my voice was flat. "I used to do all my shopping by boat."

The car banged away back down the road. I've learnt a lot today, I thought. Organic, sweat lodge. I learnt I don't like men eyeing me up and down. Not now I've been away from it for what seems like a very long time. But I didn't have to worry about that when I was back inside the willow fence with bears and angels.

I pushed open the garden gate. I was glad to see Virginia sitting on the wooden bench behind the potting shed. This was a shady spot and a favourite haunt of ours when the sun got too hot and we needed to rest. The bench was long enough for two and wide enough to put a writing book beside you. I sat down beside her. Her eyes were closed. I studied her face hoping that she didn't know I was there. Her forehead and the space between her eyebrows was a criss cross of lines and brown colours. There was a faint circle of pale skin right where her hair started. Usually her hair fell over her face but today it was tied back in a tight pony tail leaving her face exposed. Her eyelids and the tip of her nose were red. Her lips were pale. Her cheeks were dark brown and I could see tiny blonde hairs growing down the side of her ears. She had no make-up on. No posh hair do. Big, silver loops of earrings. Virginia had told me she was fifty something. She'd forgotten quite what. I hoped I looked like that at fifty something. I think at fifteen something I had looked a lot older. Virginia's lines weren't worry lines though, not like I'd had, they were her age lines, the lines of her life. The lines of her character and when I looked at the lines it told me who she was. Her lines said I am Virginia and this is my life. Every face said something all the time. I think that is why there is a word for it. Expression. Virginia's expression was always kind, saying I am your friend. She opened her eyes, smiled and all the lines changed direction.

"Oh, you're back," she said.

"I was looking at your lines. They're lovely."

"Well thank you Jess. Lovely lines, what a compliment. Better than lovely wrinkles." She rubbed her hand over her face. She wasn't smiling any more. But the lines were still lovely. "How was your trip?"

"I liked the shop. Cora said it was all organic. Like our garden. But I didn't like the blokes that served in it."

"Why not?"

"I don't know. I think they were eyeing me up and down. I didn't like that."

Virginia turned her head and looked at me. "I wouldn't worry. It's a bloke thing. They're nice really. I don't think they would mean any harm."

I closed my eyes to think about what she said. Eyeing up and down to me meant harm.

"You need to find your power centre. Right deep inside of you. It's there. And if you believe that it's there then those kind of things can't get to you. You can stand in yourself in a safe way."

"Not when you are a little girl you can't," I said.

I didn't know about that kind of power. I'd had some kind of power when I ran. I'd had some kind of power when I got the bus. I'd had some kind of power when I'd hid in the back streets and not let people get to me. But that was all when I was full of fear.

"My power was always there when I was frightened," I said to Virginia to try to get her to understand.

"Mine used to be like that as well. But then I got to know myself better, I got to learn about love and other things. You'll get there Jess."

That night I dreamt about walking on frozen ice. The ice stretched out in front of me till it reached the sky. When I nearly reached the sky the ice started to break. Cracks started darting in front of me like flashes of lightning. I had to walk between them. Then there was no ice, just water. And I sank into it and screamed for help. There was nobody to help me. Then I saw the great bear that sleeps all winter in front of me and his great bear paw was stretching out towards me. I woke. The word was back in my head. Transformation.

I told Virginia about my dream. She said she would think about it, it sounded good, but Alice was much better about all of those kind of things than she was. Maybe I would ask Alice next time she invited me to help her carve.

"Kate is going to bottle some tomatoes today. So we have to pick them. And I think Cora brought some fresh pasta from the shop yesterday so we need some courgettes and peppers too, so she can make a sauce to go with it for dinner."

We got baskets from the potting shed. Yellow tomatoes in one. Red ones in another. Beef size ones in another. Plum ones in another. Soon we had four baskets to carry to the kitchen.

Kate clapped her hands when she saw our harvest of goodies. "I need some help here girls. How about it?"

Virginia pulled a chair to the table. "We're up for it. You sit here Jess. Kate is going to give us instructions. So we must listen very carefully." She winked at me. It was great to be in between these two women bantering away and laughing. Making the lines of their faces change with every smile and every word. I watched and listened. Skinned red and yellow tomatoes. Put them in the bowl for Kate. I could smell garlic and basil mixed in with the sharp, sweet smell of the tomatoes.

"Is that a pungent smell?" I asked.

"I suppose it is." Kate stuck her nose in the air. "Maybe it's too sweet for pungent. Why pungent?"

"Jane Eyre smelled pungent," I said.

"Did she? Gosh. Jane Eyre had it tough." Kate was mashing tomatoes in a big brown bowl.

"Did Jane Eyre find her power centre?" I looked at Kate and Virginia. Virginia told Kate about our conversation in the garden.

"I think she did," Kate looked at me. "In the end I think that she was in complete control of her life. Even though she had to look after Mr Rochester."

"So it's about control as well. Your power centre." I needed to know about this power centre so I wouldn't be frightened of the wrong look.

Virginia stood up and went over to the yurt door. She straightened up and then bent her knees and put her arms and hands in front of her.

"Push me Jess. Go on, push me." I stood next to her and gave her a little shove.

"Harder. Push harder. See you can't push me over. That's because I am strong in my centre. Balanced. I am in control of what you can or cannot do to me and I am in control of my own power." She closed her eyes and started to breathe really deep. The lines softened. There was a lovely calmness all round. It was power. Nice power. Power where you looked after people and didn't push anybody around. Power where nobody pushed you.

Power was dropped and Kate told me about how she had always loved cooking but her parents had pushed her into university and she had been a history teacher for a long time. She hadn't liked that. Now she was happy. She could cook for ever more if she wanted. She could do that with her silly leg that had pins and pegs in to make it go. But if she didn't want to cook that was fine too. Everybody else who lived here would be happy to take their turn. And everybody else did things for her that she didn't want to do. Kate looked happy. She had happy lines all round her eyes because she smiled and laughed so much. Virginia said she was sometimes in a lot of pain with her leg. But it didn't stop her being happy.

The tomatoes were bottled. The lovely sauce was cooked. I had learnt a little bit about power and more about Kate. This was transformation. The ice was cracking. Each day brought more melting moments in the ice. But it didn't break open. Not like in my dream.

The day arrived for the sweat lodge and there was a lot of moving around amongst all the women. Carrying wood, stones, towels, drums, branches, feathers, pebbles. Everything but the kitchen sink as they used to say where I came from.

I said I would go because they had been kind enough to ask me. How could I know whether I wanted to be sitting in a sweat lodge? I didn't have a clue what one was.

I heard Virginia say to Kate that Freya would be preparing herself for the ceremony. Ceremony. That's a word I knew, but I always associated it with weddings and sometimes they happened in Venice when there was a special festival day. That threw a little bit of light on what was going to happen. It wasn't just about sweating.

I could see smoke and there was great chat amongst the women between the yurts.

Alice said that it would all start about five o'clock. "First of all we have to bless the tent and then we bless the fire."

When it was time, I followed her to the sweat lodge. I didn't think anything of it. I didn't think that it would be anything unpleasant, not with these kind women. I had done bigger, stranger things in my life and thought what did it matter if I died doing them. Because I hadn't died, a sweat lodge it would be.

All the women stood around the tent. Freya made funny noises then she waved a smoky stick around. It smelt of sage. Strong sage. Into the tent we all went. My friends took off their clothes and sat on the benches without a stitch on their bodies. I'd never seen an old body without clothes on before. I tried not to look but I couldn't help it. They weren't shy about it. I was though. No way I was going to take my clothes off. My body didn't look like their bodies. Although it was a little plumper because I was eating more, it was still pretty neat. There were life lines on their bodies as well as their faces. But they had everything that I had even if it all had dropped a little bit.

Freya lifted the smoky stick into the air and moved it from one corner to the other. She started to chant and the tent got very hot. She walked round the fire and her wrinkly bottom hung down the back of her legs. It got even more hot. Somebody poured water on the stones and steam blew off in great swirls. Then Freya stopped chanting and sat down. The smell in the lodge was so powerful it made you feel dizzy. Nobody spoke. Cora rubbed herself with drops of oil. Virginia stroked her arms with thick cream. Kate rubbed some dry leaves between her hands and held them to her face. Minutes passed. There was a sound of heavy breathing. Then Willa stood up and danced around the fire in the most peculiar way stamping her feet and moving her arms up and down in the air and twisting herself into circles. Alice started banging on a drum. Cora made funny noises. Sort of wailing. Then everybody started to wail. I didn't know what to do, so I started to wail. Way up high my voice went, louder than anybody else. Then the wailing stopped. But I couldn't. My wailing noise got louder and louder. I was up on my feet. Wailing and throwing my arms around. I didn't care that everybody was watching me. On and on it went. Me, wailing away. I was out of control.

Then the words came. "I'm not a silly cow. My name isn't silly cow. It's Jess. My name is Jess. Take your hands off me. You're hurting me." Then I threw myself on the ground. "I'm just a little baby." I curled up into a little ball. I could feel grass on my face. "Don't do that to a little baby." What was I saying? I was choking. I screamed. Nobody moved. Nothing was said. I wanted somebody to say something. Choking noises came out of my throat. "I'm just a little baby. Save me. Save me." Mammy doesn't come. Mammy's lying on the floor. She's groaning. She didn't save me. He didn't save me. Images flashed into my mind. Horrible images. Then a little girl runs through a door. She has no clothes on. She's screaming. Words were coming out of my mouth. What was I saying? I didn't know any more. Bad things. Very bad things.

Things that should not be said. Shame. What shame on a little girl. Spoiled. Run Jess, run. Never stop running. Running from the faces, running from the shame. Then I screamed. I screamed and screamed. "Don't hurt me. Let me go." Scream. Out it all came. Screams from the depths of my body. Making my body hurt. Making it shake. On and on it went.

Then, slowly it stopped. I lay on the ground. I saw the ice give way. Tears came like waterfalls out of my eyes. Somebody lifted the top of my body and held it in their arms. Cradling my shaking, hurting body. I felt skin on my cheek. Soft skin. Gentle hands stroked my head. Arms rocked me backwards and forwards, backwards and forwards. Sobs shook me. Spit came out of my mouth and my nose was running. But the arms didn't let go. They held me tighter. My arms went round the body holding me and I clung on whilst more and more sobs came out of my mouth. Someone held my feet. Now, there's a circle of bodies around me. Hands are stroking my shaking body. Calming the sobs. Letting the tears flow all over their bare bodies. I'd opened the wounds bleeding inside of my body and all the blocked up pain flowed out into the sweat and the fire and the wrinkly old bodies.

"Let the healing in," a voice said.

How, how could I?

"Just let it in." I looked up into the face of Freya.

"Have I spoilt your sweat lodge?" I said.

"My dear girl," she said. "You have given us yours. That is a great honour."

Chapter 14

Fire

I didn't understand what had happened. None of it made sense to me. But to all these women, with their old wrinkly bodies, what happened to me in that sweat lodge made perfect sense. I obviously hadn't done anything wrong, because they all wanted to hug me and kiss me and hold my hand and say how brave I was and how sorry they were that all those bad things had happened to me. They had understood the words even if they were all jumbled up. They knew what the words meant.

For me, something changed. I let them touch me for a start. I cried. I didn't just cry, I screamed and wailed and threw myself on the ground and all that crying flung itself out of my body like it was dying to get out. It just couldn't wait to get out, but I had never been able to let it out. It was out. What did that mean? It meant I could talk and I did. I talked and talked. Alice, who told me she used to be a doctor in another life, listened. So I talked to her because she wanted to listen to the stories. Each time I finished a story she would say something and then I would dream a dream and tell her all about it and she would make sense of the dream. I always felt lighter after a story and a dream.

I would smile and say good morning to everybody. I didn't half look at their faces and just say hello. They would ask me how I was. They didn't want to tell me anything bad. And they would tell me how they were and maybe talk a little more or have a little hug or maybe sit down at the table and have a cup of coffee. Whatever it meant, it was different. And I liked being different.

I had writing notebooks and books on the little table beside my bed. Kate had given me a book about healing your life. It was full of little stories and things you could say to help you feel better. Affirmations, they are called. I started writing my own and carried them around in my pocket. Every morning when I woke up I would say my affirmation about healing my life. Every time I had a bad thought I would read one of my slips of paper with an affirmation on. I was starting to understand transformation and my life took on a rhythm.

I got used to going to the shops to buy groceries. I managed to smile and talk to the men in the shop and ignore the looks that they gave me. That was progress. I still had no direction to go in and that worried me. I tried not to think about it but it would torment me at night. I would toss and turn and run over in my mind things that I might be able to do. But the thought of stepping out from that willow fence with a bag on my back and nowhere to go scared me stiff. My notebooks were full. Story after story had been written. There were nice notebooks in the grocery shop and every time I went there, Cora bought one for me. I soon filled them up. I wrote about the seeds that I had put into the ground. How many times I watered them. When they started to push their little heads through the ground. This was magic to me. With Angelo I had never seen little seeds growing, even though the boat was full of vegetables and apples and oranges and fruit of every kind.

I hadn't really got to know Charlotte until there was the fire ceremony. She asked me if I was free and would I like to help her? I didn't know what with but now I was starting to understand that everything had a meaning here and it all seemed to be good. So I told her I would.

"Let's gather some wood," said Charlotte. She was quiet was Charlotte. Seemed to think a lot. She looked younger than all of the others and stronger. She was really strong. I saw that when we went into the wood on the other side of the dinner table. She found really big branches of trees that had blown down and lifted them up without any bother. I started picking up the wood and putting it into the wheelbarrow. She told me what sort of trees were in the wood.

"That's an oak. That's a beech. That's a willow. All of those are olive trees." She picked the leaves and showed me the difference between the patterns and the shapes. Trees had always just been trees to me. I had never been in a wood or a forest and as I've said before, my knowledge of the countryside was limited to Tynemouth beach and I don't remember any trees there. Then she got all scientific and I had to tell her that I didn't understand any of it.

"You've lost me," I said as I stuck my fingers into the holes of an oak tree, but I did get the bit about rain forests being very important and how if you hugged a tree it would become your friend. That their roots went down miles into the earth and that they could breathe.

I looked at trees now in a completely different way. All of that happening right there in front of me in the oak tree. "This tree can be my friend," I said.

"Give it a hug then," said Charlotte. "Tell it that you want to be its friend."

That is exactly what I did. Put my arms around that oak tree and then I didn't want to let go. It just kept hugging into me.

"Good stuff," said Charlotte as she lifted the handles of the wheelbarrow and went back to the edge of the wood where there was great activity. Willow branches had been tied together to enclose a circle. Stones were being carried and laid in the centre. Charlotte started to empty the wood into the circle. I copied her.

"Like this Jess," she said. "It all has to be specially placed for a fire ceremony." I had a new respect for a twig after that hug with the tree. At first I just watched her putting down the wood. Then I noticed that she was putting it in different directions. I copied her. It was like sitting with Freya. Calming.

Backwards and forwards we went, Charlotte and I, picking up branches and carrying them to the fire place.

"That's enough," she said after a while.

All the wood was in the right place and Charlotte told me she had to prepare herself for the ceremony. "I am the Keeper of the Fire," she said. "I had to train especially for this role. In America. With the native peoples."

"Great," I said, "that's really great." I didn't know whether it was great or not but it sounded great. Really great.

Charlotte smiled. "You can be my apprentice Jess, if you like. You can train with me. Then every time we have a fire you can help."

I smiled back the way I did now. I'd never been an apprentice, I'd never been anything other than full of heaped up and blocked up emotions, apart from when I was on the barge with Angelo or singing in the choir in the Pieta. Now I was training to be the Keeper of the Fire.

"Sounds great," I said. I meant it because if being a Keeper of the Fire was as good as hugging the tree then I was satisfied with that.

Now I had to prepare myself. Virginia said that it was important to dress up for the fire ceremony.

"Express yourself," she said. "Anyway you like. Get feathers. Wear a hat. Gather some stones and bring those too. Bring your angel." That's what everybody else seemed to be doing. As apprentice Keeper of the Fire I must make a big effort. I went into the garden and picked some flowers and sat on the chair and tied them up with some string. I hung the string around my ear. I took a scarf from one of the hats in the potting shed and wrapped it around my head. As luck would have it I spotted a feather lying among the lettuces. I couldn't believe all the different colours that feather had. But then, like with the trees, I had never really looked at birds and feathers before. But I was looking now. Maybe it was good I was only looking now. If I'd looked before, I would never have seen what I saw now. Like the tree, like a song.

From the garden, I could see the women gathering at the fire space. I thought maybe I looked daft with the flowers and a feather hanging from my ears. I needn't have worried when I saw my women friends. Daft didn't come into it. Pretty barmy was more like it. I didn't recognise Alice who had painted her face with black and red stripes and stuck great big feathers all over a ribbon which she had tied round her waist. She carried one of her wooden poles with painted figures on. She stood at the opening of the willow circle with the fire in. Freya was already sitting at one of the benches beside the wood and the fire. Her long, grey hair hung loose down to her shoulders. She wore a long cream robe. Her feet were bare. Her eyes were closed. I knew she was thinking with her inside eyes that saw a lot of things, even when they were closed. Virginia carried a little bag in her hand. She had earrings on that were made up of little shells. When she sat down she opened up her little bag and took out some pebbles. She placed the pebbles at her feet and then she closed her eyes. I sat next to her and put my little wooden angel on the ground besides her pebbles.

Then Cora walked into the fire circle and sat down next to me. She looked really wild. She had tied her hair up with lots of pieces of coloured ribbons. She had painted her eyes black all around the outside. She wore pink, flowing trousers and a little white strappy top that only came just below her bra. Her ribs pushed out into the bare brown skin. She wore a leather belt around her waist and brown leather sandals on her feet. Her toe nails were painted different colours. Willa sat opposite to me. She had put some white stripes on her face and wore a huge scarf full of bright coloured stripes round her shoulders. Then Kate arrived carrying bunches of herbs and willow. She had tied the willow to the front of her body. A dark blue scarf was tied around her head. Coloured ribbons were woven around her walking stick. Now there was only Charlotte.

Everyone sat really quiet with their eyes closed. I couldn't close my eyes. I wanted to look at all of this for as long as I could. Crazy as it was, the scene in front of me looked like that new word I had learnt with Alice. Serene. Like queens on their thrones. I could see what serene was when I looked at all the colours and how my friends created this amazing atmosphere, sitting there at the fire ceremony with stripes and tattoos and feathers, shells and pebbles. Then in came Charlotte. She had yellow ribbons round her head. Red ribbons round her wrists, green ribbons at her waist and blue ones around her ankles. Ribbons everywhere. Serious Charlotte looked wicked. She bowed and placed a stone at the entrance of the circle and sat down next to Willa. Then Freya started to speak. She asked the spirits to bless this ceremony. Silence. I still couldn't close my eyes, I was looking for the spirits who were to bless us.

Angel spirits, stone spirits, tree spirits, animal spirits, bird spirits, every spirit in the world was mentioned and asked to come and join us. Charlotte stood up and placed wood around the fire. Freya asked the spirits of the four directions to bless our ceremony and Charlotte moved around the fire as Freya called. North, south, east, west. When all that is done, she lit the fire and put wood onto it from one of the piles we had specially arranged. Then she took her seat again. Willa, Alice and Cora hold hands. And then I feel Virginia take hold of mine. So I then take hold of Kate's. Only Freya is not holding hands. She is praying. Then she asked us to look into the fire and to tell the story that we see in the flames. Try as I could I couldn't see a story. But Alice could. She told a story of a dolphin rescuing the world. Virginia told a story of the sun. Willa told a very long story of a special spirit who had come to heal people after a great famine had arrived in their land. Even though it was very long, I listened to every word because it was a great story and she told it so that you thought you were right there. Charlotte told the story of a tree spirit that was here now with us in this circle and said what a special circle it was.

Kate lifted her bunch of herbs and threw them into the fire. They crackled and flared on the red embers.

"My story is to give back to the earth what we have taken from it," she said.

Cora said that her story was to thank the fire and the circle for the peace and harmony that there was around the fire and for the wonderful friends that made up the circle and that she was so grateful to have found these friends when her life was falling apart. She felt only joy at this fire.

It was my turn. I couldn't see a story in the flames. I looked at Freya. She looked at me. I could see her thinking, there is a story in you Jess. It seemed an age that I sat there looking for a story. Then I clicked. I couldn't see a story but I saw a song. And I could sing a story. So I sang my solo song. There was no organ to lead me in. No chorus to lead me out. But I knew the words and the tune off by heart. And I was sure even if I didn't understand the words, they were a story. Slowly I hummed until I got into the right key. There was no rush. I closed my eyes and there I was in the Pieta with candles flickering all round me and all the abandoned little girls in their long dresses swirling around. I did it. I got that precious sound that had earned me the place up there behind the railings. This time singing to wild wonderful women who had saved my life, and tree spirits and shells and totem poles and stone spirits and a special fire. Once I got going I didn't want to stop. I couldn't stop. My song went on and on and when I got to the end I went back to the beginning and started all over again. Eventually my voice started to crack and I stopped. I raised my eyes from the fire. Tears were falling all round the circle.

"I've made you cry, I am sorry. I never wanted to make anybody cry."

"We're crying because it is so beautiful, Jess." Virginia grasped my hand in hers.

"Thank you," said Freya. "You brought your song. We were truly blessed."

Then I started to cry. "Please don't make me go," I sobbed. "When a good thing happens then a bad thing does. Don't throw me out." Back to words full of fear.

"Trust Jess," said Freya. "It's okay for you to be here."

"Besides," said Charlotte "you are my apprentice Keeper of the Fire. You can't leave." Everybody laughed at that. Then Alice got her drum and started drumming. Cora stood up and started to do this wild belly dance. Her hips and belly moved like nothing else on earth. So much for old people not being able to dance. Cora could. Better than anybody I had ever seen. They weren't old at all these women. Just older than me. One by one we stood up and started to dance and we all danced like crazy for hours. The sun went down and the moon came up and we carried on dancing. The fire gave out glows and shadows. Voices made strange sounds. We danced till we couldn't move. And I danced the longest and sang the loudest and was allowed to put the wood on the fire in that special way that Charlotte knew because I was training to be the Keeper of the Fire. I took my training very seriously with these crazy, barmy, wonderful fire women.

Kate often sang about rhythm when she was in the kitchen cooking. And I got it, I really got it. I got rhythm. I liked having it as well. Every day had its ups and downs but it all happened in the rhythm. I always knew where I was and what I would be doing next. The rhythm took up all day. I gardened and washed and cleaned and chatted and sang and then there was a little ceremony or a big ceremony and I fitted in well with it all.

Then change came knocking on my door again.

Chapter 15

New Life

I didn't know anything about having a baby but I knew I was having one. I'd seen the signs with others in the hostel and the care homes. I'd heard the curses when the machine turned blue. That's what happened to people like me. Having babies was considered getting landed. It meant a house. But it didn't mean anything else. Because you weren't in control. You'd never learnt that you had to have control if you wanted that baby to be just right. Now I was landed. And I wasn't in control. And there wasn't a housing association down the road to give me a house and no social worker to sort out the mess of an unwanted pregnancy.

I rubbed my hands over what I knew was a swelling belly. I lay in bed and frightened myself to death with the thought of what would happen to me now. How could I tell my kind women friends that I was having a baby? How would they react? Was this the nail in my coffin? Would I have to leave now because there was no space in the yurt life for a baby? I had become the apprentice Keeper of the Fire. I was learning to carve wood, tend a garden. And now this happens. Yes, that's what happens to people like me. Just when you think you're getting it, you lose control.

Sleep didn't come quickly, not now I had let the thought into my mind. I could pretend I didn't know, maybe it would come and they couldn't throw me out. I could leave without saying anything. But that would be really horrible considering all the kind things they had done for me. It wouldn't solve the problem. The problem of the baby.

I lay in bed till I couldn't lie any longer. I was too restless. I wandered around outside. The sky was full of stars. I walked to the willow fence and opened the gate into the potager garden. I lay on the ground and looked at the stars. I loved being in the potager garden because it was full of things growing. Just like my belly.

My growing belly. I was back to the problem. Did it have to be a problem? If I didn't see it as a problem then maybe it won't be. The stars twinkled up in the sky. I stood up and walked over to the wood. I stood beside my friend, the oak tree. It was strong. And good. Like my Angelo and this was Angelo's little seed in my belly.

"What now?" I sighed into the bark of the oak tree. Trust. Why did that word come into my head. Did the branches whisper into my ear?

That was the last time I ever thought about my baby as a problem. The last time I felt landed. Like the oak tree held me, I would hold this baby in my arms. And those arms would always be there, the space always open to come back in, whatever and whenever. My baby was to come into this world with every ounce of love that I could give. I didn't know how much then, but I do now. It would be looked at and talked to. It would be listened to and fed at proper times. It would be given a bed and never ever would I be far enough away that it couldn't hear me singing. I would sing to my baby.

It would always hear my voice. I sang right there holding on to the oak tree. Must be the best place for a baby to hear its first song. A lullaby.

I could make amends for bad things happening to me and to Jane Eyre by loving this baby. Somehow I had to work it out. I had to think hard.

I was shocked by how clever my brain had become. There was so much stuff in it that wasn't there before. Talking stuff. Gardening stuff. Tree stuff. Reading stuff. Fire stuff. Sweat lodge stuff and shopping stuff. Alice said it was called knowledge but if I wanted to call it stuff that was fine. I thought knowledge was a better word.

I have knowledge in my head now instead of all the space being taken up with memories of what can happen to a little girl who has no one looking out for her. Instead of watching to see who was going to have a go at me next. I could think about other things, but the biggest thing I could think about was love, what I got and what I could give. That was a huge bit of knowledge. It almost spun out of control when I looked at my friends and saw it weave around the circle and in and out of me like a ribbon through a straw hat.

But I said nothing. I had put my growing belly into my heart Nothing in the whole wide world would change that now. Everything that I had in me was about loving and protecting that little baby But I didn't know about little babies growing and what they needed right now. Love had to be enough until I got the strength to tell.

So I carried on like I had before. I felt the more I knew about carving wood, growing food in the potager garden and spending time in the kitchen watching rice being boiled and vegetables being steamed was all the better, not just for me but for the baby. I blocked the practicalities out. I could learn more, there was still lots of space in my head. So far nobody had asked me to leave. I hoped that wouldn't change. I spent most of my time with Virginia in the garden and I watched Alice carve the wood and helped Kate in the kitchen. Alice made me laugh. She encouraged me to laugh and to be funny as well.

"Act the fool," she would say. "Let go and have some fun." It didn't come easy but I was finding my funny self very slowly.

I talked to Alice after my sweat lodge. She said it was important not to close up again. Bury it all back inside me. But she also said that I should only say what I wanted to say and only if I felt safe. Feeling safe with Alice was not too hard for me. All those totem poles and big winter bears came with Alice when we had our talks and sometimes she hugged me and held my hand. I could let this happen now, since the sweat lodge and the fire.

"Fire is transformation" said Virginia. I could see why. Because after the fire was when I could laugh and carry on a bit and sing just because I wanted to and I could move around the tents without feeling afraid. I could ask Virginia questions about the garden and Kate about why this was good and that was good. Which herb went with what.

Surviving was not in the day to day running here. I think all these women had done their surviving one way and another. Not like me maybe, but one way or another. Once or twice I wandered outside the willow fence and walked down the dusty road between the rocky hills. Sometimes I walked down to the little church. But I didn't go in. I wasn't that healed. I couldn't bear to look at the choir stalls and the altar. At the places where the singing went on. When I told Alice she said that sort of association was common but that I would get over it. I couldn't see that happening. How could it? How could I ever get over that wonderful night? Bad associations were different to good associations. I said that to Alice. That the bad associations were better out than in. But happy associations I never wanted to let go of. Not when you had so few to hang on to. I never wanted to associate anything in the whole world with my singing night up behind the railings in the Pieta with Angelo watching me full of pride. Before he discovered who I really was. Alice said I was protecting myself too much. That's a habit, I told her. That's what all my life had been about. Running and protecting. Protecting myself against hurt, pain, shame, badness. Alice said that something would have to shift or I would never be able to live my life. I could have said then that something had shifted. That my heart was full of a little baby. But I didn't.

My notebooks were filled with my activities. Every day brought some new knowledge. Every day I got closer to these women. Even Alice, who liked to spend a lot of time alone. Sometimes you could tell from her eyes that she had been crying. She often went into the sweat lodge tent with Charlotte and I think they talked a lot. They liked being in there. It was like a little nest. Cosy and calm. But that is where I screamed out the pain and cried out the horror. I could still smell my fear in there so I didn't go in. Not to sit and talk like Alice and Charlotte.

Sometimes I went for a walk with Cora. She liked to go over the rocks to a stream which had some deep holes in. She would take off all her clothes and swim round and round in circles. She'd ask me to go in as well. I didn't know how to swim so I just dabbled my feet in the freezing mountain water. But I also didn't want to freeze the little baby in my belly. Tucked up warm in its little sleeping bag. She said she would teach me to swim. Not today, I'd say. Then she would sit at the side of the stream and watch the water falling over the rocks. She closed her eyes and listened to the sound. I could see why she did it. It really calmed you down. One day I listened so hard I could tune my voice into the sound and I made humming sounds to go with the water sounds. Cora liked the sound. She lay on the ground and put her hands over her heart. Tears would squirt out the side of her eyes. I never asked her why she was crying because you could see it was a private thing. I reckoned that by the time you got to Cora's age you had got nearly all your stuff out. So if you were crying it was more about something you wanted and didn't have, rather than what was hurting you deep inside from your past. On the way back she always tucked her arm inside mine and told me little stories about her life. She liked to talk about her mother and said they had spent a lot of time together and her mother always encouraged her to do what she wanted to do with her life. Cora said that when she failed in her life, her mother was always there to support her and she was heartbroken when her mother died. They were so close. After that happened, she came to live here.

Could I be that mother? I hadn't had any training. Everything went scary in my head when I even thought the word. I never thought that Jane Eyre was lucky. I never thought that she got the best of the deal between the two of us. But she could dream of how wonderful her mother would have been. I couldn't. She never took care of me, my mother. She never washed me and changed me like other little girls. Then maybe someone would notice and I'd be taken away for a little while. She always got me back. I don't know how. Why did she want me? Bad things. Bad, bad things. Bad things I couldn't say to anybody. "Your mam's tried really hard this time Jess." That meant it was time to go back. The words were black and heavy on me. I was just a little girl. Her trying hard was more important than me being safe.

She was only good at one thing. Telling lies. And the woman I called Nan, who was kinder, lied for her and made it all worse. I always had to go and I always had to come back. Till I took to the streets. From there I could run. It was better. Then I was an angry runner. Police, care homes, social workers, foster parents. That's what they saw.

Anger. Black anger. It turned against me. My mother tried hard they say, but I am too angry to deal with. So I am put in care, suffering in anger and she is dealing on the streets. Nobody worked it out. I did. And Mr Vivaldi.

When Cora talked about her mother it was good. It gave me an idea of who a mother could be. What a mother could do. She thought it would upset me, but I told her I loved her stories about her mother. Cora was nearly old but she still cried for her mother's love. That's why the tears came. All those years of loving her mother and her mother loving her. What a dream for my life. To love my child properly for as long as I lived.

Chapter 16

Telling

Round and round in my head the telling went. Should I tell Alice first? Or, maybe Virginia, I could write it. That might be easier. Or should I wait for the right moment in the circle. In the end it didn't matter what I thought because one morning, before one single person said anything at all, Freya said "I think Jess has something to tell us."

    I went bright red sitting between Alice and Kate. Everybody looked at me and that made it worse. I went beetroot. It was like being in the sweat lodge. Then all the colour drained away and I started to shiver. I got a bad feeling. I didn't run. Alice took hold of my hand. Nobody spoke in the time my face went from red to white and it seemed like years. Then I thought there is no shame in my baby, there will never be shame in my baby. I put my hand onto my belly and said the words. Still nobody spoke. I looked around the circle hoping there would be a smile.

Then, after a long space, Freya spoke. "I think we knew Jess, because we could see the signs. Now we have to decide what will happen. As you know we make decisions as a group and the group have to talk about this matter. We have to come together and have a special talk. In this talk we have to think about what is best for our community."

I didn't like the sound of that. Still nobody smiling. Still silence from everyone. Alice kept hold of my hand and gave it little squeezes.

"Thank you," I said. What else could I say? But then I did think of something else.

"I didn't plan to have this baby. I really didn't know it was coming. And I don't know anything about having babies. I only know one thing. This baby will be mine and I will give it all that I have. At the moment it's not a lot, but it's more than I ever had. I'll never ever feel bad about it even if you don't like it."

I took my hand out of Alice's and left the circle. Outside in the fresh air, I took some deep breaths. I didn't know what was to happen now that they knew.

I went into the garden and weeded and gathered vegetables and salad leaves like I always did in the morning. I pulled some herbs and sat down on the ground and rubbed them into my hands. One thing for sure I had nowhere to go and because they were my friends they would not make me leave. But I knew there had to be money for a baby. There had to be nappies and prams and little baby clothes. A cot. I didn't know what else. Blankets and teddy bears.

Virginia came into the garden. They had talked.

The talk had gone like this. They were a community of women who had not had children. They felt that this was one of the reasons why the community worked so well. Not that they were against children, but just that they were each free to make their decisions without a family involvement. And no matter how much they wanted me to be here, no matter how much they sympathised with my predicament, there were other things that had to be taken into consideration.

By now Virginia had sat down on the garden chair. She waved her hand, she wanted me to sit beside her. But after those words there was no way I could sit down. I stood with my hands full of lettuce and stared at her. I couldn't believe the words.

"I'm not going back to England. I can't go back. I don't want to go back. I never want to go back. How can I love my baby and take it back there. I've nowhere to go to there."

"But you will be looked after Jess, there are support systems, you will be given what you need." Virginia was very calm. How could she be calm? Didn't she understand what she was saying? All these words coming at me. But still, I didn't run. I wasn't just thinking about me now.

"I thought you were my friends," I say. Full of hurt.

"We are Jess. Absolutely your friends. It's just too difficult for us to have your baby here. We are too old to be made vulnerable. You could go back to the father and see if that makes a difference. Register the baby with him."

"I can never go back. He'll never want me again."

"Are you sure Jess, are you absolutely certain?"

"I am. That Jude told him what my past was like. And he was so perfect. So good. He just loved me."

"Well then he probably still does. Maybe he is a windhorse man. They are kind of special. You should trust him."

"But he can't trust me. That makes it different."

I didn't know about windhorse men. Was he one of those? Would he be a windhorse father? Was there such a thing? I could do all the loving of my baby. I could do the best for it that I could with everything that I had. Having a father meant something different to me. No protection, no safety, no money to keep me warm. So father did not come forward as the best thing in the world for my baby. Being a good mother was going to be a big plus for my baby.

I couldn't go back to England. I couldn't risk it.

I would have to run away again. That was my next thought. Virginia was talking about giving me the money for the fare and one of the women had said that she would pay for everything the baby would need to start with.

I let her talk. It wasn't going to happen.

How hard after this conversation to go back to the me who helped and washed dishes and sang and walked with my friends. I felt like I had just been a play thing to them. When it suited them they wanted me, when it didn't, they didn't want me. Horrible bitter thoughts in my head. But later, when I really thought about it, I realised they were right. I would have to register the baby. I would have to find somewhere to live. And no matter how angry I was now, this baby and me were not their responsibility. They'd never had babies, why should they want mine? These women had rescued me from starvation, given me food and care and taught me lots of knowledge. My head was so full now of new things that the space might be running out. I'd a lot to be grateful for.

Eventually I told Virginia that I could see their point. She was sitting on the grass writing.

"I'm not glad about that Jess. It's just a situation that cannot be resolved. For us it is very hard too. We like you here, we knew it couldn't last forever. So we will miss you. It is a no win situation for us both. There is no rush though, it's not as though you will have to go tomorrow. You have time to make plans and Alice will check you over to make sure that everything with the baby is healthy and that you are in good shape."

"I'm in good shape for my baby," I said. "I'm in the best shape that I have ever been and that is thanks to you all." I meant what I said. But I also told Virginia that I wasn't hungry and if it was all right with her, I would go and lie on my bed for a while and think for a bit.

Think for a bit, trying to work it out. Where to go. I held my belly trying not to let the baby hear my thoughts. It mustn't know that this was not the best start for its little life. But I didn't run. I lay down on my bed and thought. But the more I thought the more I couldn't work out what was the best thing to do. I lay all day in the circle tent on my bed. I didn't think bitter thoughts about my women friends. I understood. They had saved my life. I could not expect them to do it again. Not when it was against the rules of the community. So next morning in the circle, I went to each one and hugged them. Cora cried, and Alice clung on and Charlotte showed a fist and Virginia held my hand and Kate hugged me like she was never going to let go. Willa said she would miss me. Freya said the same words she had said before. "Trust Jess. Just trust." And then, funnily enough, things went back to normal.

Alice examined me and said she thought I was quite far on. I was so tiny, she said, it was hard to tell. She measured my belly and then measured it again a week later. She could tell that the baby was growing.

Nobody said where the money had come from. But there was enough for everything the baby would need and enough for me to stay somewhere until I got fixed up. It was a lot of money. I couldn't give it back because I didn't know where it came from.

Alice told me about baby care and feeding. She talked me right through the birth thing, breathing and pushing and holding. There is not one single thing they did not help me with. But I still had to go back to England, back to Newcastle. Back to seeing people I didn't want to see and a life that was full of painful memories.

Chapter 17

Preparation

Inside every day for me there was joy and there was torture. The joy was the sun on my belly warming the growing little body. The torture was the dark form in front of me of the return.

Alice and I had a little chat together everyday about how to do things. I told her I was sorry that I had made her go back to her other life. She said she didn't mind but I could tell that she did a little bit. After all I knew how I felt about having to go back to my other life. Why should she feel any different? She had been hurt in her other life and who's to say her hurt was less painful than mine? But when she rubbed my feet and massaged my back she got really happy and smiled a lot. These were things she liked, she said. Not all that doctor medicine. This kind of medicine.

She said when she got sick she took herbs and homeopathic pills. I didn't understand the explanation that Alice gave of how it worked. But I trusted Alice so I trusted homeopathic. Sometimes when we had our talks Alice carved her wood. She would hand me a bit of wood and ask me to get it ready for carving and I would shave and chip till it was ready for her to make her animal or figure or another totem pole to place on the willow fence. I would hold the pole up for her and she'd carve a shape and tell me about panting and getting the milk to come down. Then she'd ask me questions to see whether I understood it all. I did. I took it all in. Alice was pleased. She said I had been quick to pick it all up. I thought about this and told her that not having an education probably had been a good thing for me because now I was learning things that I really wanted to know, and nothing got in its way. My knowledge had increased from carving, gardening, the keeping of the fire and reading to baby knowledge. Alice said it made her very happy that I could think that way. I was pleased with myself that I'd made Alice happy.

Kate bought some soft cotton sheets and made some baby wraps and a couple of little vests and Cora bought three organic cotton baby grows at the grocery shop. She thought it would be a good thing to have them in my case so I was ready and besides she wanted to buy a present for the baby. This made me cry. It made me cry so much that Alice had to give me some rescue remedy to calm me down. Presents for the baby and it wasn't even born. What did that mean to me, who had never had a present till the library man bought me the notebook and Angelo bought me Christmas presents? Already this little baby had presents. I folded the presents up and carefully placed them in a little bag and put them in my rucksack.

A decision was made about the date for my leaving. Cora would buy a ticket in the town the next time she went shopping. I would fly from the nearest airport and land in Newcastle two hours later. It would be that quick. I would be back in the other life two hours from leaving this life of love and care and new knowledge.

Landing in Newcastle. What did that mean? Where would I go? I had money. What would happen next? Even with money? Social Services. Those words hit me hard. They would take care of me, Alice said. Not like here. Not real care like I was getting now. I felt sick when I thought about it.

In the potager garden I'd rub the little white chamomile heads in my hand and put marigold flowers behind my ears. I helped Virginia pick herbs to make oil and I watched and learnt how to do it. With the oil she would make soap and candles. The best time, she told me, was when the herbs were fresh and young and full of life and energy.

"You can do all this in Newcastle," she said. That I had to trust that somehow I would find my place there and use all my new knowledge. She kept saying this till I almost believed her. There were probably places where I could be happy. I only knew dark streets and hard times. But there were other things there. I just had to find them like I had found this. I could go to the library. I might find them there, the way I had found the Pieta.

I was healthy like I'd never been. I ate rice and vegetables and seeds and fruit. I walked to the stream with Willa. I worked in the garden with Virginia. I felt strong. My hair was thick and unruly. Sometimes Willa cut it for me but she wasn't the best hairdresser in the world. But what she did suited my face and suited me as I was now. I didn't know what the social services would think of my hair. But I wouldn't change Willa's style for anything. She always made me laugh when she was attacking it with her scissors which were not really sharp enough for my thick lumps of hair. I wore trousers that wrapped around my tummy, baggy things, much more comfortable than my tight jeans, and long cotton tops that Kate gave me. Old things that she didn't wear anymore. They covered a growing bump. A very quick growing bump. Alice said it really was time for me to get back to have the baby. She was probably right. I could make it work. I'd done it before. Look at me now. All different from a year ago, nothing was the same. But that didn't stop me crying when I thought about losing my friends. No matter what they said it still made me cry. Then Alice reminded me that I had to let my baby hear me sing so that it would be happy in its little sleeping bag in my tummy. I sang like anything in the potager garden and Virginia joined in to help me remember happy singing. Sometimes, I would sing and instead I wanted to howl. Right out loud. Howl and howl. I didn't though. I watched Virginia weeding and planting and listened to a little weeding and planting song that she wanted to teach me. She knew lots of songs, Virginia. We sang in the potager garden the morning before the day I was due to leave. She praised my voice up to the heavens. She said she knew I would be fine because I could use my voice to bring my life on in Newcastle.

"It's special. It's one of the finest voices I've ever heard. You know how to sing Jess. Your voice will carry you through."

I don't think Virginia had ever spent time on a council estate in Newcastle. You didn't have any big singing opportunities. I said this.

"I know," she answered. "But life can change. You have. And people are kind."

Chapter 18

Leaving the Sanctuary

I'd never been in an airport before. It wasn't like the bus station and it wasn't like being in a potager garden. It was a shock and it was too sad for me. I couldn't say goodbye. I was angry and I was frightened. Scared stiff. That made me take off like a bat out of hell towards where the man in the uniform told me to go, so I could show my ticket and go through the glass doors and away from my friends, my sanctuary, my happy me and my happy memories. I did everything I was told and got on the plane. I was choking. Choking with anger and tears. Choking so much every part of me hurt and I had to hold on to my belly and tell the little baby that it would pass and it musn't get upset. I didn't like being on an aeroplane and I'm sure my little baby didn't either.

Then I was there. Back in Newcastle. Hurting so hard inside. Wanting to rush to the potager garden. Desperate to pick a lettuce. Instead, Jess back where she belonged. But it didn't feel like here was where I belonged. I took a deep breath and told the baby that somehow I would make it turn out alright. That we'd find our own place in this life. No matter how I tried, I couldn't imagine that it was here.

"It might all fit into place," Kate had said.

"Just give it a try," said Virginia when she gave me a hug.

"It's your journey," Freya had said.

And Charlotte, serious Charlotte, who didn't like babies, whispered in my ear. "Don't suffer Jess. Come back if you have to. Please don't suffer."

How could I do anything other than suffer? I had left my beautiful friends. I had lived in a beautiful city, loved a beautiful man and sang in a beautiful church. All I had was memories of little spaces in my life where special things happened and I was lucky.

Perhaps I should be focussing on luck. Hope that luck would happen again.

I found the way to the metro and took a train right into the centre of Newcastle and I found the hotel that my friends had booked for me. I had enough money for a month. They thought that I was owed this money for the work that I had done when I was there. So typical that they would try their best to make me feel better about taking it. Somehow I would pay them back. That thought made me feel better. It gave me something to go forward for. To show them I was grateful for all that they had done even though my anger and my fear had been the last thing they had seen of me.

I was back to square one and would soon be back in the hands of the social services. Just for a while, I told myself. Just for a while. I hadn't looked at the faces of the people on the train and in the street. I didn't want to see. Old life. Past life. But it's not the same, I said to myself. It's different now. I knew about therapy. I knew about transformation and ceremonies and totem poles and singing just for the sheer pleasure of it. It was not the same, I kept saying over and over again. Unpacking in the hotel room with the window overlooking the river, I could see the concert hall if I strained my neck. The one where I sang and said to myself, I am going there. I am going to the Pieta.

By this time I was so hungry I felt a bit sick. I had left my rhythm behind. That wonderful rhythm of eating and planting and singing. I didn't want any other rhythm in my life. But I had to eat. I picked up my bag and walked up Grey Street. I went into the first sandwich shop I came to and picked up a box of salad. I held it up at the counter. The coffee machine hissed. There was a strong smell of roasting beans. I watched the slow drip of rich coffee. It reminded me. Guiseppe's. A pavement table. Talking, dogs, sun. Ciao Guiseppe.

"Is that all?" A strange voice. I was remembering.

"Hello, anybody home. Is that all?"

I stared at the person talking to me. I lifted my arm and held up a five pound note. I took the change and left without a thank you. I turned back down the street, walked onto the quayside and back along the river until I reached the hotel. I sat on the bed in my room and ate the salad. Probably it was the state my mind was in, but there was no real flavour in the salad. It tasted like the cardboard box it was sitting in. This was not what I wanted. I wanted lettuce that I could pick myself, herbs that worked in my body like medicine and flowers that I can put on my table.

I could say that tomorrow. Then they'd know that I wanted something different in my life. That I knew about other things. I would ask for a house in the country with a garden. There were bound to be little houses outside of Newcastle where I could live and grow vegetables. I knew how to do that because I'd had some very good teachers. Maybe, just maybe, I could get a job in a garden or something. Yes, those were good things to say when I went to see the social services.

The smell of the coffee lingered, filtering in and out of my nose. I used the bathroom in my hotel room. There was a hard smell in there. It caught my throat. I was used to soap made in the potting shed with lavender freshly picked from the garden, water to splash on your face that had been infused with rose petals. Cream made from calendula and candles full of herbs and flowers that were gathered at the height of their potency. This smell was all about chemicals that hurt you when you weren't used to them any more. I would be able to say this too in my interview. That I could make soap and candles and use words that sounded very scientific. Words I had learnt from Kate and Virginia when I was their apprentice in the garden and the kitchen.

I lay in bed thinking of all the things I could say that would impress. Words that would get me the little house in the country. Perhaps there was lovely country around Newcastle. Just as beautiful as anywhere else. How would I know? It wouldn't be like a barge in a lagoon or a yurt village in the Spanish mountains with a big golden sun every day.

I hadn't slept inside a room for a very long time now. Not since my bedroom in the Pieta. There was a lot of noise and there were a lot of thoughts in my head, so sleeping didn't happen very much. That meant I was back on the pavement early next morning and heading towards the social services building. Facing that familiar building, walking through the door, asking for the woman who had been my care worker. Waiting in the grim, open room with all the other people who, like me, needed help. I stared at the floor. I didn't want to look around, take it all in. Just in case I lost what was there in my head, ready for discussion. When I was in her office, she didn't look straight at me. She looked down. Noted the shape of my body.

Did she not notice how comfortably my hand lay across the roundness?

No. She was sorry I had got myself into trouble. Disappearing, everybody worrying about where I'd gone. Not knowing whether I was dead? Did I not understand the concern I caused? I looked at her. I felt my lip go down into a sneer.

"Who cared?" I asked. "Tell me their names?"

"Well there was your mother for a start. And your nan."

I laughed. "You must be joking," I said. "My mother would only be interested in the child benefit that she could stuff into my pocket and send me along the street to buy whatever it was she was on. My nan just stood back and let that happen."

"Your mother has voluntarily gone into rehab. She's making good progress and if she gets clean and back on her feet then we can monitor the situation with the baby."

"What baby?" My hand gripped my belly. Holding. Protecting,

"The new baby. Your little sister. Did you not know?"

"No, I've been away. Where is she now?"

"With foster parents. Being well looked after. Thriving."

"Can I see her?"

"We'll talk about that later. Let's see what's going on with you."

Marigolds and candles, lettuces and herbs, dramatic whiffs of best coffee, totems and dreams of gardens disappeared into the pit of my old life. Just like that. Gone. All my fine words would be wasted here. Another little girl was heading towards the fate that had been mine. My sister.

She talked on. My father had been sent to prison. She didn't know for how long. She would have to make some calls. Another appointment was made for me to have an interview with her in three days time. Then, she said, we would talk about emergency accommodation for me, where I would have my baby. Whether I would be able to look after my baby. My family history had to be taken into account.

"I will look after my baby. Get a little house in the country with a garden. Or a little flat. Maybe somewhere I could get a job in a garden." I stared at her when I said the words, hoping she saw the truth in what I was saying.

"We need to keep an eye on you and the baby first and foremost. See how you cope."

She hadn't heard.

"I'll cope. I've moved on from all the stuff in my family. I'll cope."

She looked straight at me. I could see sympathy in her eyes. Feel it in the movement between her hands. But her face was all authority. That scared me.

I rushed back to the hotel. Not that I wanted to be there. Where else could I go? I didn't want to hang about on the street. I didn't want to go into a bar or a café even though I was hungry and very thirsty. I bought water and some soup in a carton because I knew I had to eat. But mostly I wanted to think. And then I didn't want to think. Because thinking was really going to upset me. I didn't care about the person they called my mother. I didn't care that she was in rehab or out of rehab. So what? I knew what love and care was now. I knew that I got none of that from her. I knew that you could get addicted to being treated badly. That you could go out and actively seek it. That's what they expected to happen with me and my baby. Never on this earth that would happen. But it wasn't just me and my baby I had to think about. There was a little sister and I did care about her and I did care that she didn't have the same life as I had and I did care that I had some sort of responsibility towards her. I could have burnt down houses with the fire in my head. No house, monitored, history repeating itself. A little sister. This was not the passage into a little house in the country and motherhood that I had started to plan. I was a bright girl, the social worker said. But not bright enough to be listened to when I started to say, it's not like that for me. My mother was bright enough, she could fool them when she made up the stories about my problem behaviour. As soon as they were gone she'd let them in. The groomers and the abusers. That's when I learnt to run. Sleep under stairs. Behind bins. They tried hard to tame me. But I bit and scratched and fought till I got away.

"She runs away all the time," my mother said. Nobody asked why. Nobody asked me why.

I was measured by my parent's behaviour. All the stuff that happened before I left crowded into now. And the new counted for nothing. I looked down at the round swell of my belly. You will be a lucky little baby, I said. I will keep my promise that I made that night in the garden.

I was young, still very young. I could sing. Really sing. Sing my socks off if I wanted and sing other people's socks off if I tried really hard. What was happening now made me forget that one night, long ago, I was the star turn in the Pieta. The space I was standing in now held no magic for me. It was a hotel room. It had a view of the river. I tried to work out the difference between arriving here and arriving at the Pieta. What was the difference between the rooms? One bed, one chair, one desk, one wardrobe, one window, one door. There was a decent breakfast. A choice. The difference was I had no place to go. I had no sense of belonging. I had no feeling that something could happen. I had no images of angels, singing behind railings, voices floating around a beautiful painted ceiling. It was never going to happen here. What was I bringing my baby into? Nothing that I wanted in my heart.

I put my bag onto my back, pulled on my shoes and left the hotel room not knowing where I was going and not really interested. I had to walk. I found myself up on Northumberland Street. I went into shop after shop looking at baby things. Prams, cots, baby hats with bows on and little boots with ribbon tied to the side. There were pictures of happy little babies with perfect looking mothers and fathers standing proudly beside them. I couldn't see myself in any of the pictures. I didn't fit in with the pictures. I didn't know what my picture was.

I walked down the street, stopped to look in the windows. I felt a movement against my back. Thinking somebody was pushing past me I took no notice. Another movement. Then a tap on my shoulder. I turned around quickly as my body reacted with an old signal. Danger.

It took seconds for the face to register. There was no change in the eyes. No change in the movement of the mouth. No change in the hunch of the shoulders that held the threat of violence. None of it had changed.

"Prison," I said. "You are in prison."

I took a step back. My heel caught on the pavement edge. I stumbled but managed not to fall. My hands went to my baby. Protecting. Not wanting it to feel the threat that I was feeling.

His hands looked at mine. "So you're caught. Bun in the oven. Just like your mother. Use for only one thing."

I couldn't move. I couldn't open my mouth. Run Jess, run. My legs didn't get the message. I wanted to put my hand out. Hold on to somebody. Anybody. Shoppers walked on unaware of the drama they were passing by. I was going to sink to the ground. Breathe Jess, breathe. I did. I started to walk. Shaking inside.

"Don't you bloody walk away from me." The words spilled onto the street as I walked. Menacing, insulting. Word after word of threat. Abuse. Following me down the street. Now people looked. Then looked away. I started to run. The words were still there. "No good piece of rubbish. Telling tales. Little liar." Round and round my body they went. I went faster. The words came faster. "I'll get you. I'll get you back. Tell tale piece of rubbish. Silly stupid cow. When you went missing they started on me. Asking questions." On and on it went. I ran down an alleyway. Angel, angel please help. I mouthed the words over and over again.

There it was in front of me. Not my angel but the next best thing. The library. I squeezed in through the rotating door and past the man in black. The big man who stood on the door. The man whose label said, security. I went straight to the moving staircase and held on to the rail as tight as I could. My breathing was heavy. My mouth was dry. I was shaking so hard that I could hear my teeth chatter and feel my heart pounding. I stood at the top of the staircase. No sign of him. He wouldn't walk past the big man in black with security written on the label.

I walked deep into the reading room, slowly moved around corners till I found a table and chair that was empty. I sat down, pulled a magazine towards me and bent my face forward, pretending to read. Safe. Nothing could happen to me in here. This had been my sanctuary in the past. I hoped it would be again. I'm safe. But for how long? How long could I protect myself from the hatred? I was born into that hatred and it was back to haunt me. The horror story was back. I put my head down onto the magazine. Poor Jane Eyre. Poor Jess. Poor little sister. Poor little girls. Tears streamed down my cheeks. I lifted my head to wipe them away, hoping nobody was looking. I put my head on my arms trying to get myself back in control. What now? What a mess. It couldn't be worse.

A voice. Another tap on my shoulder. A quiet voice. I didn't lift my head. I couldn't trust the voice. Then the voice said my name again. My proper name. Jess. Just a whisper.

"Jess is that you?" I lifted my head Through the tears I saw the hair. Then the earrings, then the expression. That in your face look. I wiped the back of my hand across my face.

"It's you," was all I managed to whisper.

"What you doing here Jess? What's going on?" She sat down next to me and put her hand on my arm. I slowly drew my arm away.

"It's okay, relax," she whispered. "Can I help?"

Through the blur of my tears I stared at her. "Help. You're the reason I'm here in the first place. It wouldn't have been like this if you hadn't opened your mouth."

"How long have you been here? Where are you living?"

"I've been here for two days. Two days too long. I don't know why I ever came back."

"Where were you before that? It's been months since you left Venice."

"I know exactly how long it is. You don't need to remind me."

"So what are you doing now, sitting crying in the library?"

"I met a man on the street."

"He made you cry?"

"Not at first. He never made me cry. I couldn't cry. Then I learnt how to cry and now he's made me cry."

"You're not really making any sense, Jess. Do you want to grab a coffee somewhere? Then we can talk."

I looked at her. Jude. Last time we grabbed a coffee it changed my life. My lovely life on a barge. This time it couldn't change anything. Couldn't do any damage. Couldn't harm me one way or another.

"A coffee. Yes, why not?" I stood up. Looked around. Pushed my chair back. Looked around again. She stared at my round bump. But she didn't say anything. Just turned and went in front of me. We went down the elevator. Past the security man. Through the revolving door. Down the street.

"We'll go to The Tyneside. They do good coffee there." She led me across the street. And there he was. He saw me. I turned to run. "Bitch. Come here you bitch. Bitch girl."

Jude stared. He grabbed my arm.

"Get off her," she screamed and grabbed my other arm. "Help," she shouted.

That did the trick.

"You bitches," I heard as he turned and ran. "I'll get you. Bitches."

By now she was pushing me across the road.

"Quick down here." We walked like our life depended on it till we got to a car.

"Get in quick." She opened the door and pushed me in. Then we were on the road. Driving. Away. Away from danger.

"What you doing being involved with a man like that?" She looked at my bump.

I knew the thoughts that were going through her head. My fault. My problem. My behaviour.

"I'm not involved with him."

"Didn't look that way to me."

"I don't care how it looked to you. I'm not involved. He's the man they call my father. I'm not involved with him."

She drove so fast, it stopped me thinking. Weaving in and out of cars and buses, crossing lanes of traffic, going through lights until we were on a straight stretch of road and then she really went fast. Overtaking every car on the road. I was scared. I didn't like it, like I didn't like the plane. I watched everything. My feet moved with every sudden turn of the wheel. We slowed down. We were back to streets and shops. She stopped the car outside a red brick house in a terrace. It was quiet. I hadn't said a single word the whole way. She hadn't either.

Jude turned to me. "I know this seems a bit crazy but this is where I live. I think you should come in and tell me a few things and then we can think about what to do next."

I didn't move. I thought of Charlotte's words. "Don't suffer," she'd said. My lovely friend with the straight, serious face. I pictured us gathering wood together for a fire ceremony on a moonlit night, with stars shining as we sat together singing special songs for the earth.

My legs were like jelly when I got out the car. I followed Jude in through the door of her house. What was happening to me now? I had set out with a clear motive in my mind, determined that everything would work out for me and my baby. A little house or flat. A garden. Eventually a job. Now I was walking into the house of a woman I had never wanted to see again in my life. I had been threatened by my father and been in the situation of yet again running. My social worker thought that I might not cope with a baby and even though I had never thought it would be easy or great when I came back, I didn't think I would be catapulted back into the old horror story. I was suffering. I was really suffering. Charlotte, I'm suffering.

"Sit down Jess," said Jude. So I did. She could have said jump in the sea and that's what I would have done. In twenty four hours, back here in Newcastle, I had lost my will.

"Do you want to talk?" she said.

"About what?" I said, not being very pleasant. Charlotte, I'm suffering.

"Okay," she said and left the room. I heard a tap running. Then she shouted through the door. "I'm putting the kettle on. Do you want a cup of coffee or tea? Or maybe a glass of water or juice?"

I thought for a while about what would be best. Chamomile. That is what I drank in the potager garden when I felt a bit tense.

"I wonder if you have any chamomile tea? That's what I would like."

Her head came through the door. Her hair hanging down like bunches of grapes.

"Chamomile? Really?"

"Really," I replied. There we go again, she's thinking how can I know about chamomile. After all, I don't suppose many people who had experienced the person who was my father would think that chamomile tea was in the equation as well. Two steaming mugs appeared on the table and Jude sat down. I looked at her.

"I'm sorry about this," I said as I put my hands around the base of the mug. I felt cold. Chilled.

"Angelo looked everywhere for you. Did you see him again?" She swung her leg around, backwards and forwards. I felt more chilled.

"No," What else could I say? I looked at my cup. "I don't want to talk about him."

"No explanation Jess? I think you owed him that." She looked at her cup. She didn't look at me when she said that.

"I don't think you have any right to say what I owe him. What I don't owe him is knowing that that man you just met outside the library is the man who is my father. I never wanted Angelo to know that. To know that is my history, that is my past, that is where I came from. He's just out of prison and my mother is in rehab. Do you think he needed to know even a tiny bit of any of that? Because I don't. I wanted him to see just me. Jess. A person he loved for who she was. Jess who could sing. Jess who could help deliver vegetables and who looked inside a dictionary and loved to get presents. Not a pathetic, social misfit from a shit family who was excluded from school and slept on the street before she was a teenager. Do you think that is what I wanted him to see? He was better than that was Angelo."

"You never gave him the chance to understand," she said, still not looking at me.

"You never gave me the chance to tell in my own time," I replied quick as a flash. "I think I better go now. Thanks for the tea." I stood up.

"Look Jess, I don't know where you've been or anything. And probably I should never have said anything. But I did. Now, you need help. Let's try and sort things out. Please. Let me help you."

Something in her voice made me stop and sit down again. There was a softness there that I had never heard before. And I believed her. I think she was sorry and I think she did want to help me. And I was a bit stuck now. I didn't know where I was.

"Can we start again?" Jude held out her hand and touched mine. This time I didn't pull my arm away.

"We can try," I answered and sipped my tea. "You haven't got any honey for this have you?"

Jude went into the kitchen and came back with a jar and a spoon.

"Honey we have." She put the jar down and I spooned a lump of thick honey into my cup.

"I have to go and pick my child up from the child minder, so maybe you can just sit and drink your tea. Take your time. I'll be back in five minutes. Then I'll make some food and we can have a good chat. Lulu will be happy to watch a video. It doesn't happen very often, so it will be a treat for her. How does that sound?"

I answered that it would be alright. I could see she was thinking that I was going to run while she was away. But I wasn't. I needed to talk to somebody. But it wasn't like my friends in Spain who just let me find my own words in my own time.

So I drank my tea and stayed sitting in the chair. I was still as tight as a board. I couldn't have run even if I wanted to. I felt frozen to the chair. I looked around the room. I presumed this was a normal room in a normal house. Something I had never known apart from an occasional spell in a foster home, but they were always full of children and I was never there very long. I sat at a table which was wooden, there were wooden chairs around it. There were wooden boards on the floor which were painted a deep red. The curtains were deep red as well, with huge yellow swirls painted on. There was an open cupboard with shelves. On the shelves were bits of china and pottery, photographs and postcards. The walls were covered with paintings and drawings. Some looked like they had been drawn by a little child. Pictures of suns and little people with stick bodies. Drawings that I would be able to put onto my walls when my little baby was old enough. I had only thought about protecting my baby, giving it all the love in the world. Babies grew up and drew pictures. Pictures would then be put on the walls. Then other things happened as well. Things I didn't know anything about. It was good to look at those walls and take in what could happen in the life of a little child. Good things.

I heard a door bang. I stopped looking at the paintings and looked back at the cup. The door opened and Jude came in with a little girl.

"This is Lulu. Lulu, this is Jess and she is going to stay for tea." The little eyes glanced at me and then the child ran out of the room. I heard her going up the stairs. I watched as Jude put down a bag and took various books out of it. She laid those on the table. Then she went into the kitchen and came back with a glass of juice. She put that on the table. Her actions were revolving around the little girl. Her needs. I was watching this because I needed to know. I was once a little girl but I didn't know any of this. The little girl appeared again. She pulled out a chair and climbed on to it. She sat at the table and picked up her glass and drank some of the juice. Then she picked up a book, opened it and turned the pages. I was watching, frozen to the seat, still holding my cup. Jude said that she was going to get some food together in the kitchen. She asked her child if she was alright sitting there. The child looked at me and nodded.

We were left on our own together. The child started to hum a tune. After a while she asked me if I could sing.

"I can," I answer.

"What?" she says. "Do you know Bah bah black sheep?"

"No. Can you sing it? Then I can join in."

After two verses I started to hum. I hummed and she sang for what seemed a very long time. Now I was humming, feeling came back. I could move my hand and touch the skin stretching over my baby. I was back in me.

"You sing a song," she said.

So I did. I sang one of the fun songs that we used to sing around the table in my yurt home. After a while she joined in with words that didn't belong, but she had picked up the tune. Soon we were both laughing at the song.

"You have a lovely voice," she said.

That is the one good thing I knew about myself, and I was so happy that she said it.

I tried to eat the food that appeared on the table. Omelette and salad with big hunks of crusty bread. I wanted to hold on to my cup. Like a security. I pushed a fork in and out of the food, but it was hard to swallow and painful to force.

Lulu went into another room to watch the television and I was left with Jude. She made another drink of chamomile tea and I moved my hand quickly from one mug to the other. Now it was time to talk.

This time, she didn't push it, demand that I speak. She seemed less intense when her child was there. She freed up a bit. So I did talk. I said I was staying in a hotel down at the Quayside. That I had got there from the airport. That I had arrived in a plane from Spain. That my friends in Spain thought it was the best solution. That my friends in Spain, although they had been wrong, were the best people in the world and they would not want me to suffer. That they had rescued me and taken me in. That they had taught me so much. But now I was having a baby. It was Angelo's baby. But it was my baby.

"Who were your friends?" she said.

I don't know how long I spoke for, or how much I told about Freya being quiet and gentle and Kate doing the cooking and Virginia in the garden and Charlotte and the fire and Alice with the wood and Cora and Willa behaving like clowns. I told her about what I had learnt, carved totem poles, what colour the tents were, how big the fence was. I reeled it all off without taking breath.

"Sounds fantastic Jess. I'm almost jealous. Don't you want to go back?"

"They think it's best for me to get a little house and have the baby here. And there are no children there. It wouldn't be right. It's not that sort of place."

"So what now?" Jude sipped her tea. After a moment or two she looked at me and said, "I think you should stay here tonight and then we'll talk some more in the morning."

Before I could answer, she got up and went into the room where her child was and disappeared upstairs. I heard giggles and then a bath running and some more singing.

When she came back into the room I had not moved from the seat. I had not taken my hand off the cup. Not since I came into her house. I felt okay being there. I felt safe.

She said she had been thinking about what had happened to me. It would be stupid to go back to the hotel. We could go and get my things and I could stay with her till I sorted myself out. I knew this was a very generous offer.

The chamomile tea was working. I relaxed my hold on the cup. Eased myself out of the chair and followed her upstairs where she showed me a little room with a bed in and lots of books. There was a chair beside the bed with a lamp on. It looked like a very cosy little room and it had a feeling in it of being loved. I said that. She told me that it had been her room when she had come to visit her grandmother when she was a little girl. That she had loved being here, listening to her grandmother's stories, going to the beach for picnics. She hadn't changed it since then.

I told her I thought she was lucky to have a little room that she had loved for so many years. And now, there was no point in holding back so I told her about where I slept when I was a little girl. How I was never put to bed, never read to, always afraid there would be an intruder into my room and I would have to start fighting and spitting and scratching, run and hide. School was no place to be either as I was called stinky and when I sang nobody heard me. It all tumbled out. Care homes, hostels, courts, all of it jumbled out of my mouth. For the first time I said a lot of the words. What was the point of hiding anything after yesterday? Words that had been hidden inside of me. The pain had come out but not the words. The words were my words. The words were my memories and I had never said some of them before. I didn't spare her and I knew the words I said were hurting her. I wasn't being cruel. This was what I had to say. And she was the one who listened to the words I had to say. The words I had never said to Angelo or even my friends in the yurt tents. They weren't the words of Jane Eyre.

I could see her face pucker at the words and a tear or two escaping down her cheeks.

"You should write a book," was what she said.

"It's already been written. It didn't change anything." Poor little Jane Eyre.

Nothing more was said between us about my life. We went back downstairs. Another chamomile tea appeared and she suggested that we should go to bed and talk again in the morning. That she would be out early in the morning to take Lulu to school but would come straight home. She gave me a nightdress and a toothbrush and hoped that I would have a good night.

I closed the door of the bedroom. Took off my clothes and stood with nothing on. I looked down at my growing tummy. Baby tummy. All my body was changing now, still thin, but not skinny. Did it feel different now that the words were out? I couldn't tell. Perhaps it would take a long time to leave the words behind. Perhaps it didn't make any difference. That the words of my life would be with me forever. That they were embedded in the scars and would never go. I ran my hands over my body. At the moment all that mattered was that I was safe. Tomorrow would bring something different. Whatever had happened today.

When I woke next morning. I heard music. Beautiful music. Music that I knew. It was by Mr Vivaldi. Daylight was bursting through the curtains. I looked around the room I was lying in. It felt old, this room. It felt like a lot of things had happened around this room. A lot of people had read the books. People had read and talked in this room. I think only good things happened in this room.

Happy things around little children. My baby should be born in this room I thought. With happy things around it. It needed that start. Born into happy memories surrounded by books. Even if they weren't my memories.

I got out of bed and walked into the bathroom. Jude appeared at the top of the stairs.

"Hi," she called. The way she did. In that high pitched voice. "Here's a cup of tea and I'll show you how to use the shower." She fiddled with the knobs and hot water came steaming out of the shower head. I sipped the tea from the mug. Now all I wanted was to get into the shower, wash off yesterday, wash off what I didn't want in my life. I thought I had already done that, long ago in a beautiful city.

When I got downstairs there was some cereal on the wooden table. And milk. And honey. I was hungry. I smiled at Jude. The smile was back. And she smiled at me.

"Do you like the music? I put it on specially for you."

"Thank you. Thank you for listening last night. That was the first time I ever spoke the words. Not all the words but a lot of the words. I don't want to say the rest of the words. I don't want to remember them. They hurt too much. And I don't want to have those memories. Not when I am carrying my little baby."

Then I started to chat. I asked her about her little girl. Asked her about her work. Did she like living here? She chatted back. Lots about her little girl. And yes, she did like living here.

"It's hard for me to say this but once upon a time I don't think I was a terribly nice person. Bit of a little rich bitch. Spoilt. Married to Lulu's father. Life was all about great works of art, spa days and shopping. I didn't care too much what was going on in the rest of the world. Then, when my grandmother was dying I sat with her for a long time in the hospital ward. I learnt a lot about other people's lives. And I got humbled. My arrogant attitudes got really challenged. I could see the depth of the lives of the other women in the ward. I thought I was the bees knees. In there, I learnt I wasn't. Then hubby decided I wasn't the bees knees any more so off he went and I had to find a new way to get through life. Get me and Lulu steadied into something different. And this was the answer. Being here. Feeling history, my history."

She picked up a photograph. "That's my grandmother. Meg."

The face in the photograph looked kind. Sitting proudly on a chair. Looking right at the camera. Family picture. I'd never had any of those.

She went on to say that whilst she was still rich and probably always would be because she inherited a lot of money and she would inherit more money, she wanted to have a life that was about not being outside of things because of her wealth.

I think I understood. It was completely different to my life but I knew about different lives. How it all could change. Mine had happened without knowing. Hers had been with a knowing.

She talked about how she loved the countryside. The beach, the moors, the hills. How she took Lulu out whenever she could. Having picnics beside a waterfall. Taking a boat to see the puffins. Walking up hills to see the wild goats.

"We can go out into the countryside if you want. Today. One of the advantages of being rich is that I can choose when to work and when not to. Today, I choose not to. We shall do something together. I'll just check my diary."

She opened a book that lay on the table. A diary. Her diary was full of bits of paper. She glanced at a page.

"No, not a thing on today. No meetings, no telephone calls. Just have to get back to pick up Lulu. Let's go out."

"I don't have to check my diary, so that's fine by me." I was going to the mysterious countryside. Maybe I would end up there with my baby. I felt a surge of excitement.

"I think you should stay here for a while. Till you get sorted out. We'll look for somewhere for you to live. Sort out stuff with the social services. Get you signed up for some money. I'll help. We'll go and pick up your stuff from the hotel before we head off on our countryside adventure."

Jude went back into the kitchen and hummed to the music which was still playing. I left the table and went upstairs. I put on the clothes I had worn yesterday. They didn't feel right on me. They felt as though they had been touched by something I didn't want. Something I wanted to leave behind. I went back downstairs.

"I hope you don't think I am being cheeky. Could I borrow some big trousers and a shirt or fleece or something?" I didn't say why.

"No problem, give me a minute."

Off she went and came back with a pair of trousers with a ribbon around the middle. They fitted perfectly. Then she presented me with a cotton top, stripy with a hood. Perfect as well.

"I feel normal," I said as I rubbed my hands through my hair.

"What's normal?" she said.

"I don't know, I feel like a person in nice clothes living in an ordinary house. It's never happened before."

"And what's even more normal is we are about to go out for a run in the car. That's terribly normal." Jude picked some keys up off the table and I followed her out of the door. First we went into Newcastle and picked up my things. She stood at the hotel desk and argued with the receptionist about a refund which she eventually got. So that was a bit more money in my pocket.

When we left the hotel and stood on the quayside I kept looking around, just in case. Where I couldn't see round corners I moved into the middle of the pavement. Ready. Always ready.

I watched people having coffee on seats. Moving over bridges. Nothing stirred me. Nothing made me think, I like that. That's nice. Not even when we passed the big glass concert hall where I had sang on the stage. That seemed like a long time ago. Another life time. I remembered the spark. The determination to get there. To Mr Vivaldi's church with the railings. Not knowing what would happen next. I never knew what would happen next. When I thought I did, it didn't. Perhaps I had never been able to think about what would happen next. Could you plan what happened next? Next week I shall do this, next week I shall do that. I had never thought like that. It all just happened in my life. Bad things, good things, bad things.

Jude talked about her family when we were back in the car and on our way to the countryside. Her mother and father. Big houses, holidays, running on the beach. Books and dolls. Woods to run in.

"That must have made you very happy," I said.

She didn't know whether it did or not. Didn't help her make the right decisions about relationships. That didn't turn out well.

At least you had a choice, I thought, but didn't want to say in case I was being rude. In my world you didn't know that there were such things as choices because you thought there was only what you saw around you. Because you were just a little girl and the world wasn't big enough yet for you to know anything more. And when the world around you is just made up of hard, black holes that you are always going to fall into unless you sleep behind the bin or run behind the stairwell, you don't think there's an awful lot more on offer. Because nobody has shown you any different. It wouldn't happen like that for my baby because even if I end up with nothing, I could show my baby a flower. I could read her a story. I could sing her a song. It was simple. The right thing to do.

"I wasn't loved like Angelo loved you," she said.

"I know," I answered. Because I did. I knew that.

"You always clam up when I mention his name. Is it not easier to talk about him?"

"No," I said.

"Why?"

"It's too precious."

Then I turned my face away. I could see my reflection in the car window. I saw his face next to it. That was my picture. Nobody else's.

"So, where we going?" I turned my face back to her.

"For a walk to somewhere special. I like to go there. I think you will too."

Chapter 19

The Stones

We drove for about an hour past fields and farms and tiny little streams and across a river by a stone bridge. We passed a forest, then hills and went down leafy lanes till we pulled up beside a hedge. The sun shone through puffy little white clouds. There was beautiful countryside here. I stared at it all. Not knowing it existed till now. Jude chatted about what we saw, the names of hills and rivers and villages. She was good at explaining it all. I took it all in. This is where I could be with my baby, I thought.

"Now we have to walk for about an hour." I think she forgot there were two of me walking because she went at such a pace. I couldn't see where we were going to and I hung back a bit.

"It's not going anywhere this path," I said, not trying very hard to keep up.

"Every path goes somewhere Jess, it doesn't have to be to a shop or a garden, they can stretch for miles and the pleasure is being on the path."

I pushed away the feeling that she thought I didn't know anything. That I didn't have my own knowledge. I don't think she meant to be preachy. It's just the way she was. I did have my own knowledge. I just didn't know about paths.

We went past huge, big corn fields, yellow with seeds waving in the wind. I knew about seeds and planting them. Now I was on familiar territory. I stuck a head of corn behind my ear. Just like my friends and I used to do when we did a fire ceremony or dance to say thank you to the moon goddess. Now I felt at home on this path. I didn't know where it was leading to but it was okay for me. Round a curve and up the path. Then round another curve and up another path. Then a hill. A round hill. Like one of Kate's pudding bowls. Jude marched on in front of me, climbing up the pudding bowl which was covered in wild grass. When we got to the top there was a circle of huge stones standing like totem poles and praying to the sun. There was a tall one. It looked like a warrior. Next to it there was a smaller one with a big round bottom. Just like Alice's wooden figure of the goddess that sat in front of the potager garden. There was one that seemed to be pointing the way and one that had drawn a cloak around itself.

I went into the circle. I didn't know where Jude had gone. On her own journey I suppose as Freya would have said. I moved towards the stone with the cloak. Without knowing why, I put my arms around the stone. I felt the cloak wrap around me. Protecting me. Whispering in my ear. Saying my name. Holding me in its stone heart. I opened my eyes. Jude was in front of me. The woman who betrayed me and then saved me. Always there when the drama was happening.

"What are you doing Jess?" she said.

"I don't know. It's like the stone is asking me to get inside. Can you see it's got a cloak."

Jude said that she did feel that about the stone. That it reminded her of a sculpture by a very fine artist.

"Her name is Kathe Kollwitz. She did this amazing figure of a woman cradling her dead son. This stone is like that figure."

"What's it called, that figure?"

"It's called The Pieta, Jess." Jude stroked the stone. "Isn't that amazing?"

"The Pieta." I looked away from Jude and put my hand on the stone. "The Pieta," I said again. "My Pieta, my lovely Pieta."

"The sculpture is of the Virgin Mary cradling Christ her son. Pieta really means sorrow, compassion and pity."

"I never knew that. I never thought about the meaning. To me it meant little girls being rescued and singing with Mr Vivaldi."

The Pieta. It all fitted into place when I stood at the stone. Holding on to its heart full of compassion and pity and sorrow. I went to the Pieta as a pilgrim with pity and sorrow in my heart. I lay in the arms of the Pieta and they protected me in my sorrow and my pity for all the little girls like me and Jane Eyre.

Now I felt like the person who knew. Who was cradled. Who learnt past the sorrow and the pity for herself. Who grew into love in many different ways. What luck. What luck to be here and have this lesson. I couldn't save my little sister yet, but I would. I was young still and now I know. All those bad years behind me, were behind me. I would go forward with my baby and my baby would go forward with me. Protected.

"I'm going back," I said bluntly to Jude.

"Back to the Pieta?" she asked.

"Back to my friends and teachers and then who knows what?"

"Why there?"

"They see me," I replied.

That was it. I was going back to my friends. I couldn't see anything else in my life but that. Back to where I felt love and could give it. This was me making a choice. Planning what's next. For a little while anyway. Then I would choose what's next after that. But there was one more thing I had to do.

"I have to see my mother first."

"Really? How will you do that? I suppose you'll have to go back to your social worker. She'll know where she is. We'll do that tomorrow. We'll have to hurry. I must get back to pick up Lulu. You're full of surprises Jess. What's made you want to see your mother?"

"I have to tell her not to take the little baby back. Let the little baby go where it will be loved. She owes me that. That promise. It's all I'll ever ask of her. If she says yes, it's all I ever got."

Don't suffer, my friend had said to me. Come back if you have to. I have to, Charlotte.

So we left the great circle of standing stones and drove back to her house. She asked me question after question about why I had to go back. What would happen there with the baby? I couldn't answer the questions. I only knew one thing. That the stone with the cloak was telling me to go back to love. To go where I felt wrapped in the cloak of love.

We picked up her daughter from the child minder. In Jude's kitchen we drank tea and talked about my future plans. There were a lot of disturbances as Lulu was keen for me to sing. And I did sing. I sang every song I knew. Lulu danced and screamed and laughed as I sang. She put hats on our heads and we played pretend. I loved to play pretend. I had never played pretend before. I had all that before me now.

Jude came with me to visit the social worker. She spoke up for me. She could say words that I didn't know. Words that influenced peoples' minds. The decision was that I could visit my mother. A telephone call was made and we left the office. I was moving things along. Each step going forward, out. Like when over a year ago I got a passport, bought a ticket. Not planning. Just doing it. Knowing that each step was the right one.

Jude came with me into the hospital. I walked into the special wing. Through the locked door. I said my name.

Daughter visiting mother. Seeing her face. Looking at her body in a bed. Helpless. Blank eyes.

Sorrow, pity, compassion.

I had to say my name. I had to say I am your daughter. I had to say you didn't have a heart for me. Have a heart for my little sister. Please have a heart for her. Let her be loved. Do you understand? She nodded.

"Never let him touch her," I said. "Do you understand?" She nodded.

Sorrow. Pity. Compassion.

I choked on the words. Did she understand?

"I'll never come back," I said. "Ever. Do you understand why?"

She nodded. Helpless, powerless, lifeless.

Sorrow. Pity. Compassion.

Words started to pour out of my mouth. Unplanned words.

"How did you get like this? Were you a little girl once upon a time? You were never a mother. I'm sorry that I came when you could never be a mother. That's why I have to go. Because I can't be sorry any more. I could be your daughter. But I choose not to be. I will be a mother. And I pray my daughter will always want me to be her mother." The tears spilled over and streamed down my face.

I cried our tears. Our mother and daughter tears. I cried the tears she never did, in front of her. There was one flicker in her eyes. One little movement of her finger. Was that as much of her mother love that she could show? Or was that something else?

She turned her face away. I'd never know. I stood to leave. I had said what I wanted to say. I had said the words. I looked at the bed. I didn't see my mother. I didn't see the neglect or the cruelty. I saw a person. And for that person I felt more pity, more compassion and more sorrow than I felt for myself. I was moving on. I had a way out. I couldn't see one for this poor woman. I turned away from the hospital bed and walked out of the ward without looking back.

Half way down the corridor, before I went through the locked doors, I stopped. I wiped my hand across my face. I turned and went back to the ward. I went back to the bed and took the hand still lying there on the top of the sheet. I put my little wooden angel into the sweating palm. Closed the hand around it and turned away again.

The sadness spilled over into the car. I exploded with tears, I squirmed with sorrow, pity and compassion. But it was over.

We went back to the social services and Jude talked to the social worker about my life, about the baby sister who should never be sent back to the hell of my family. The social worker listened. It took a different sort of voice to get her to listen. One that had authority in it. One that didn't have my history in it. Steps would be taken, the social worker said. It would all be taken care of. The proper steps taken. Too late for me but not too late for the baby sister that would only be abandoned if she was given to my mother.

"Have you got a number for your friends?" Jude's question penetrated the silence in her kitchen. Broke into my wandering thoughts. Had the social worker listened? Had my mother listened? Would that little sister be safe? How could I tell? One day I would make sure she was. One day I would tell her who I was. But now I had my own little one to make safe. I had to keep that promise.

"Yes, why?"

"Let them know you are coming. We can text them." Jude picked up her phone.

And that's what she did. Sent the message. "Jess coming back. Is that okay?"

Two hours later a message came back. "Yes, Jess. We miss our apprentice. Perhaps there are some things that you can teach us."

Chapter 20

Arrival

Cora met me at the airport in the little yellow car.

When I left that morning. I had thought that I would be happy as anything as I passed through the security and the customs. But I had images in my mind that I knew would not fade and a new memory of the darkness that had hung over my young life. Once again I was aware of danger. There was a new sorrow too. The sorrow of the pathetic image of my mother. Unresponsive to her daughter. Unloving and unloved. I didn't love her and it wasn't hard for me to say that. Everybody is supposed to love their mother but I had never felt love as a child. I didn't know what it was. I had never learnt it. Maybe that was the biggest tragedy of that life and not the blows and slaps, the threats and the nights spent freezing. Not the isolation and never getting a present.

Now I was back to love. I had to be with love from the moment my baby was born, so it would feel love the very second it took its first breath.

I was back. Cora bumped down the sandy road asking questions, telling me how much they missed me. That Alice was going to make appointments at the hospital and that somehow they would be able to make a new space for me and the baby. A new yurt. They had talked about it after I'd gone. They felt they had abandoned me. I loved Cora for all of this talk. I was wanted. My baby was wanted.

I told the truth about what had happened to me in Newcastle after all the hugs and kisses had been done, Charlotte held my hand and told me I was the little treasure of the community. They were sorry that they hadn't realised that. I told them about my father. About the Social Services. How I would be monitored and how I had a little sister, already in care. That my mother was in rehabilitation and I had visited her. How I had been held in a stone that was about pity, sorrow, compassion. That I had been rescued by the woman who had betrayed me and how she had helped me. I told them everything and they listened in silence till I had got to the end of the story of my return to Newcastle. Then I was exhausted. Too much to tell and too much to remember. I think it was too much listening for my friends. They all said that they wanted to go to bed early and I was glad of that. But I think they felt sorry that I had gone through what I did. I didn't want them to feel that. Why should they? And perhaps I needed to know and needed to give my mother the only thing I could. My angel.

I was back in my space in the circle tent. Back into that little bed. My friends came and went, kissing me goodnight, telling me how glad they were I was back. I couldn't wait for tomorrow.

After breakfast sitting under the apple trees at the big dining table, more plans were being talked over. I asked Alice if I could make another wooden angel and Virginia if I could help her in the potager garden. These were the two most important things for me to do. I was longing to be back amongst the lettuces, smelling herbs and seeing what had grown while I had been gone. Perhaps some of my own seedlings had grown. Longing to talk to Alice about baby things, feeling safe with her knowledge. Sharing it with me.

The sun was hot. The sky was blue. I pushed open the gate. I saw Virginia with her mad hat on sitting on the bench in the shade. I walked over and sat down beside her.

"Apart from the Pieta, this is the most beautiful place in the whole world," I said. "It's really, really lovely to be back. Thank you for having me here."

"It's lovely to have you back. You know Jess, we didn't realise how important it was to have you here. How much you actually helped us. Me in the garden, Kate in the kitchen and doing the shopping with Cora. You help us a lot. And you sing to us. And once you stopped being so angry, your energy made us feel more alive. I think Charlotte missed you the most. Who would have thought it?"

Not me. But then I remembered her whisper. "Don't suffer Jess, come back."

Virginia stood up and walked over to the shed. She picked up a hoe and handed it to me. "Back to work, you weed, I'll plant." I picked up the hoe and started on the weeds. She chatted about her plans for planting and some new vegetables she wanted to try.

Then, standing right in the middle of the lavender bed, I gasped. A huge gasp. I grabbed Virginia's arm. My legs opened without me telling them to. There was a great big surge in my body and water dribbled out from the bottom of my trousers. Virginia stared. She looked down at the ground and then at my face. She couldn't move and I couldn't move. I put my hand down in between my legs. Everything was wet. Soaking wet. I had wet my knickers.

Virginia started to shout. "Oh my God," she said. "Your waters have broken."

I knew what that meant. Alice had told me all about false labour pains and waters breaking. But my baby lived inside of my belly all safe and tucked up. That's where it was supposed to stay. Now I realised that I had not really thought about the baby coming out. It had all been a dream. A lovely dream. Now it was going to be something else. I didn't want it to be real. I wanted the dream. This baby was not supposed to be born. But it was going to be born. Now.

Virginia propped me up against the fence. "Don't move," she yelled. "Don't take a step. Breathe."

By now I was having contractions. Not massive ones. But I knew what they were. Virginia stood at the garden fence and screamed. Alice came flying through the tents towards us followed by Cora and Willa. Alice took hold of my hands.

"Hospital," I heard her say. "We have to get her to hospital. Lie down Jess, let me have a look up there."

Trousers down and off, legs open right in the middle of the potager garden. "Crowning," she shouted. "Quick into the tent. Towels Kate."

She got me up off the ground and Cora and Willa helped me to walk back to the circle tent. No knickers and huge contractions. This baby was coming fast. I lay down on my bed and Alice opened up my legs. "Pant Jess, pant push. Pant, pant, push." I did exactly as I was told. Panting and pushing and stopping and breathing and letting my body do its work.

I could hear someone singing and I turned my head between a pant and a push. It was quite a scene. Freya was dancing in a corner. Dancing and singing. Alice was showing me panting and pushing faces. Charlotte stood by the door with a huge frown on her face. Kate sat on a chair next to the bed and held my hand. Willa was laughing at Alice and Cora was rushing around putting towels in different places. Virginia lit a candle and held it close to my head so I could smell the herbs. One big push. One big pain. Then a noise. A little noise. A whimper noise. I stopped panting and looked.

Alice put her face very close to mine. "A little girl, Jess. A perfect little girl." She held the bundle up to my face and then placed it on my belly. I put my hand on the little girl and stared at Alice. I had given birth. Just like that.

Then I saw Freya with her long grey hair move towards me. She took hold of Alice's hand who took hold of Kate's hand who took hold of my hand till everybody was holding hands, even serious Charlotte who was holding a tissue up to her eyes. Then Freya chanted and everybody joined in and, in complete shock, I started to chant and for all the world you would have thought the baby chanted too. I was now a mother. It took less than two hours, Alice told me. She'd never known anything quite so quick.

So there was no hospital. No knocking on the door of social services asking for a place in a mother and baby home and a single mother flat. Alice cut the cord and the baby was wrapped up in one of the cotton sheets that Kate had made. I sat like a queen with my head propped up on pillows and a little baby girl in my arms.

I don't know if I lay in my mother's arms. I don't know if she felt like this. I don't think so. I don't think you could feel like this and then allow all those hurts to happen.

When the chanting and hand holding stopped and the practicalities were taken care of, I was kissed a million times by my friends as they left. All except Alice who kept looking under the sheet and between my legs and checking the baby's temperature. "You'll need to rest now," she said.

"Not on your life," I said to Alice. "I want to stay awake and watch this little head and this little body squirm and squidge about until I can't keep my eyes open any more."

The little body snuffled and sniffled and whimpered and opened and closed its little mouth. I put my finger between its lips and felt the tiny tongue working away like everything else was working away. Little eyes blinking, little nose breathing, little heart beating. Little feet pushing, little toes wiggling. Eyes staring, huge great big eyes, deep brown eyes with lashes so long they already curled. So dark against the little red cheek. Angelo's eyes. The eyes were all his. But the lips were all mine. Thick and full. Little ears lay flat against her head which had two or three spikes of dark hair dotted around.

I asked Alice if she needed to be fed yet and Alice didn't think quite at the moment but when it was time she would show me how to do the job. Then she left us alone. I sang to the baby. The same lullaby that I'd sung when it was growing in my belly when I told her how much she would be loved. Great eyes looked into mine as I crooned away. When Alice came back the little eyes were closed but I still held her close so I could feel her breathing next to me.

"We have to weigh her," said Alice. "She's got to be early Jess because you didn't look full term."

The wrapped up baby was popped into the black steel basket of the weighing scales from the kitchen and Alice started putting the round weights onto the scales. Baby came out at a very small normal birth weight.

"Not quite a little premmy, but close. She must have been neatly tucked away." Alice wrote the weight down in one of my notebooks and placed the baby back into my arms. "Now you could try her with some milk, Jess. Let's see if we can manage this between us. It's not my speciality, but I understand the academics. See if we can put it into practice."

So I fed her and felt quite content and thought that rice and vegetables and seeds and mint and chamomile were good things to get your life going on. Better than heroin and various shades of alcohol. I sighed deeply as she sucked.

Not with pleasure but with huge satisfaction that all this goodness was her first grasp of life.

Possession took me over that night. Big as anything. No sleep for me whilst I guarded my baby. No handing her over to strange arms. No letting her go as I perched on the toilet or drank tea. Kind women with open arms turned into baby snatchers. Every movement beyond my bed was an act of sabotage. Nobody would come between me and my new baby. I snapped and snarled at anyone who wanted to interfere in my bonding. I refused to sleep, wouldn't eat and no way allowed any touching. A fierce monster grew inside me. Even Alice, kind, kind Alice was rejected. What would have happened without Alice, I can't think. But my thinking now was anything but kind. Old Jess, back to survival. But there were two of us now so my frantic attempts to hold the baby as close to me as possible took on mammoth proportions. I resisted any attempts to help, all reason left me. My friends came and went but they never left me alone. Kate sat quietly knitting, Alice carved, Cora read, Virginia wrote. Each quietly sat with their activity whilst I cooed over my baby and growled if anyone came near.

After some hours Alice came close to my bed. She told me with a very gruff voice that if I wanted to behave like a wolf mother that was fine but she needed me to drink all that water within the next two hours. She placed a big jug on the table beside the bed. I saw her glance at the sleeping baby quickly but after that she turned her back on me and left the tent. I did drink the water. And then I fed the baby. And then I fell asleep. I desperately tried not to. All trust had gone, so I didn't know what would happen if I was not awake to protect the baby. When I did wake, the baby was gone out of my arms. I threw the covers back ready to scream, pounce, charge. There, right next to me, sat Freya, stroking the baby, moving her hands over the little body this way and that, humming away. I didn't hiss and spit. It was Freya. You couldn't hiss and spit at Freya.

"Child," she said to me. "You are in our hearts and this new little life form is in our hearts. You are safe and she is safe."

She passed the baby back to me. Baby didn't seem to mind at all that it had left my arms and been in the arms of another. I drank some more water and lay back. Now I was really tired. And I didn't know what to do. When to feed and wash my baby and when to change its little nappy which was just a sheet cut into lots of pieces. Alice came back and took Freya's place.

This time I watched Alice looking at the baby. There was no threat in her face, no wish to harm. "I need help," I said.

"I know. You were very dehydrated and confused. And also the birth was a big shock to your body."

"More than that," I said. "Once the dream was over, the dream of the baby, the reality made me really frightened. I think that's what happened." Alice said it made perfect sense to her and it was time to get going on a nappy lesson.

Nappy lesson over, we then did a feeding lesson, after a feeding lesson it was all about checking baby's temperature, making sure it was warm enough or not too hot. Then washing and bathing with all the wonderful baby gifts that Cora had been shopping for. A little plastic bath. A baby shampoo and special lotion. A little bar of baby soap. Holding the little head and dabbling the water over her little tummy was the best baby learning experience. Her first bath was a community event with happy whispers and smiles.

After that, Alice told me, it's all instinct. Alice held the baby on her knee, and I slept. Not a lot, but enough to bring in a new day with a great feeling. My instinct then was to get out of bed and get hold of my baby and take her into the garden. It hurt a bit when I walked and my body felt loose and light. But I cradled baby in my arms and walked around the willow fence, showing her totem poles, little carved bears and strange figures made out of clay.

"This is where you were born," I whispered. "You are a clever little girl, waiting till we got back. You could have been born in a mother and baby home but you knew you didn't want that didn't you? You wanted to be here with the power animals and the sweat lodge and the Fire Keeper."

I paraded her around the willow fence and into the potager garden. Virginia was weeding. I presented my baby to her. Then I thanked her for all she did and said I was sorry about being such a horrible person. I told her what I told Alice and she said she understood and felt that she would feel exactly the same if she were me. That made me cry and kiss Virginia. Forgiving me like that. Especially when I had jiggered them all by having the baby here. The more I walked the more I could walk, so I went to the kitchen to see Kate who was making lunch. I showed her the baby. Then she cried. I think she had wanted a baby and that was why. She stroked her little rosy cheek with her finger and her tears fell onto the sheet. I wasn't quite into sharing my baby yet, but I did say she could hold her for a little while. She sat down on the chair and took the baby into her arms.

Even very serious Charlotte who said she wasn't into the baby thing at all, said she had to admit she was lovely but she didn't want to hold her because she'd never held a baby before. And she didn't want to particularly start doing that sort of thing at her time of life if I knew what she meant. Maybe I did. But I kissed her anyway and said thank you.

My healing your life book said that it was always important to show gratitude for the things that you had. But saying thank you to Charlotte had nothing to do with that. She could have said no, she could have decided against me. She could have been cold about me. But she wasn't. She was strong and she was clear. I think she was a little disappointed about me not being her apprentice any more. So I told her that she now had two apprentices. Charlotte said that although she didn't want to touch baby, or do baby things, with baby it would be a good idea to have a ceremony to welcome her into the world and to give the baby a name if I had thought of one.

Of course I had. From the very first moment that my hand touched her when she lay on my belly, I thought of angels guarding me. I thought of a beautiful man on a boat. Angels and Angelo. Her name was Angelina.

I walked around the tents, talking and showing off the baby. Kissing people and saying sorry. Alice said it was amazing. I was like an Amazon. Producing a baby just like that. Being strong enough to walk and talk and hold the baby.

Looking good. It was all down to her I told her. Her help and advice. Better than any in the whole world. For me it was over, the birth thing. My baby was here. Now we could get on with our lives. I didn't want to hear Alice talk about infections and injections and other sorts of official stuff. We could just go on as we are.

Alice said it was early days.

Then the longing started. I tried to brush it aside. Not think about it. I got back into a rhythm. Eating and sleeping and changing and weeding and washing the dishes. Sometimes I read when I fed. The baby lay happily in the cot in the garden whilst I gathered leaves and weeded. I put little bits of chamomile in her bed or lay marigolds across the sheet. I strapped her into a harness when we walked with Cora and happily let Alice handle her to check her progress. But the longing got worse. It grew into a fever. It burned my head at night. Every time I looked into her eyes the longing got stronger. When I looked into her eyes, I saw her daddy's eyes staring back at me. I longed for

Angelo. I longed to show him his daughter. I longed for him to hold her and me in his arms.

Chapter 21

The Grandmother Naming Ceremony

This was her thing, Charlotte told me. Doing ceremony. She'd never done a naming ceremony for a new born baby before. It would take a bit of research. She wanted to get it right. She said it was important to welcome the baby into the world. That is what I wanted too. A real welcome into my life and the world. And it would all be as good and loving as I could make it. Freya said they wanted to welcome the baby into their life as well. That they had been given this opportunity as a community. She said she didn't know where things would go from here but now, at this time, in this place, the baby was welcome and a ceremony would be a very blessed occasion.

Everybody thought it would be a good idea. Willa said she was really looking forward to it. Gave her a chance to dress up and act daft. She liked acting daft. She made funny faces for the baby to look at. She clicked and rolled her tongue, holding the little eyes in the sound.

Then Freya did what Freya always did after making a statement, she went back into her yurt tent. Charlotte said that Freya meditated in her yurt. That she prayed for the world and the beauty of the earth and all the animals. I think if praying worked, the world would be alright. She prayed so much. Freya never frowned and never laughed. Freya knew things. She could see things and she could see things in me. So I thought then that she could see things in everybody. But she didn't speak about it. She'd seen my hurt and she'd seen my baby without me ever having to say and so I thought her words came from a deep feeling thing in her. If rescue remedy didn't work when I was remembering a pain or longing for a man on a boat or a railing in a church, I would sit at her feet and that worked. The remembering became calm and I could think of other things. Freya blessing my baby was special. I knew that. It added to my love.

The naming day was chosen and Charlotte and I collected wood for the special ceremony. It was fine for me now to leave my little baby with Kate or Cora who were happy to hold her or push her around in the buggy if she was sleeping. I think she was a content little baby. She slept and fed and sucked her little lips and sometimes there was a whimper, but I was never far away. Like I told her before she was born. I would always be there to sing to her. I learnt new songs from my friends to sing. She'd watch my lips as they moved. Virginia said, when we were weeding one day, that she was a lucky little baby. I hope she feels lucky and I hope she is. I would try my best for lucky to be in her life. That she wouldn't have to wait for lucky like I did.

Charlotte lit a fire in the sacred fire space. This fire was to bring all the earth and tree spirits into our community for the blessing. I fed the fire with wood in the way that Charlotte had told me. Bringing in the energy from the four corners of the universe, the north, the south, the east and the west and my energy would be in the fire too and that would bring in baby energy. I did this exactly as she said. Collected special wood and placed it on the fire. That was fine by me if that was what Charlotte said.

The fire burnt for twenty four hours before the ceremony took place. We gathered at the table. A feast had been prepared. Fruit and cakes and even cherries covered in chocolate. It was all laid out on a white cloth and lovely bright flowers from the garden were thrown everywhere over the food. Each of my friends came with their own gift. A wooden carving, a poem, a book, a painting, a crystal, a photo. For this ceremony, there was no wild face painting because they did not want to frighten the baby. No crazy dancing. There was a peaceful circle around the fire and I sat in the centre with my baby. Freya waved an eagle feather around us and then wafted us with burning sage. Then she asked me to tell her what the name of the baby was to be.

"Angelina," I said, so proud.

"Welcome Angelina, may you have many blessings. May you honour your mother Jess and all your blessed ancestors. May you know that you have many grandmothers to watch over you. We, gathered in this circle, are your guides and your grandmothers and we will always hold you in our hearts."

That was it. The baby was named Angelina and was truly blessed in her naming ceremony. We circled the embers in the fire and Charlotte stood chanting as we all moved around. Then each person touched Angelina and said something special to her.

Around the table we ate our feast of food and sang and Charlotte played a tune on her guitar. Willa got up and danced to the music, moving her arms around above her head and dancing around the totem poles. As she danced she made lovely noises. The sparkling sound echoed through the trees and Angelina fell asleep in my arms as I hummed to the tune.

She was still asleep in my arms when the longing started again. My arms were full of Angelina, but they wanted more. They wanted the man who she belonged to. Would he want me? Could I risk even thinking about it? When did he stop looking for me? Was he still looking for me? Or had he forgotten all about me? Had he a right to see his child? I couldn't stop thinking about it all. How was I to know about a child's relationship with a father?

This longing disturbed me. I had moved through a million mind zones in a short time and I was ready not to move my mind for a while. It was enough to look after Angelina and do my little jobs. Could I not be settled here? I knew that my dark old life was gone although the memories hadn't. Talking with Alice taught me that the memories might always be there. But as the good things happened then the bad memories would go further back. Good memories. The Pieta. Angelo, Angelina. My friends here in the yurt community. Could that not be everything for me at the moment? I didn't think run any more. I did not think bad things about my friends here. I didn't believe any more that they would reject me or plot against me. In this little secluded world it all happened in the best way possible for me. There was no longing for lots of money or to meet men or to have a proper house all to myself and Angelina.

Sometimes a warm feeling swept over me. It surged into me. I can't even explain that feeling but it was good. It was about feeling lucky. It was about feeling love and it was about being grateful for the gift of being here. I knew it couldn't be for ever. I knew that there were rocky roads ahead and I knew that whatever happened, my promise to Angelina to keep her safe for ever would not be easy. But something special happened when she was born here instead of where she was supposed to be born. Every day I read my healing my life book. It worked. It made me feel different about me. About my shame. About my fear. I could think about it without getting angry or hating where I came from. I couldn't forgive my past but maybe one day I could.

But the longing stayed with me. It was still there the day after the naming ceremony. Even stronger. Feeding my lovely child in the garden, right next to the sunflower that Virginia had planted on the spot where my waters broke, tears poured down my cheeks. I couldn't help it. It was a soft cry. Not full of frustration, not full of wounding. Soft tears full of longing. I couldn't help it.

When I told Virginia what my longing was she said she would give it thought. Next day in the circle, Virginia spoke about my longing. Freya closed her eyes and hummed in the way that she did when she wanted to see things. The circle was silent.

"There is a calling," said Freya. "You are calling each other. A windhorse man can know in his heart that he is still in your heart and he can feel your longing through the wind. We shall all meditate on this to find a solution."

I said thank you to Freya and thank you to the circle. I knew that the solution would be about what they thought would be the best thing for me.

So I had to leave them to meditate and talk about it all without me. I trusted their talking and their meditating. They were good at that. They would come up with the best idea. They were good at ideas.

Their idea was that I should go to Angelo. That my longing was about my love for Angelo. That they did not want to lose me or Angelina but I was young, and I had to find my own place in the world as they had. That they would always be in their place and there would always be a place for me there.

I discussed with them that Angelina had to be a little bit older before I made the journey and I needed to be stronger and more confident in my role as a mother. I listened to what Alice had to say when I raised my fears and concerns. I became the expert in bathing and feeding. I learnt to listen to the sounds of my baby. I could tell the difference between those that were about her needs and those that made me nervous. There were always willing arms to hold and help when I needed it.

Angelina's cot had a place in the kitchen and when I was helping Kate to make bread and salads, I listened to her when she told me stories about her life and her experiences and what had brought her here. I talked back. I liked talking now. I could chatter and laugh and use words easily. I could think about things and ask questions without fear. I was part of this community. For now. As long as they were here, Angelina and I would have a home. That gave me confidence to go ahead with my plans. To go back to Angelo and the Pieta. Because the longing got stronger and stronger. If going back didn't happen in the right way then I could come back here. That was clear.

Angelina lay happily in her pram in the potager garden so I could still help Virginia with the weeding and planting. She would read to me her latest piece of writing. I learnt to listen and to think and to understand the words. I loved learning.

Then it was time. Angelina was thriving and I was ready, strong enough to make the journey. My mind was full of anxiety, but my heart was full of the leaving, my longing and my love.

Chapter 22

Return

Every face was a mixture of tears and smiles as the small yellow car set off down the dusty road. The willow fence disappeared from my glazed, hazy view. The totem poles were gone. My friends had said their goodbyes.

My goodbyes were still stuck in my throat. But this was how it had been chosen, the solution to my longing. It could be risky this journey. If Angelina was discovered we may be deported because she had no passport. She wasn't registered anywhere. We hadn't thought about this until not long before our planned journey. But we had talked it through and I had decided that this was the risk I would take rather than try to find another way. That was why Charlotte was chosen specially to drive the car. She could speak all the languages, she was used to dealing with officialdom. She could stay cool. She was the best person to help me and Angelina and my longing. I trusted that Charlotte was the best person to do this journey and I listened carefully to everything that was said. My instructions were clear.

Charlotte agreed to drive the car. Serious Charlotte. Strong Charlotte. Charlotte who did not want babies in her life. Charlotte was moving my destiny along with her strength. It was probably going to be needed.

Angelina, strapped in the back by a special belt, was sleeping. Everything had been packed and planned with what Virginia had called military precision. There was no room for error, Cora had said as she placed the buggy underneath the spare wheel. My bag and Charlotte's bag were then placed on top. I took the baby changing bag into the front with me and blankets were laid across the back seat. Plastic containers, filled with salad and fruit and bread that Kate had made that very morning, were packed, along with tea towels and flasks of tea and coffee, into a picnic basket.

My friends had thought things through thoroughly for the journey.

Charlotte was quiet as she drove. Thinking. That's what she did. Serious thinking. She was the Keeper of the Fire. She lived the matriarchal life, she said. I asked what the matriarchal life was and she told me about women being strong leaders. Goddesses who were worshipped. Women living in their own power. She didn't want to talk about past things. That was not her thing, she said. She'd had her pain. It was over. Her life suited her now and that was that. She drove with her eyes on the road and her mind on her task. I stopped asking questions and thought about what my other women friends would be doing now. Would they be sitting in the circle talking, planning? Would they have dried their tears, got on with their tasks? Would Freya be praying for the world? Quietly sitting in her yurt seeing things that I couldn't. Freya was wise. Old and wise. Wise was good. I hadn't known about wise. But I had seen wise when I sat with Freya. So now I knew about it.

Would Virginia be writing in the potager garden? Would she be looking at my butterfly?

Would my butterfly be looking for me? Wanting to tell me of transformation. Transformation had happened to me. I could cry. I could smile. I didn't run. I was a mother. I learnt about growing things. I learnt about how to have friends. I learnt about letting it out. Pain and hurts and wounds and terrible remembering thoughts. I learnt about words and reading and writing. I learnt how to dance in the sweat lodge and I learnt about fire and how it spoke to the earth. I learnt about trees and the little spirits that lived among them. I think all of that was transformation. I learnt to share my voice. I learnt how to cooperate without hitting out. I learnt that things can work.

Alice gave me a little coloured totem pole to keep us safe on our journey. It was painted green and blue with a yellow eagle on the side. I had it in my pocket. It would work. I also had an angel in my pocket. I had given my mother my first angel and I hope it kept her safe. The new angel was like the old angel only I had carved a little face, a smiling face. Alice had showed me how. Lovely Alice. Alice who cared for me and who first held Angelina. Angelina couldn't wait to be born. She knew she could be born into nearly the best place and with the best people in the whole world. I think the angel made that happen. Pushed her along and out of me into Alice's waiting hands and the smiles of my friends. Lucky Angelina. Born lucky. I hoped the luck stayed with her. If it was up to me it would.

The bread made the car smell lovely. Kate had made it specially. She didn't rate my bread making very highly.

"Not your best skill Jess," she said. But then she said that I always picked the right lettuce and herbs for the kitchen yurt and brought lovely flowers for the kitchen. So I didn't worry too much about not being the best bread maker in the world. I could do other things.

Cora and Willa would be having a bit of fun somewhere. They had often tried to make me laugh when I was stuck inside of my own horror. They dressed up and sang silly songs and read funny poems. I didn't understand poems at first but as I got to know them I started to like them. They would try to get me to write a poem. That was another thing I wasn't much good at, like bread making. They would read the poems out at the table when we were eating and sometimes I felt angry at that. Old Jess would boil away inside when I thought they were making fun of me. But they weren't really. They were just fun people and in the end it helped because I learnt to trust that not everybody was making fun of me. They were just trying to get me to see my fun side. My fun side was not a lot in evidence at first. Cora and Willa were not much good at carving or cooking or gardening. Singing and dancing and playing made up instruments and organising dressing up for the fire and getting things ready for the sweat lodge, was their thing. This was as important as anything in the yurt sanctuary. My sanctuary. How hard it was to leave it. But the longing was big. Bigger than the leaving.

Charlotte broke into my thoughts and said that it was time to eat and to try to feed Angelina, who was still fast asleep in the back. We were nearly at the border, so we must make sure that she was fed and changed and back to sleep again. This was part of the plan. She drove down a little side road until we found a grassy patch to sit on for our picnic. I lifted Angelina out of the seat in the back. She didn't like that. I stroked her and moved her up on to my shoulder to coax her to wake up. Charlotte cut up bread and placed salad and fruit and big hunks of cheese on the tea towel, which she had spread onto the grass. I shoogled Angelina until she took my breast and started to suck. I knew Charlotte didn't particularly like all of this carry on so I turned my back to her and she ate the food in silence. I didn't mind. I respected how she felt. I had my stuff. She had hers.

I got the nappy bag out of the car and changed Angelina. She kicked her legs and made little sounds with her lips. I wiped her bottom with the special baby wipes that Cora had got in the organic grocery store. Everything that Angelina had was organic. Soap, towels, nappies, wipes, cream. All bought for her by my friends. Every time I changed her, I told her how kind our friends had been and that organic was better than anything for her vulnerable little body. Alice had told me all about a sore bottom and how to look after it. I wondered how often my nappy was changed. Did my bottom see soothing organic cream? The thought made me shudder and I always made specially sure that Angelina was soaped and changed and creamed in exactly the way Alice had told me.

Charlotte read a book as I walked around in circles patting Angelina on the back and stroking her legs. At last she slept. Then, as planned, instead of going on the back seat of the car, the special seat was placed on the floor of the car behind my seat. The picnic basket was put onto the back seat with lots of coats and blankets and just as we reached the border into France, we carefully put the coats and blankets over the little car seat so Angelina could not be seen. She had no passport. She had not been registered. This was the scariest moment for me. I was like wolf mother again. Ready to run with my young. I started to shake violently. I couldn't breathe properly. I could smell the fear like an animal when in danger. I was in danger now. What would happen if the plan went wrong? I had been willing to take the risk. Now I was sorry. This was too much risk. I should have been satisfied with what I had. This longing business was going to finish us off. Me and Angelina. And what would happen to Charlotte if it all went wrong? Smuggling Angelina across the border. Charlotte pulled the car into the side of the road and told me I looked guilty as hell and I had to calm myself down if we were going to pull this off. She gave me three drops of special rescue remedy and slowly I felt my breathing start properly again and the awful shaking stopped. I put my passport onto my lap.

"Just keep quiet," said Charlotte with a cross voice and an angry stare. She started the car again and we went a little further down the road and then joined a queue to go through the border post into France.

I hoped that Freya was praying as hard as she could. I hoped that Angelina wouldn't snuffle or wake up and cry. I hoped with all my might that I looked like any ordinary tourist out for a trip. The border guard had a gun on his hip. And a very serious face, that looked as though the worst would happen to us if he discovered our secret. I pulled myself up in my seat. I had to be as brave and bold as I had been when I got on that bus and it went past the Angel of the North. I put my hand into the pocket of my jeans and held my little wooden angel in my fingers as tight as I could. Charlotte talked in a very friendly way to the border guard. I didn't understand a word of what she said. She picked up my passport and opened it up at the back page. The border guard looked, nodded and waved us on.

I don't know how many times I sighed with relief. I wanted to hug Charlotte and kiss her. But I knew she didn't like that. So I didn't but I did say thank you lots of times. She said that it wasn't over yet, we had a long drive and then we had to get across the Italian border.

We pulled into a café car park to uncover Angelina and put her onto the back seat. She was still sleeping and looked very content. Charlotte drove on. After about three hours she stopped at a hotel and booked two rooms for us. I had been practising trying to speak Italian every day with Virginia in the garden. I had been practising writing and reading and knew that I could use language in a different way than what I used to. But I didn't have a clue what Charlotte was saying when she spoke French. I stared in amazement as she blabbered away with strange sounds. Then forms were signed and keys handed over and Charlotte marched on ahead as I followed on with Angelina in my arms. As Kate would say, Charlotte is as Charlotte does. I didn't understand that either but I think if Kate was here that is what she would say.

My room was tiny but there was a bed and a table and a very small bathroom and that was quite enough for us. Back inside four walls again. It was strange. But the bed was clean, the pillows were soft, the towels were fluffy and there was water, a glass and flowers on the table. I fed Angelina and changed her. I took her outside in the harness for some fresh air. It felt good to walk. I was trying not to think of tomorrow. The evening sun fell on my face as I walked around the garden in the hotel. Where would I be in the evening sun tomorrow? I couldn't think about it. I could only focus on every moment, looking after my baby. Keeping going.

Charlotte marched across the garden and said it was time to eat. We went to the restaurant and sat down at a table. Charlotte ordered lots of food. She said that she loved to eat all the things that she didn't eat at home. Then she went to the bar and ordered a glass of wine. I left her chatting to the bar man and went up to the bedroom. Every moment of non action increased my anxiety. Angelina cried so much I spent half the night in the garden so no one could hear her. She could feel my heart racing. Beating like a drum. I whispered to her that maybe soon she would meet her daddy. Did he want us? Was he calling like Freya said? Would he still be there? Would he be alone?

I couldn't eat breakfast. I had spent all night trying to comfort Angelina, feeding, changing, holding her to me. It was hard. It was the hardest night I had spent since the little thing was born. But that wasn't surprising, I'd said to Charlotte. She didn't know where she was. She missed our friends, her grandmothers, she didn't know where she was going.

"Not having second thoughts?" Charlotte said. "You better tell me now before we go any further."

I told her I didn't, but I was worried. My worry increased as we got nearer to the Italian border. Charlotte stopped the car and yet again we covered the special seat with blankets and I held my passport in my hand. Angelina started to cry. I reached my hand down the back of the seat and touched her. It didn't work. She cried louder. Charlotte swore and turned the car around and went back down the road until we found somewhere we could stop. I took the crying baby into my arms and walked around the car. Louder and louder her screams got. No Alice to comfort me. No Alice to check my Angelina over. Charlotte kept on swearing which didn't help me to feel reassured.

I got back into the car and tried to feed her. Nothing would stop her crying. I was starting to panic. How could I do this to my baby? Put her through this. Make her unsafe. What was I thinking about? The plan was going wrong and I was crumbling.

"Jesus Jess," said Charlotte. "Calm down. Let's get a drink somewhere." She started the car again and we went along the road till we found a café. By now the crying had stopped and once again, I changed her and put her back into the seat and hoped that she would sleep.

It wasn't long before I realised that I had lost my passport. In the panic, I must have dropped it when I got out of the car. Charlotte's anger was brimming over and we flew down the road in the car at such a pace that I had to hold on to the door. Was this my luck running out? All my happy thoughts on the first part of the journey had gone. I couldn't believe I had been so stupid. When everything in the plan had been talked through with me in mind, I had spoilt it. My eyes strained the road ahead. Charlotte stopped the car at the spot where we thought I had dropped it. No sign of a passport. We took everything out the front of the car. No sign of a passport. By now I was in tears and Charlotte was as grumpy as anything. I opened the back door of the car. I was reluctant to disturb the sleeping Angelina again because I think that would have sent Charlotte over the top.

There amongst the blankets was a tip of red. I pulled the blanket back and there was the passport.

Charlotte smiled and took my hand. She had calmed down. I was forgiven. "Let's go for it," she said. "Head up. Smile."

And off we went. Angelina slept. The passports were stamped. The border guard yawned as we passed through. He wasn't bothered about us. He didn't even look into the car. He was already looking ahead before he gave us our passports back.

I was back in Italy. With my baby. Charlotte put her foot down and we tore along the road at a great speed. She started to sing. I joined in. One more stop for a coffee and to feed Angelina before we got to Verona where Charlotte was going to visit a friend for a few days. By now she was in a very good mood and seemed very happy about her visit.

I wanted to do the last bit on my own. I had to get my focus back. This was where we would part. Charlotte found the railway station in Verona and parked the car. She went into the station. I lifted the buggy out of the back of the car. Assembled the seat and put our belongings onto the tray underneath the base. We had practised this and everything fitted in neatly. I also had a rucksack on my back. All I had to do now was lift Angelina into the buggy. Charlotte came back with a ticket and told me there was a train to Venice in five minutes.

Then Charlotte wasn't as Charlotte does. She took me into her arms and hugged me tightly. She told me that it had been difficult for her, but then she was a difficult person. That all the women at the community held me in their hearts, including her. That if it all went wrong I was to go back. They would be there. She said they had all appreciated my contribution to the community even though none of it had been planned. And that I would always be her apprentice Keeper of the Fire. I sobbed and held onto her. That was too much for Charlotte.

"Enough's enough," she said gruffly.

I took hold of the pram. Checked my pocket. Money, passport. Ticket.

Chapter 23

Home

One hour on the train. Thirty minutes on the Vaporetta. Three bridges and thirty steps to the Pieta. Past the Arsenale. Three bridges to Garibaldi. I pulled the buggy over them with fierce determination. I didn't look ahead. I knew the route by heart. Ten more minutes to go. I didn't look at faces or buildings. I didn't want to see familiarity unless it could be mine. I didn't look until I was there.

The landing space was empty. I stared into the lagoon. Empty.

What now?

My thinking got muddled. I was hot, tired. I had a baby to see to. Maybe I should have stayed where I was, cushioned from the world outside.

Nestling inside a willow fence. Now I was just another single mother up against the world. Abandoned. Old Jess surged up through me. Run Jess, run. But I couldn't because I hadn't got rid of the longing. It pushed at old Jess. Pushed old Jess out. The longing was right, I knew it was.

I sat on the wooden pole that he tied the rope around. I held onto the buggy. I pushed the buggy backwards and forwards. How long could I stay? Not for much longer. Or all night. What should I do?

I did what I did at times like this. I sang. Softly, gentle sound coming out of my lips.. Angelina snuffled underneath her cotton sheet. She could hear me. I remembered my promise. That made me think hard about what I would do. There were places I could go and the Pieta was one of them. That would be my plan. A little while longer and then I would find my Pieta angel. She would help. Charlotte had given me a number to ring if it all went wrong. She would be in Verona for three days. That was another thing I could do.

I stopped listening, I was thinking so hard. I was looking at my baby. The purring sound of the engine was loud when I looked up. But I didn't have to look up. I knew that sound, that engine. The front of the old wooden barge was pointing straight at me. It slowed. It swung round. It bashed against the side of the jetty. Angelo stood on top of the hold and stared. Then he looked at the buggy, my knuckles were white with the grip of my hand as I held it. He threw the rope. I caught it and wrapped it around the pole. He jumped from the barge to the jetty. He kept on staring. Then he lifted the buggy onto the barge and held out his hand to me. I took that one last step from the jetty onto the barge. I was home.

I looked at Angelo. "Were you calling me?" I said.

"I call and call Jess. I still call for you."

"I heard you," I said.

Down the wooden steps. Nothing had changed. My old brown leather dictionary was still on the table. My rubber boots still in the corner. I walked into the big room and opened the cupboard door. There was my dress, pink and silky. I sat at the table. I lifted my baby out of the buggy. I cradled her as I looked at him.

"Your baby. Our baby. Our Angelina."

Angelo stood with his hands by his side. Tears pricked at the corner of his eyes. Big, strong, beautiful Angelo.

We took the barge into the lagoon and sat together with our baby between us. At first he was afraid to touch her with his big hands that lifted crates of apples and oranges. I knew those hands would only love my baby in the right way. We watched the sinking sun and the rising sun and the sinking sun again. There was no time here. Only a space to hold and touch. A space to watch and take care of our baby.

Chapter 24

Filling in the Gaps

I knew that Mr Andreotti was the right man to tell Angelo my story. He would do it properly. He would translate it well. Sitting beside his old wooden desk, I told him the full story of what happened to me when I ran away from Angelo and the Pieta. There were so many tuts and stops to shake his head, that I thought we would never get through the story. At times Mr Andreotti wiped his eyes. At other times he would comment about what I had said.

"A fire ceremony. Ah yes, I see. It's good. Ah yes. I know of it."

But I think he faithfully told the full story to Angelo, who listened to every word without moving. Until I got to the birth. Mr Andreotti threw his hands in the air. Angelo grasped my hand and leaned over the desk towards our story teller to urge him on.

"Quick Quick. Very quick. Oh wondrous. So lucky, little Jess."

I told Mr Andreotti how much I had learned with my friends, that each friend had taught me something. That they had cared for me and been kind to me. That I would always be grateful for everything they did. And then I told Mr Andreotti that my life as a child had been a painful torture, that I had been put into the care of the authorities, but that they had always given me back. That I had spent most of my young life running from some pain or hurt. And that is why I ran, that was the only thing I knew. But that I would never do it again. I had learnt not to run. I knew that I would never do it again because my head was full of different stuff, my head was full of knowledge. And the knowledge was good for my life.

Mr Andreotti continued to tut and say oh dear and shake his head and then say the words to Angelo. Now Angelo knew everything. I didn't have to struggle to make him understand any more. Mr

Andreotti had been a faithful friend to us. He gave me a book by someone called Marcel Proust to read. I think he misunderstood my use of the word knowledge. It was a very difficult book to read.

Without fuss and without ceremony, Angelo and I were married in the registry office. Mr Andreotti was there and Mama and our baby. No more authorities, no more not belonging. I had the best belonging.

Angelo put a wooden railing around our boat and my life took on a rhythm that would please my women friends. I would get out of bed with Angelo when the sun was just rising and we would sit at the wooden table and drink coffee, eat muesli and delicious bread from the local bakery. Then we would take the barge out to market. I would feed and wash and change Angelina whilst he bought the fruit and vegetables. Then by the time we were slipping out of the market and into the canals, I would be there on deck. Angelina knew all the palaces before she was one year old. She knew the square where the angel appeared and a church was built. She knew Mr Andreotti worked in the beautiful palace near the Academia bridge. She knew the fine statue in Santi Giovanni. She knew the tree lined avenue leading down to the university. She knew the wonderful wooden door of the Pieta, she knew the angel on the ceiling and she knew the music of Mr Vivaldi. This is what Angelina learnt for her little life.

Mr Frandetti was thrilled to have his favourite soprano back in the Pieta choir. He kissed me on both cheeks and pushed me back into my place in the choir stalls.

"The best soprano I have ever had," he said. "Back, back in my choir."

His words made me feel a bit awkward but Mrs Sabotini said that it was a better choir when I was there, so they all were happy. Very soon people came to hear me sing in the Pieta. I never left the Pieta choir, even when I was asked by the choir master of the Frari and the director of the Fenice to audition.

We rented a little flat in Campo Sant' Anna. Close to the mooring place for the barge. We needed the space for Angelina and for her to be safe. She could play in the square with other children. We shared our life between the boat and in the flat. Granny Monique still stood in the square and screamed at her husband and her sons. Then she would scuttle into her door until she felt it was time to come out again and insult whoever was passing by. She loved Angelina though, and would always stop shouting when she saw her and lean over the pram and her face would break into a huge toothless smile. We had our peace on the barge. Our magic barge. That was really where we lived, with a small wooden table and an old stove.

Chapter 25

Ceremony Two

It was the best morning ever. Angelo had moored the boat at the station steps. Angelina was asleep in her buggy, well secured in the alleyway between the hold and the side of the boat. The sun shone onto the steps. Tourists poured out of the glass doors of the station and sat down with their maps and their rucksacks. Cases with wheels made loud noises as they were bounced down the steps.

The barge swayed with the waves from the traffic on the water. One after the other, vaporettas banged into the stops against the station steps. Police speed boats darted in and out of the river traffic. Gondoliers turned their gondolas into quieter waters. I stood up and then I sat down. I stood again and peered into the throng descending the stations steps. Then I sat down again and tweaked one of the flowers in the pot next to me. Angelo had fastened painted wooden pots all around the railings and I had filled them with marigolds and basil and thyme.

Another surge of people pushed out onto the station steps. Another train had arrived. I held onto the railings and stretched as far as I could to see into the crowd. They couldn't be mistaken. Seven women stood at the top of the steps. Loose trousers, long skirts, leather tanned skin. Beads and feathers and sandals. Long hair and feet with henna tattoos. My crazy, odd friends were here. I jumped onto the jetty, ran up the steps two at a time till I reached them. Their faces burst into smiles when they saw me and and they all held out their arms. I rushed into them, trying to kiss each cheek, acknowledge each friend. I took Freya's hand gently in mine and led her down the steps. We all gathered on the jetty and I held my arm out towards our home.

Angelo greeted Freya with a shake of the hand and a kiss on each cheek. He took her hand

and put his arm under her elbow and guided her onto the barge. He led her to the seat we had wedged in the back especially for her. Then Cora, then Willa, Virginia, Kate, Alice and last of all Charlotte. Each looked at the sleeping Angelina in the buggy, even Charlotte. As each one climbed onto the barge Angelo greeted them.

"Thank you for saving Jess," he said as he helped each one to their seat. He had asked for the proper words. He was saying them with real gratitude. They told him that it had been an honour and how happy it had made them to help and be part of my journey. He smiled and nodded and took his place at the back of the barge. He started the engine and glided away from the jetty with his precious cargo.

We sailed down the Grand Canal like royalty. I pointed out the House of Gold and this palace and that palace as we went. Then we chugged under the Rialto Bridge and then under the Academia Bridge and past the Palace Franchetti where Mr Andreotti had his office. On past the steps leading to the Salute. Then we floated past the Lions and onto the Riva. Angelo pulled into the jetty outside the Pieta.

I didn't feel important being in charge of this wonderful procession to the Pieta. I felt honoured. But the words I learnt from the women in our procession had taught me were important. Trust, rhythm and transformation.

Angelo helped them all onto the jetty and I invited them to come with me. I didn't go into the Pieta. Not yet. I led them up the side and into the pilgrim's hostel. I had booked all the rooms for their stay. Then I took them onto the roof terrace and ordered teas and coffees and anything they wanted. We looked out over the roof tops of Venice. I asked if they'd had fires and sweat lodges and who was looking after everything while they were away. I was so proud. To be back in the circle. To hold Virginia's hand. To share what I had with them as they had shared with me. Not just their home but their care, their wisdom, their potager garden. I could never pay them back. Feeding me when I was starving, Alice bringing my baby into the world and teaching me how to look after her and Charlotte taking risks to get me back here. The list went on and on.

But today was my day. I wore my pink dress. I put the scarf around my head. I placed the little pink slippers on my feet. Angelo looked fine in his white shirt and grey trousers. Kate had made a dress for Angelina from cream organic cotton with embroidered flowers all over the top. It was perfect.

They were all there at the door of the Pieta. Angelo went in first, with Angelina in his arms.

I took Freya's arm and we walked down the aisle to the front of the church. Behind me were my friends, my maids of honour. Truly honourable.

Father Pietro smiled as I took my place next to my husband and my child. The blessing was given. The candles flickered in the darkening light. Mr Andreotti stood up.

"Bella, bella," he shouted and clapped his hands in the almost empty church. Then I left the altar and walked up the steps to the balcony with the railings to sing my song.

When you walk through a storm. I looked up to the ceiling. "Thank you," I said to the angel. *Hold your head up high.* "Thank you," I said to Mr. Vivaldi.

And don't be afraid of the dark. "Thank you," I said to all the spirits of the abandoned little girls floating in the rafters.

Then I walked down the steps and back to the altar. I took Angelo's hand. We sang together. *Walk on. Walk on.*

"Thank you," I said to my friends. "Thank you," I said to Mr Andreotti. "Thank you," I said to Mr Frandetti.

"Thank you," I said to Angelo as I looked into his big strong face, his arms holding our child.

Angelo sang loud with his big baritone voice. *You'll never walk alone.* I was glad he had been a fan of Liverpool football club. He knew the words off by heart.

You'll never walk alone.

I sang with my heart open wide. I sang till the tears poured down every face.

I was a woman who could sing with a fine soprano voice. I was a woman who was loved by a windhorse man. I was a woman who lived on a boat in a beautiful city. I was a woman who was an apprentice Keeper of the Fire. I was a woman who knew how to tend a garden. I was a woman who had a child. I was a woman who had received the best of care from women who cared about the earth and the animals and tree spirits. I was a woman who met goddesses and angels. I was a woman who learnt about healing the wounds that closed your heart.

In the end, Jane Eyre and I triumphed. We were the lucky ones.

In the beginning, I was a girl with a Geordie accent who got on a bus.